What if?

Written by IronWil

AuthorHouse™
1663 Liberty Drive
Bloomington, IN 47403
www.authorhouse.com
Phone: 1-800-839-8640

First published by AuthorHouse 03/01/2011

ISBN: 978-1-4520-9815-9 (hc)
ISBN: 978-1-4520-9814-2 (sc)
ISBN: 978-1-4520-9816-6 (e)

Library of Congress Control Number 2010917789

Printed in the United States of America

This book is printed on acid-free paper.

Dedication

This book is dedicated to my mom, Maria E. Alcocer, for guiding me to God and for teaching me what is important in life. It's not so much the material side of life, but the faith and hope to one day enter into eternal glory which must be the focal point of our lives. In addition, I give thanks to my sister Guadalupe for taking my hand at an early age and encouraging me to read. She encouraged me to get lost in what I read, for even that short while can be an incredible journey. Blessed is the one that believes and trusts in the Lord.

Contents

Introduction

What if the *Bible* were manipulated over time, changed? How would we know what we are reading is true if certain parts had been manipulated for what is to come? Changed not for our benefit but for whose? If it were changed, why would anyone in his right mind go to all the trouble to change the word of God? Don't they realize that it's a sin to change even just one word, but to change numerous parts would be like asking for a free ticket to damnation. We need God in our lives and in our hearts in all that we do. It's sad that we are weak. Even in our modern age with all the technology that is available, we don't have the courage to say no. Evil thrives on our weakness. What makes us grow the weaker, the mind, is easy is to manipulate. Temptation is all around us growing by the moment, but do we care? Some of us do but most don't care or are in denial.

We enter the twenty-first century and after a brief scare not knowing if our technology is to crash or freeze, we manage to see January 2, 2000. Society evolves at a rapid pace over time; rules disappear out the window. We become a nation where everything is accepted. With the explosion of the computer revolution in the late 20th century, we linked up for the very first time in history... in the beginning using only laptops, tweeter, the I-pod, satellite dish, GPS, and cell phones connecting all over the world. Then, came the interactive games including X-Box, Play Station. Yes, we evolved at a rapid pace. Now we are cooking. We are all connected the whole world over. If we stay on the right path following the rules that were set back in the days of Moses and the Ten Commandments, we will benefit. Practicing them will bring us closer to GOD.

Instead, Man takes a path; greed and selfish desires feed the need for him to venture and in his own egotistical way, he starts creating life.

Now, playing GOD, Man thinks he can make his own rules because he is creating. He can set the rules at his discretion for his benefit. Some people back in the day that trusted in GOD remember saying that it felt as if the devil broke his chain. It was so much information knowledge; so much good could have benefited mankind. Diseases could have been cured but corporations had other ideas. Even when they had the means, they refused to help because it would lower their profits. Therefore, they only kept it under control to keep people coming back for more. It's like people are on a fishing line, and they reel you in a little at a time. Every time you think you are able to escape, they yank on the line and pull you a little closer. That's how they operate. Sure, they give you the good stuff and then you have hope. Then, they drop the dosage or substitute a placebo without your ever knowing. Bam! You're back to square one so it never ends and their profits continue growing. The bottle with the cure is right there just teasing you waiting to be used.

The oil giants are the same: they cut production to raise the price because profits are into the billons. They justify that they have problems that are causing spikes at the pump. At some point the economy is so bad that they have no choice but to lower the price; however, it is soon raised again. It has taken many years for the country to steer away from fossil fuels, but it has been worth it. Batteries and electric cars have put a stop to the abuse. Say good-bye to the pumps. Currently, a battery lasts for five years and will go four hundred miles on one charge. The next generation will have regenerating batteries that will last up to ten years. The stored power will be used only as it's needed and then switch off. Maybe if we had a president that cares and doesn't have his own agenda, we would not be here. Instead, Mankind in my time has evolved again now facing Armageddon in the future for the mistakes of the past. When will we learn?

We have passed through the sky and entered the depth of outer space. Will we still have our differences? Will color of skin still be an issue, or will it be where it has been since the swearing in of first-rate President Obama? Standing next to President John F. Kennedy is the beloved President Obama. The statue still stands inscribed in stone the words of President Kennedy: "Ask not what your country can do for you, but what you can do for your country." President Obama's plaque says that when he took office, he pledged that from that day forth there would be change. We did change and on his first annual State of the Union address, he thanked the American people for their support. Then, he said the magical words that are written forth today: "I wake not as a black man but as an American first." This will be a strong nation from this day forth. I decree affirmative action is no more. I promised change. That is what is happening now. We, the people, will get satisfying results from our performance, from crawling to standing to becoming responsible. Working together as Americans we can succeed. It will take all of us to reach our goal. That is how it should be. Promotions will be based on merit and face-to-face meetings saying this is a win-win situation. Only people complaining are the ones wanting this great nation to be divided." He asks for help pledging our word to rebuild the foundations of America. It's hard but not impossible.

From this day forth, people will be held accountable for their actions. President Obama mentioned that some people don't like him because he won't bend; others because he cares so much for this country that he won't sell out. Had he run for another term, maybe he would have finished the movement he started. People still had a choice even at this point in time to change remembering the rules. President Obama took ill the last year in office due to a rare case of tuberculosis. He was confined to bed two months before leaving office. President Obama worked on a list implementing programs to save jobs. We, the people, need to work in order to live and to have high self-esteem. Our number one concern as workers should be to produce so that the company profits. Quality work is a priority that should not be taken lightly. If we give back by doing good work, we can then ask the companies for better benefits. We should help keep costs down by not having so much rework. Giving an honest day's work is a start. Maybe then the companies will decide to stay once more in America. Do this thing, for the next door that we knock on will be in the hall of Congress. The people will be heard!

President Obama continues speaking to the people. "Today comes change. We must pass laws that benefit the people. From the poor to the middle class to the rich, we must beautify our country for America is becoming a garbage land. What is so sad is all the foreigners that come to our country are littering our streets. Neighborhoods are being destroyed without regrets from these foreigners that mistreat our country and property. You people come and ask for a better life, and then you do this act. We promise when you are caught you will lose your right to live in America. No courts will save you. Signs are being posted in all languages so no excuses. I promise from this day forth to create jobs to help clean neighborhoods, like I said earlier. Jobs will be created from fines. Some infractions will cost more than others so beware! I'm passing a law that anyone caught littering not only pays a fine but also automatically becomes enrolled in community service. The first offense is five hours. The next punishment is ten hours linked to an overseer to make sure that it's maximized to its fullest potential so the free ride is over. You litter and get caught and you will pay heavily!"

Being the intellectual man that he was, at first even his own people resented him. Thinking back, the public cried foul that he had sold out. That is why the people loved him; he had not caved in. He stood his ground, knew he was right, and asked God for guidance for the people to see that it wasn't his choice, but the right choice to make. For once in their life, people needed to take responsibility to help turn this great country around. What a president! He was sadly missed. When he was buried, people cried for they had lost a hero.

Can Mankind rise to what is right meeting head-on encounters that wait for Man in the distance? How will people represent Mankind when venturing out further into space? Man did not just land on the moon. He built a space station…just a matter of time before he takes his leap into history.

Programs that President Obama started were not completed. Who benefits, you ask? What happened to the man-hours and supplies? It's odd no one questions, especially about the money. You ask how long a country doing this kind of business can exist. When so much revenue is invested for no real reason, its funding stops. Programs that were to benefit the people are eliminated. Why I ask you? This is just the beginning. In the year 2008 the banking industry nearly collapsed. The housing market fell to record lows. Just two years before, the market was booming. Money was being made hand over fist. To this day people will not fess up to the truth. The bubble was waiting to explode. President Obama took office January 21, 2009. He took charge immediately by freezing wages, giving no bonuses, and making banks responsible and accountable for their actions. On the present day July 22, 2025, asking the wrong people about the past can get you hurt or worse…. did I say disappear? Some things never change, especially in politics. It always comes down to favors. What's in it for me?

For the record, the big three auto companies of the past fail to exist in 2012. Had they cut ties with the refineries, had they explored new technology like Honda and Toyota, they would still be here running on batteries. They cried like little girls when their dreams came crumpling down. Fossils fuels will be outdated in the year 2018. A bill is signed into law prohibiting continued research on drilling, and they will begin capping the remaining wells. The president at the time says that we could truly never stop the crude, for there will be needs but not like before. A vehicle life span is determined by the following: any vehicle powered by fossil fuels ends at the time when it's unable to be retrofitted with an electric motor. Congress also signs a law that prohibits the sale of a vehicle powered by fossil fuel to any country. Mandatory fines are in place. We will not continue to contribute to global warming. Scrapping is very lucrative so for once the pubic is behind it. Why did we have to stop there? We would have been better off if we would have continued not only ridding the giant oil barons of profits but also implementing measures for others to see that this country was not putting up with Congressional pork spending anymore. We should have followed the you-break-the-law-you-pay philosophy, and we as a country would not be here facing a dilemma. We have not functioned like a country since President Obama. Something has to change.

Same sex marriages have evolved to the point where adopting children is okay. How? Are children supposed to adapt to having two moms or two dads? Where is the logic? Children are already confused just dealing with peer pressure. Then, by no choice of their own, they have to adjust to a decision or a situation where they must adapt to same sex marriages. With so many straight couples willing to adopt but not having the clout as say, for example, celebrities that have so many resources at hand, kids are growing up not learning about giving thanks or being grateful, to say the least. We need rules to function as a country. To be a great country people need morals, discipline, and prayer to meet the challenges that await. We have the means to make a difference, not just the celebrities but all of us. Helping Americans that need our help, helping soldiers returning home after serving our country, and helping the less fortunate people that want to succeed but need a boost.... come on, we can make a difference; we're all Americans. Let's open centers to educate the people to give them hope to feel important and provide day care centers for working parents that get out at different times of the day. We need to provide extracurricular programs for children in the summer or anytime there is a need to save our youth. Do understand that we need to help other countries, but let's take care of home first. If celebrities were to contribute, others would follow. This would have a positive impact causing other countries to follow suit. It takes time and effort but the results would be phenomenal.

That is just the tip of the iceberg. Then come the scandals and the scams causing the public to lose their life savings to corruption and greed. Investors are ruining people's lives with no remorse when caught. Where does it end? Are we being set up like Sodom and Gomorra? What happened to the compassion and the principles that were the foundations of this great nation? Are we, the people, so blinded that we can't distinguish between right and wrong? What happened? Where are the values and all the morals that we were taught growing up? Has our technology advanced so much to turn us as frigid as a cold winter day, walking along and not noticing the homeless and the hungry. I ask what happened to "Love thy neighbor." Was that just a speech or was it to comfort our soul? This story is about what happens to a country when it loses its purpose and veers from God. It shines no more; only vanity creates the "bling." To be looked to for direction and to be on top for so many years with other countries imitating us in so many ways, we had charged forward, always first. What a Country! This book is fiction, but even in fiction there is truth.

So it begins

After my second cup of coffee, I am ready to leave for work. As I'm leaving, I hear about another bombing, casualties numbering in the hundreds, and what's odd is no one is taking responsibility. Even more ironic, it's the third one in two weeks. Effort is being made to bring justice to an unstable Middle East. Fighting has broken out with different factions, the country is in disarray, and the F.B.I. and C.I.A., including a number of different agencies, have been assigned to investigate with no real lead. Effort is being made, but as I'm hearing the radio, there is no progress at this time. There is so much loss, but there has to be a reason. Someone is going to a lot of trouble to desolate the area to drive the people away; it's concentrated in a specific quadrant. What is unique about it? The Middle East is known for its oil; that's why we are there, not only to stabilize the region but also to keep an eye on a commodity of high value. However, in the future the barrel will drop to ten dollars due to a lack of demand; therefore, who benefits?

Troops were starting to withdraw. Our President Morgan kept his promise to the people when he took office. People were in awe of the speed of his aggression being in office only ten months and keeping to his agenda. The troops were coming home. People now stop in their tracks when he speaks. It's like being hypnotized. His voice paralyzes the masses for it generates hope and everyone loves him. It is odd no one questions him; Congress follows like lost puppies looking for reassurance. Before he became president, he was pretty well-liked. He worked his way up the ranks like so many before him. Once it became public knowledge that he was running, he became our hope… our salvation. Our country was in chaos. We needed a strong figure like President Obama. We needed hope. One day he was just a typical man, but the next he was giving us courage to move forward in this great nation. All the countries praised him. They sought his guidance. I did not think he had the experience before he took office. He could be next to me in the subway, and I would not know him. Now you see him everywhere… so popular. There was one concern. When asked about his family, he would steer away from the subject saying his parents died when he was fifteen years old. He said he had been an only child raised by a trustee appointed by the institution where his father was CEO.

President Morgan was married, had no children, and became a widower two weeks after taking office. His wife Rita was killed in a drive-by. A massive man-hunt was mobilized to capture the assailants. Rewards were posted, doors were being kicked in, and the media was in frenzy. The people cried-out for justice; the country was turned upside down until her killers were found. Hiding in an empty warehouse is where they found her killers. The S.W.A.T. team moved in and immediately killed all members. At the time, the public praised the actions taken, but that would all change. For now, justice had been served. President Morgan had closure and then a country mourned. President Morgan thanked the people and buried his wife, Rita. It was odd that at the funeral there were no tears. Even though he was wearing sun glasses, he never removed them to wipe his eyes. Watching the coverage from home on all of the networks, the news anchor says they have been married for ten years. (Heck, I remember crying when Bruno, my dog, was dying.) At the time, people were saying some morn differently than others. (I'm not married but I would like to think that if I lost my honey, I would hurt for a long time.) Since his loss, he has never spoken of her in all his time in office. Some say that all of her pictures had been taken down. Anything that was related to her was gone. Some say it was because the memories were too painful. (I find it hard not to keep some memory of a loved one.) Rita was from a well-to-do family who had lived in Hartford, Connecticut. After the funeral her name was seldom mentioned.

Robert was working on his Master's degree and had transferred from Cambridge, England, where he had gradated in business and economics. He did say one day he would return to claim his home. Robert was a man who could not remember when he was not in school or being educated in some manner, but he did miss living here in the states. After receiving, his

Master's, he worked for a firm where he met Rita. They had dated for many years, marrying at the age of forty-two. Two years later, she would inspire him to enter politics just like her daddy. All she wanted was for Robert to fit in and he did. Her dad took him under his wing and taught him the ropes. Feeling sorry for him having lost his parents, her dad learned to love him as a son. It was ironic that she was their only child. When Robert decided to run for governor, it was no surprise that her dad, Frank, endorsed him and all political connections tied to Frank helped vote Robert in.

Having served only two terms, he told Rita the next stop would be the White House. Robert continues to develop and in recent years has learned how to sustain his composure under pressure. Frank marvels at his protégé. Had Frank been blessed with a son, he would have wanted him to be like Robert. He loves Rita but she was no son. She notices how Robert and her dad have bonded. They were spending hours conversing about the next strategy because there was no time for mistakes. He was determined to get to The White House and with Frank's influence there was no stopping him. Little did Frank know Robert's real agenda!

Yes, Robert was a fine president. He was easy to get along with. Although his lips often smiled, his eyes never did. The eyes were cold, so serious. (I compare them to a shark dead calm, the kind that sends shivers down your spine. When I was mentioning it to some friends, they thought I was suspicious for nothing. Once when I was speaking to Father John, my priest, I asked him if he had noticed the eyes. I was not ready for what he said next, "The eyes of a demon!") Father John explains that his sheep are blinded by false hope. How could that be? This is America. (I was starting to regret ever bringing up the subject, trust me. I was getting scared and did not need to know anymore.) Father John asked me to come over for dinner because he wanted to show me some articles that would explain what he was about share with me. (I had no clue. I wasn't real sure about even coming back. Should I be as the sheep and just accept what was?) Dinner was set for three o clock. Which is worse, knowing what is to come and to prepare or just to lie down waiting for it to happen? As I was leaving the parish, I asked God to enlighten me. I remember what my mom would say, "Trust in the Lord for He is our salvation." She always said that He would not let us down. We would only let ourselves down because our weakness is being greedy and materialistic and not having honor. Malice comes to mind because we don't think of others, only of ourselves.

Father John was waiting for me. He seemed sad but glad that I had come back. Not much was said over dinner. I wasn't very hungry. My mind kept wandering because it was hard to focus. We went to his office. Father John waited until he was sure that no one was around. Then, he produced a brown envelope. I reached for the envelope and sat down while Father John took hold of his Bible and opened it to almost the end. He gave me a chance to familiarize myself with the articles. They were about President Morgan and his family.

Father John started from the beginning wanting me to fully understand what is at stake. The Morgan family had emigrated from England from a town named Yorkshire. Robert's parents ran in some distinct circles. It was mentioned that he was involved with the Freemasons, and that he was also not surprised to find that he had been acquainted with the Illuminate. Bruce Morgan was a hard man who was educated but ruled with an iron fist. The land that was leased out was to be charged rental for the said home and the crops. People paid and if for any unforeseen reasons they were late, out they would go losing their crops and all that had been invested. Bruce even rented farm equipment at a discount to his tenants to ensure his crops were tilled and his bases were covered. At times he hoped they would fail for his profits would be even greater. The general store extended credit in the same way. Many were not able to go anywhere else for the next town was twenty-five miles away. Anytime credit was used, another ten percent was added to the bill. The store items were already overpriced, but Bruce relied on the fact that he was the only one nearby.

Bruce had two sons. The oldest died from fever and complications. Little Bruce did not make it to his second birthday. Father John says that was when their problems started because Elsa became ill after little Bruce died. Doctors said it would be impossible for her to consider having another child so there was a possibility that Robert was not going to be born. Bruce could not fathom the idea of not having an heir. How can that be? He needed to have a son and that was all there was to it. Poor Elsa struggled to get better. All Bruce cared about was another son. He watched over his wife but for his benefit he told his staff to watch over her while he was away. A strict order was given that Elsa was to remain in bed until his return. His staff knew better than to cross him. At the time, Bruce didn't know what was in store for him, but he made his mind up that no matter what the cost, he would not return empty-handed.

The Price of an Heir

Bruce traveled to Manchester to meet with some undesirables who then introduced him to a man from India. He was taken to a place like no other. It was as if India existed in the here and now in this building. From the people dressed in customary wear to the belly dancers to the erotic feast, it was like nothing he had ever imagined. He was here but not able to indulge it. Bruce was on a most important business mission. The Indian motioned for Bruce to walk to the back of the building, down a stairway, and to take a seat as they entered the room. The room was empty but had the smell of stale air. After a few minutes a woman appeared and led him to another room. Finally, after a cup of tea the woman asked him, "What is your problem?"

That's when he explained about his son dying and not having an heir. She took his hands one at a time, turned them over, and started to read his palm. When she was done, she asked what he is willing to sacrifice. He was thinking that since he is well-off, money would do the trick.

She replied, "What I want is to bring a new beginning. We are entering a new era. I have my reasons but I think we can come to some understanding. We can form an alliance, a common interest that will bond us forevermore."

Bruce asks, "What does that have to do with my problem?"

She looks into his eyes, "Do you accept?"

It did not take long for him to reply. He never bothered to ask about the consequences. Oh, so selfish. Maybe had he prayed? Had he asked God, maybe just maybe, Robert would not have been born the way he was, without a soul. Now, the woman leads him to another room. It's elegant. She tells Bruce that there will be no more questions.

"Make yourself comfortable. This room has a big bed, and I will return shortly."

Bruce couldn't believe his luck. He was considering spending half his fortune, but to think that the woman didn't want a dime was shocking. When she returned wearing a red robe, the woman had a bottle in one hand and two glasses in the other. They drank without speaking until the entire bottle was consumed. At this point they were exploring each other's body. As Bruce's mind became delirious with lust, he desired more. He would take, mount, and thrust into her for he was a lion, an animal. He didn't have a clue as to what was in the drink. All he could think was that he was alive and invincible. This woman was like no other. She mounted him and rode him until he was ready, and she took him in her mouth until he was spent.

Once again she left the room. To say how long she was gone was irrelevant in his state of mind. When she returned, she was wearing a black robe and had two small bottles. As she opened the first, he noticed how beautiful she was… perfect in every way except for her eyes. They were cold. It was odd that she had an olive complexion but blue eyes. She toasted to their future son. She put her hand on her belly and said she needed his seed in her. Once again he mounted her. She moaned as he penetrated her. She reached behind to have more of him inside her. She was incredible. Then she rolled over. Bruce thrust hard into her womb. He had no idea how many times she came, but it was great. Again when she sensed he was getting close, she greeted his thrust with her movements until his seed was deep inside her.

He looked at the bed soaked with their sweat. She says there is one more bottle they must drink in order to consummate their agreement. Therefore, this toast is for the change that is upon them. They indulge to the fullest. She straddles and rides him like a mad woman. Then she cries as she comes. By now her body is shaking as if she were having convulsions. Turning over, she tells him to put it in her ass and not to stop until his seed is deep inside. Were they performing a ritual? Completely spent, he closes his eyes and sleeps. While sleeping, he hears voices chanting. Although he can't make out what they're saying, it's like something won't let him open his eyes. He remembers smelling incense and sage before falling into a deep sleep.

When Bruce awakes in the morning, the woman serves him a cup of tea and says it is done. "By the time you get home, your wife will be expecting," she commented.

Bruce asks her how that can be possible. She smiles and says, "For I'm she. I have many names." A shiver runs up his spine. She says that she is a disciple of Lucifer, and that one day when Robert is older, someone will contact him. When Robert turns sixteen, he will start his training. There was one last thing she mentioned. Neither Bruce nor Elsa was to interfere when the time came. She reminded Bruce that because of her, he was getting what he had come for, an heir. Before he left he asked her how Elsa could conceive being in the state that she's in.

She replied, "As we speak she is already carrying your son." He left in disbelief wondering how that could really be and a chill ran up his spine.

He left and the downfall of humanity started. (I have felt over time that God has his reasons for what we attain.) We ask for things, material ones being in the forefront. Some are granted; most are not. Sometimes if we wait for a little while and try again, it's the right time and we attain what we seek, especially if our wishes are realistic.

Going home, Bruce didn't know whether to rush or to take his time. For the second time in a couple of days, he was not only confused but also truly scared. Was this woman sure about what she had said? Could it be? Since Elsa's illness they had not been sleeping in the same room. His decision was made. He would get home and see for himself. If the woman had been lying in any way, he would come back and she would pay with her life. He would go so far as to torch the whole place, for no one would dare to mess with Bruce Morgan. Back in the day Bruce was considered a big man at six feet two inches and two hundred pounds. He was big, agile, arrogant, out-spoken, and a shrewd individual.

Now, he must make haste. Yearning to be home, he wouldn't stop until he reached his gate. Some of his staff was approaching as he was pulling up the drive. With excitement in their voices they yelled, "Sir Bruce, come. Hurry and see for yourself. The lady Elsa is recovering. It's a miracle, sure enough!" As he entered her room, there she was. She had a smile on her face and her color was coming back. It was hard to swallow because just a few days ago it had seemed to him that it would be a good idea to make arrangements for Elsa. She was looking grim now. He took her in his arms and, for once, hugged and kissed her like never before. Elsa hugged him back and cried, telling him how long she had yearned for his affection. It's like the man that came home was not the one that had left. She looked into his eyes and said that she welcomed the man that came back to her.

She was right; he was different. He had returned with love in his eyes. It's like the cold had melted from his heart.

Why is it that we have to do something wrong in order to find the good in ourselves? What do we do about the bad that we just did? How about the consequences, the repercussions, and the hurt that we caused? How do we fix it? Wouldn't it be better to learn from others' mistakes? Think of all the things we wouldn't have to be sorry for? We all have the gift of joy in us, but we need to bring it to the surface. Believe it or not it keeps us from doing so much wrong if only we believe. Jesus Christ died on the cross for us to have joy and freedom. Why haven't we taken advantage of the gift that he gave his life for. (I know in my heart that he was beaten and suffered so much that, at the end, you could not even recognize him.) He did that for all of us and not asking for anything in return. So what did we learn from that…nothing? Even today the abuse, the neglect, the fighting, and the killings continue. Did He die in vain?

The next few weeks were wonderful! Bruce and Elsa were alive, for once, enjoying life to the fullest. The staff was amazed at how the Morgans had evolved. Bruce stopped being a penny pincher. People actually started to like the man instead of fearing him.

One morning Elsa sat Bruce down and said that she was expecting. She had waited to tell him because she had to be sure. The only thing that bothered her was that the time frame wasn't right. She told him that she had done the math, not once but a couple of times.

"How can I be pregnant? Bruce, you were not here to impregnate me. How can this be possible, my husband? I have not been with another man in another bed. I love you, Bruce. Believe me, my husband."

Bruce was looking for the right words. He was also stunned. He had forgotten the Indian woman. Strange as it seemed, it felt as if it had been such a long time ago. In reality, it had been only three weeks. How could he explain? How could he justify his actions? Would Elsa understand his desperation? He wonders how to approach this delicate situation. "Elsa, my love, I trust you with my life. I understand that you were under so much pressure with the loss of our child that your health was failing; however, I took advantage of you when you were most vulnerable. Like a coward I satisfied my selfish needs. Please forgive me." Bruce turned away. Elsa reached for her husband and forgave him. After that, they never spoke of the matter again.

Elsa was alive with joy. It had been such a long time since he had heard laughter and singing. Bruce caught himself humming a few bars. They prepared for the baby. They even participated more in community affairs. Elsa was the talk of the town. She had the glow; her aura was at its peak. Bruce was not going to take any chances. He had Elsa call a relative in the states and ask where she recommended having her baby. It was imperative that all bases be covered. Bruce wasn't going to lose his heir. Nora, her cousin, made arrangements and found a hospital located in Chicago, Illinois, that specialized in childcare. Bruce and Elsa packed and left for the states. Oh, Elsa was so excited but afraid. She wouldn't let Bruce know she had to do the entire regimen that was prescribed by the doctor. She loved her husband, and he would have his heir no matter what. Her child was to be their anchor, and she wasn't going to be denied, come what may.

Elsa was a very strong woman for where Bruce lacked, Elsa complemented him. They made a good team. They stayed with Nora for three months and while in Chicago they ventured out to the museum and the zoo. They attended some plays. "Sheer delight" is how Elsa would put it. With all that was going on, I guess it helped Elsa keep her stress level down.

Meanwhile, Bruce was looking into investing, for he was in the land of milk and honey and there was money to be made. Onward he ventured until he found what investments suited him. Bruce and Elsa decided that in the future this was to be their home. The baby was going to be born here in the states. They would come back over time to see where they would relocate. Nora was to check for the best schools and what the area had to offer in respect to the economy and industry. Nora had majored in economics and had worked in real estate as a hobby. Her family had been in oil. When her father died from a heart attack, she had inherited quite a large sum. She didn't have to work but thought she would get bored. It was perfect. Bruce explained their intentions to Nora. She was delighted that she could be of some assistance. Telling her there was no rush was a plus so that's how the Morgans' lives changed even more so. Had Elsa not been with child would they have ever thought of relocating not even just to another town but to another country? Was Bruce already contemplating the future? Once they got back, he would arrange to speak to his colleagues about his future but for now he would give Elsa his undivided attention.

Robert Henry Morgan was born weighing only six pounds on Friday, October the thirteenth, nineteen hundred seventy-three. Bruce was a proud father handing out cigars to strangers. It was a site to see. From the moment when he held his son in his arms, tears of joy flowed. When Nora was in the waiting room with Bruce, he was a mess. Elsa was relieved when the baby was born because during the labor she didn't have a clue as to how long Bruce could hold on. The Morgans stayed with Nora for one more month. Nora had been sad to see them leave but knew that they would be coming back even if not to Chicago.

Most of the town knew the baby had been born before they arrived home. Many came to visit the Morgans. Bruce was so proud. Both Elsa and the baby were healthy. Her family who lived nearby helped care for Robert. He was raised with the finest. He had grown up fast and, time not standing still, he was one year old.

Impending Answer

Bruce received a call from Nora saying she had found the perfect home in the states. "As we speak, I'm sending you the information to see for yourself." Therefore, once Bruce and Elsa received the package, they were delighted with what they had seen. In the coming days, Bruce arranged for their trek to Hartford, Connecticut. It was a sight to see, all right. Elsa fell in love with the place. (Did I mention that Nora was there to put the icing on the cake?) Nora promised to expedite the transaction and to make sure that Bruce was getting what he wanted. It didn't take long for closing so Bruce was busy tying up loose ends and Elsa was busy packing.

Robert was to attend the best schools that money could buy. Bruce ended up buying some more real estate in Hartford and investing in Apple computers, to name a few more of his business transactions. Life was good. They made new friends; they were living the American dream. Occasionally, Bruce remembered what the woman had said. When his son turns sixteen, he will lose him to some stranger. It wasn't fair, after all, but what could he do? Robert still had fifteen years left. Bruce would think of a game plan. For now he had to enjoy the time he had with Robert.

Time waits for no man. One day Robert is one year; the next he is ten. Where did the time go? Blink and we are lighting his cake with fifteen candles.

Now, Robert is a teenager enjoying all the extracurricular activities. He excels in sports, be it football, basketball, or track. He has broken records, even some that have stood for many a year. One school reporter called him a phenomenal individual when he was just a freshman in high school.

Bruce still remembers what the woman had said even after all these years. Is it possible that the prediction could still hold up even after all this time? Just in case, he should prepare for the morrow. What weapons can he use for there is little time? How does he fight the unknown? He had so many friends, yet he could trust no one, including his wife, with such a secret. He would have to confide in someone, but whom? Would they believe him or think that he was mad! Bruce made a list of the most influential people he knew. From the list of only five names he would have to decide. He would sleep on it and make his decision tomorrow. Therefore, for the rest of the day he tried not to think about it.

Elsa had made reservations at the Bordeaux, for Nora was joining them for dinner. Robert asked his mother if it would be okay to bring a guest. Elsa asked him who his guest would be and he replied, "Roger Gant." Elsa knew the name all-to-well for they had grown up together. They had been best friends but today she said no. His Aunt had some good news to share with them. Dinner was at six o'clock.

Nora had moved to Hartford four years ago wanting to be close to Elsa. They were like sisters with Elsa being only two years older than Nora. Bruce liked Nora's being close, for he was out of town sometimes for three or four days at a time. Bruce was thankful for all that Nora had done over the years. At six o'clock they were seated waiting for Nora. She arrived followed by a tall gentleman. After the greetings Nora insisted on a bottle of champagne because she could not wait another minute. She felt as if she would burst. Just as they were toasting, she raised her hand. That is when they noticed the ring. Juan Gilbert Lopez had asked her to marry him. They took turns toasting the happy couple. By the time dinner was being served, the women were busy discussing the wedding. Elsa was having the time of her life. Looking over, Bruce thought how much he loved his wife. He had been blessed.

Juan was very intelligent. He had a degree in electrical engineering and consulted for Amoco oil. Robert talked to Juan about baseball and football. They hit it off. Juan even asked if it would be okay to join them at Robert's next football game. Robert later said that it felt as if he had known this man all his life. He wished Juan many happy years with Nora. Everyone had had a wonderful time. As they were leaving, Nora asked Bruce what he thought about Juan. Was she asking for his approval? Yes, Bruce described him as a keeper. She gave him a big hug and whispered in his ear, "I love you guys." On the way home Elsa said that Nora had indeed been asking for their approval. Tomorrow they would go shopping and make the wedding plans. A wedding involves a lot of careful consideration. They had much to do since the couple was to wed in April, only six months away. Pulling into the driveway, Bruce remembered his decision. He couldn't wait any longer. He must get some sleep because the day was rapidly approaching when he must save his son.

Robert was a warm, loving son but lacked compassion for his fellow man. Over the years Elsa and Bruce had done their best to change that. They had explained that it gave them no satisfaction to see people suffer. Elsa suggested that he volunteer in homeless shelters and nursing homes because it might help him to develop compassion. At the age of twelve, he volunteered not by choice saying he felt different over time. They could not say he had changed. Bruce feared it had just become a routine. Still feeling that change had saved Bruce, he hoped his son would see there is no satisfaction watching people suffer. If he had not welcomed change, Bruce would still be that cold-hearted man that he once was. Elsa fell asleep as soon as her head touched the pillow. With these thoughts running through his mind, Bruce was restless and found it difficult to sleep most of the night.

He waked to the smell of coffee. Elsa refused to let anyone else bring him the coffee and paper as she considered it her wifely duty. Any person in his right mind would not argue with her; saying she is stubborn is an understatement. Couples learn early in marriage what works and what doesn't. After coffee and a brief conversation, Bruce prepared for a new day. Elsa and Nora left early to make plans and Bruce was on his way to his study asking not to be disturbed. Robert left early to meet Roger. They were having an intensive football practice because a big game was coming up. Robert wanted to make a good impression so he planned to invite Juan. He was thinking that Thanksgiving is this week, and some friends would be over for the holiday so he must get his plan in motion before they arrive on Monday. That only gives him two days.

After spending three hours and several drinks going over the five names on the list once more, Bruce narrows it down to two names. He decides to take a break before he finally eliminates all but one. After much consideration Lyle Cummins appears to be the ideal choice. Lyle and Bruce go way back to his early days in Yorkshire. They met briefly in London at an auction. As fate would have it, they were both bidding on the same farm tractor. They managed to get a bit aggressive with their bidding. Finally, Bruce gave in. Lyle departed with his tractor but about seven months later ran into Bruce in a pub in Yorkshire. They recognized each other as Bruce was going to the men's room and Lyle was coming back to the bar. Lyle asked Bruce to join him for a drink which Bruce accepted. He requested from the bartender the fancy scotch on the rocks. When Bruce returned, a drink was waiting for him. Bruce suggested they toast to the tractor. Lyle remarked that tractor he had bought turned out to be a lemon, and they both laughed. Bruce later confessed that he had been pissed at him for driving up the bid to more than he had intended to pay. They laughed again. By the time they stopped they were holding each other up to keep from falling. What a night! Bruce still remembers his look when Lyle said "lemon" and over time they had become best friends.

They were the same age but back then Lyle didn't like the way Bruce treated his staff or people in general. He mentioned more than once that Bruce would be better off if he would treat them with kindness, but Bruce said that he ruled with an iron fist. That was until Robert was born. Lyle still regrets the phone call from Bruce saying little Bruce had died, and Elsa's health had declined. He did his best to console his friend; he would be there in his hour of need.

"Bruce, I'm on my way," he said after having received the call from Bruce. He stayed at the Morgans for as long as it was necessary. He was not happy about making arrangements for little Bruce, but it had to be done because Bruce was unable to function for worrying about Elsa. Bruce needed his help. He was coming apart at the seams worried that not only had he just lost his son but also his wife was going to be next. Yes, Lyle helps his friends now. Bruce needs his help again to save this son so he makes the call. Bruce does not realize at the time that it is not just his son's life on the line but humanity is also at stake.

Father John asks Steve to come back tomorrow at 3:00 because he is tired. Leaving church, Steve makes my way to the first bar that he comes across. He thinks he could use a drink, maybe a couple to keep his hands from shaking, and there will be more tomorrow!

The Call

After three beeps the answering machine picks up, "You have reached Lyle. Leave your name and number after the beep." After leaving his name and number, Bruce waited. He decided to retrieve the envelope from the safe so if Lyle decided to help, the contents would be needed. While sitting in his office with drink in hand, his mind wanders back all those years. Is it true?

The woman whose name is Sabula was she really in allegiance with Lucifer? He needs to investigate. Finding out could make a difference between living and dying. He would use all resources. Bruce Morgan was taking a stand come what may? At the time had he stepped aside maybe he would've enjoyed a couple more years with his son. Also, Elsa would've enjoyed seeing her son graduate, taking up politics, and most of all, marrying.

Little did Bruce know that Sabula had already put plans into action. Pawns were being manipulated throughout the world. What about all the careful planning? Sabula wakes. It's time that all preparations to take over humanity that began when the dark one was cast out of Heaven are implemented. Look around. The world has not really changed that much since Christ was last here. Christ gave his life for these ungrateful people that never have enough. Their greed is never satisfied. They lust for more. Had they learned so long ago, maybe they wouldn't have become such easy pickings. Killings never stopped and neither did the violence. Mankind rapes the land never thinking about the consequences of global warming and the ozone, self-centered as he is. Man has the ability to change but ignores it. It is not too late. Don't make it too easy for me. When I arrive, you'll be crying and blaming it on others. Sabula will feel at home. She will cherish and enjoy the fall of humanity especially when she is the one that the nations will seek for lust in all matters. Kingdoms will fall at her feet, and they will want more, poor souls or fools, because it all has its price. She will welcome all of them and her master will be pleased for all the souls that she gathers for him. They will know her by her name. Lust and vanity has its price; her price is but our souls. You will promise many things and some promises will be kept but most won't.

She laughs. "Enjoy the time that you have because your days are getting short and my time will be long for this will be Hell and it will be for eternity. It was all made possible again for selfishness, one man wanting something that was not meant to be, but with my help and a little encouragement, he fell into my trap. He still believes that it was his idea but it was not, just a thought that was implanted. It was his destiny. For many years we have kept watch over him waiting for the right moment. We even managed to speed up the process a little bit by encouraging his son to die a little early. Now it's only a matter of time before he begins his training, and he develops his skills and his many different talents. I will be there to teach him the fine art of manipulating people, and he will taste death with my help. He will learn to enjoy the moment and the way the body feels as it absorbs the souls of humanity. He will hunger for more and it will make him strong and one day he will rule until the dark one returns and then it will be four. The dark one, myself, Robert, and the beast, just like the four horsemen but in the flesh." Her body shivers from just the thought, "With careful planning throughout the years, finally it will come. Nothing will stand in our way. We will have our day. This time, God, you lose."

The phone rings. "Bruce, I just got your message. How can I be of service?"

"Lyle, I need to see you after the holiday. Something has come up of grave urgency. I need to tell you something that can't wait until our visit at Christmas. Is it possible to impose on a friend? I can be in London next Sunday because the guests will be leaving by Friday or Saturday at the latest."

Lyle asked if Elsa would be joining them. Elsa felt they acted like idiots when they consumed liquor, but Elsa was also quoted as saying that Lyle was like a big brother she had never had. To have one gang up on you is bad enough, but to have two, her sides were usually hurting the next day. They had a blast. They looked forward to their encounters. Maybe that's why they felt young because they were always kidding around. (No pun intended.) Over the years they went on excursions wishing to have more time together for Lyle was a bachelor saying he still hadn't found Miss Right. Elsa feels she knows him. He says there are too many pretty women out there that need his services. Lyle is a handsome man who never has trouble-meeting woman.

Lyle tells Bruce that he will get ready for his visit, and that he sends his love to Elsa and Robert and not to forget Nora. After hanging up, Bruce feels relief. He walks to the cabinet, makes a drink, and sits back thinking of what is in store and how to prepare. Lyle, not knowing what to expect, gets ready for Bruce and informs his staff that Bruce will arrive Sunday. Lyle has a good staff. Maybe that's why he is still single.

Bruce falls asleep and dreams of a woman in a far away mystic place. Erotic plants and paintings and the smell of incense surround this woman. She takes his hand leading him to another room. Bruce wants to ask something but she puts her index finger to her lips motioning him not to talk. As they're walking, Bruce tries to remember all that he sees. He knows this woman but from where? Think. This room that they walk into is huge and filled with more paintings and statues. It seems so real. Now, he can identify the incense as the smell of sage. They walk across to the balcony. The closer they get to the balcony, the louder the noise become. Bruce realizes that they're from the outside. A chill runs down his spine. He feels the sweat on his brow. How can this be? He doesn't ever remember having such a realistic dream. As they approach, he looks up. The sky looks different somehow. It's not the usual color blue; it's a yellowish brown. She motions him to look down. His heart sinks. What he sees is devastation, complete and utter chaos!

As he turns to look at her, she smiles and says, "This is what waits for you."

"What does it mean?" he asks.

"Yes, Bruce, one day in the near future this will be paradise, and you know that it won't take long to make your world this way. It is already happening on its own, and with a little encouragement it will be done in no time. People are so vain and easily corrupted. They have lost their way. They welcome me. They need me. I give them what they want, and they get eternal damnation in exchange for the good. I will make them bad, very bad, so they can fit right in."

Replying, Bruce says, "How can you call it paradise with all the killings and the pain that you are causing? No, I don't want any part! Do you understand, none whatsoever?" Bruce asks God to help him awaken from this nightmare.

She turns and says, "Look there."

Turning, for the first time he sees the Statue of Liberty, but it's on its side. Half of the statue is missing. Then, he looks a little closer and sees the Empire State Building mangled. In the distance is the George Washington Bridge. What is this? She tells him this is the place they call New York.

"You recognize it, don't you, Bruce? The *Bible* was manipulated oh so long ago. They thought that the final battle would be fought in the Middle East, but it turns out that the Middle East was only a staging point. Mankind lost, Bruce, as you know. You had better get on the winning side."

He turned to her replying, "We will win in the end."

"Bruce, that's where you're wrong, for my son will be unleashed, and he will feed on pain and more pain. He will feed his hunger and lust. Nothing will be saved. He has been waiting for so long."

"I will not let that happen. If I must take action, I will, even if it means taking his life." "How noble of you, Bruce. Do you think it will be so easy for you to kill your son? You don't have a clue as to his abilities that are now dormant, but you shall find out. Oh, you will. This is what he does to the world when he rules. He will change life as you are accustomed to it."

Then, in the distance a ruckus is heard. Through smoke-filled air Bruce sees what is approaching. It reminds him of a movie that Robert and he had seen about transformers, but they had been cartoons. Now, they were changing as they spoke. They're not vehicles any longer but machines with arms and legs and different attachments. They go on a rampage, killing and ripping people's limbs apart. Bruce did not understand how the people could still be alive for their broken bodies are still moving. She must have sensed that he was going to ask because she said that in time man would welcome death but would not find it. Then, the machines left the way they had come.

"Feel at home, for in the future your world will resemble this place," she warned.

Bruce turned and saw death at its brutal best. She laughed. All this time she had been holding his hand. He looked down because his hand felt uncomfortable. What he saw was no longer a hand but something like a slimy claw. He jumped. She laughed out loud.

"Bruce, did you forget that I am known by many names? Tell me you didn't forget."

Bruce wanted out of there. "God, help me to wake, please!"

"There is no God, for you still don't remember our agreement. Must I remind you?"

"No, what does this have to do with me? My son's time is at hand. He will be of age soon. His schooling begins very soon."

"Bruce, we have not forgotten what you did for us. We can find a place for you and Elsa here in paradise. You can live here and watch the show, for it will go on for a long time."

"No, Demon, for I shall fight for my family."

Sabula becomes furious. "We have an agreement. You are mine and so shall the rest of humanity be for my bidding." Sabula reached for his neck and squeezed hard because now she has transformed from a woman to a real demon. "I did mention that I could turn into anything so when you were having your way with me, you thought I was a woman. Was I enough woman for you, Bruce? Are you thinking you want to die?"

She must have been reading his mind. He quickly answered, "Take me, but not my family."

She looked at him and replied, "I had intended to let you live a little longer but that can change. Look at the crowd for they gather again."

"I see the people. I see them well," he replies.

She says, "Look carefully. Do you see her?"

"Who?"

"Look at the woman, the one at the center of the fire. Do you see?" The people were stacking more wood or anything that would burn around her. Yes, it was Elsa. They were setting fire to her. She was in agony. Turning to the woman, he pleaded for her to stop. She laughed and said, "Want to be the one next to her? I'm kidding, Bruce, where is your sense of humor? This place is not so bad; at least, you don't have to shovel snow. You know, Bruce, once you arrive it won't take too long to adjust. In addition, you will still have your staff. Look at the bright side. You don't have to worry too much. Friends are waiting for you. Now that they know you are the cause for Mankind's demise, you have made some friends. Bruce, you're not looking pleased. Was it something I said?"

Looking back at Elsa, by this time he saw that her flesh was peeling off her body, but yet she was still alive. The people around the fire were laughing and jumping for joy. Elsa could not find comfort in death. She was screaming. Hearing her screams and feeling as the tears running down his face, he turned to her and begged her once more to stop! She says once more that she cannot protect people if they won't do what she commands. Unable to awake Bruce hears her promising him riches here in her kingdom. She tells him he will never want for anything, but she will not be so generous in the future.

"Pledge your alliance of your own free will. Do we understand each other?" she demands.

Elsa yelling from the pain cries, "Make it stop!"

She asks, "What is your answer, Bruce?"

"Yes," he answers, looking into her dead eyes.

He awakens sweating profusely and there is a cut on his hand. He reeks of sage and wonders what just happened. If he had just awakened with sweat, he could have blamed it on a bad dream, but how could he explain the cut? He thinks he should write all of this down before he forgets. Bruce writes everything down from the paintings to statues to sage because everything could be important. He notes how everything changed with little effort including the arsenal of vehicles and the buildings of New York City. (Little does Bruce know that this is just the beginning of what is to come.)

Bruce showers and stays a little longer thinking of his beloved Elsa. What he has just experienced seeing her in such agony makes him wonder what he has done. Did he also sell her out as well? How could he fix it? Could it be put back the way it was? For once in his life Bruce is dumbfounded. He needs to meet up with Lyle because maybe, just maybe, there is something he has missed. As he dresses he notices the bruises on his neck. He wonders how he can explain this to Elsa. He calls the airline for a reservation, and then starts packing his notes and the envelope. The clothes will be packed on Saturday. Then, he goes to his study and pours himself a drink. Elsa would be home soon, and he would be glad to see her. It feels like an eternity since he last saw her. He needs to hold her and feel her warmth on him. This is the comfort he desires before leaving.

Robert gets home before Elsa. As they talk, Bruce asks Robert if he feels different than others his age. Robert says that sometimes he doesn't know his own strength. Bruce says, "Give me an example."

"Well, for instance, when I am carrying the football it seems that I can run forever, never getting tired. I mean I don't even sweat like I should. All my friends are dying from the workout the coach gives us but not me. Basketball is another example. Dad, I've never said this before but I feel invincible. I can shoot a hoop without trying. I make it look like I'm trying, but really it just goes in almost on its own. Track is the same. I run but on the inside, I have to physically slow down because I don't want to stand out like some freak. Dad, it scares me sometimes but I'm okay. Should I continue? Do you need more because lately I can't sleep. When I do, I have some weird dreams. When I sleep it's like far away places but then it's not."

"What do you mean?"

"At first I was thinking, it was like paradise, but as it continued it changed to something awful. Dad, I remember it now. It was New York City. This woman said that I was responsible for the fall of Mankind. Dad, I remember the woman being so beautiful and holding my hand. Then, she marked my right hand in the dream. I asked her why she did it, and she replied that it was the mark of Satan. Look, Dad, do you see it? The mark indeed was this symbol ^. She said that it was for my legions to recognize me, for I was to lead them to victory. Dad, I wanted to tell Mom, but I'm scared."

"Don't worry, Son. It was just a dream."

"But, Dad, it wasn't. How do you explain my hand?"

Then for the first time Robert notices Bruce's neck and his hand. "Dad, what happened to you? Are you okay?"

"I had a little accident, that's all. Don't worry, Son. I'm fine. Don't tell Mom, for she will worry too much. We will keep this between ourselves. Robert, I'm leaving for a couple of days. Take good care of Mom. I'm going to see your Uncle Lyle."

"Dad, I thought we are going there for Christmas."

"Yes, Robert, we are but I need to see him for some business."

"Tell Uncle Lyle he owes me a rematch in chess, and that I haven't forgotten."

The phone rings. It's Roger sounding excited. " Hi, Mr. Morgan, may I speak to Robert?" He hands the phone to Robert motioning that they'll talk later before he leaves. Robert acknowledges.

Now the wait. Bruce was wondering if there was anything else he might need. Elsa would be home soon. It was three o'clock and dinner would be at five. At four o'clock Elsa called saying that they would have guests because she had invited the happy couple over for dinner. The staff was notified to set two extra settings for the guests. They were delighted for they enjoyed Nora's company. Nora had blossomed into a beautiful woman. Juan is considered to be a lucky man.

Elsa arrives with the couple following close behind. They use to wonder when Nora would find her other half because she has everything going for her. She has done well in real estate, managed her finances to the letter, and is very organized. Most importantly, she fears God, a strong quality, and she gives back to the community. She is involved in extracurricular programs for the kids proving she well be a good parent.

Robert hears when they arrive. He is the first to greet them for he loves his Aunt Nora. He gets hugs and kisses. Then Bruce gets his, always being last. Life is wonderful during moments like this; it makes everything worthwhile. People must cherish the moment for time moves forward, and it doesn't look back. What we didn't do today, we can't make up tomorrow. So, people should be sure to always tell loved ones how they feel because it could be the last opportunity. Bruce's mom used to say that when a baby is born, a candle is lit. Only God knows when or for how long it will last. If one has a dream, he must not wait for it to happen but make it happen. (Many people will tell you that you are silly or a fool but that same person might just be wasting his life on what if's.) We take chances everyday so why not for something meaningful? People cannot succeed by not trying first. Many have failed and then they get scared and don't try so they end up living a meaningless life. The ones that fall and learn to crawl and then to walk are the ones that are to be admired because they refuse to give up. Many fail and then become useful doing something else because they find their niche. In the end it's all worth the wait. If they are fortunate enough to have a loved one believing in them or if they believe in themselves, it is easier to achieve their goal. Bruce reflects that he has been blessed. Listening to Elsa talking to Nora and to Juan, he truly understands that a woman can make or break a man. It's the man's responsibility to do his part by making her feel special and letting her know how important she is to him. Nora is so much like Elsa. Bruce knows that Juan is in good hands and seems to be sincere about his feeling for Nora.

Nora is so happy. She says that they ran into Juan at the mall so he ended up tagging along, of course. Juan said that they had another announcement to make as they were making their way to the dining area. Nora beat him to the punch saying she is going to be a mom. Elsa almost fell from the surprise. We laughed after we caught her. We toasted to the couple at dinner saying we would be there for them. We had a real good time. Eventually, Robert excused himself saying that he and Roger were going to the movies and that he would be home early but wants to see *Jaws.* Juan says that he will be at the game on Wednesday. Robert is happy to hear that he will attend saying that they have been practicing very hard to make a good impression. After dinner, we made our way to the parlor. The girls excused themselves, as always, for there is much planning to do.

Juan is excited about being a father saying he already has opened a trust fund for his kids' college education. They will have what he didn't have. Bruce admires the man for he does not just think of himself; Nora is a lucky lady. Juan asks if Bruce thinks that Juan is too old to have children. Replying, Bruce says that Nora is the one with child. Both laugh and Juan asks if it is okay that he joins them on Thanksgiving Day now that he's part of the family. He would like to join them for there is much to be thankful for as they have all been blessed. Juan explains that when the baby is born he will take some time off to help with the baby, and they will fly to South America to see his family. They will probably stay for a month. Bruce is invited to come along and says he will discuss it with Elsa but doesn't see why they couldn't join them. Bruce is no longer needed as much at work as he once was.

"Since I am the owner, I should not have to work the way I used to. Those days are behind me. I have a good, dependable crew and my stocks are up. I've done well. Now, I'm like Nora giving back to the community. I say and say over again how important it is to give back for how much do we really need to be comfortable? Think about it." Bruce and Juan continued talking for a couple hours, and then they join the girls once more. They couple left just before ten at night.

Finding Faith

The man awakens hearing the alarm clock. It's five o'clock in the morning. He should have returned home sooner but was too nervous and not thinking right. He listened to the radio but not much was being said about the bombing. He needed to get to work because the taxicab needed to be inspected once more. Steven Long has been a cab driver for five years. He is single at the moment and fascinated with meeting people so what better way to explore different cultures. The cab driver hears all sorts of stories, some true and some manufactured, to entice the mind. It is an honest living working a full day behind the wheel. When he cashes the check on Friday, he's proud to know that the money is from honorable work.

In the past he had always been looking over his shoulder never knowing what to expect. How many times had he stolen and someone had come and stolen back from him? All that money had been wasted on empty promises and on booze and drugs. The only thing that consoled him was that he hadn't used the needle. "Chicken shit" they had called him back in 2009. He could never understand what the big deal was about doing heroin. It just hadn't been his thing. He had lost so many friends and even a loved one to it. The thing about it was people were still sharing needles even after the scare of the '80's when so many people had lost their lives from that. It didn't seem to faze them. Then with the epidemic of AIDS, it really shocked the world. Famous celebrities like actor Rock Hudson and many others died from AIDS and that was scary because even they were not immuned. Rock Hudson had not used drugs but was a queer. Growing up, Long remembered Hudson, his hero, as a ladies' man. Who would have guessed? In general, one might think that society would have changed its way of thinking and that the AIDS epidemic would be a wake up call and the queers would stop. I guess that would have been too easy. To many this was a sign that God had intervened in their lives once more to show that Mankind needs to change to go back to the way it's supposed to be. Man and woman like Adam and Eve, not like Neal and Bob or Rosie and Betty. Of course, instead of people getting scared and changing, the situation got worse.

Yes indeed, it was worse because the church priests were not to be trusted as they once had been. Over the years the church lost so much money over lawsuits that now priests are not left alone with children. Someone has to be in the room at all times, and you know what, people accepted it. Go figure. Instead of going back to the more traditional ways, society patched it up like so many others things. That's how it's done.

In the early 1950's society had been so different. Some people were still corrupt, but most families had morals and would eat dinner together discussing their day. Parents knew what their kids were doing and who they hung out with. Of course, drugs were around but were not in the open and readily available. Even the queers were still hiding in the closet where they belong. Kids played in the park, for most part, without parental supervision. Also, kids had chores and were disciplined accordingly if their behavior was not acceptable. Back in the day, they respected their elders and if they were rude, they would get smacked and no questions were asked. Those were the days. When kids went out, people knew who they were and who their parents were during that time. Now, the youth have taken over their parents due to the lack of supervision caused by both parents working to make ends meet. Thanks to the dumb ass liberals, laws have been passed that make it almost impossible to discipline you own child. The laws have gotten worse over the years. Parents fear for their freedom because so many have been accused of abuse or neglect. Now, couples are having fewer children.

Maybe it's better not to have kids right now, for the world has changed much for the worse. It gets worse for people who don't fear God. They have lost their way. No one cares or they don't want to hear it. On TV they have programs on prime time about girl on girl or man on man. They justify it because it helps the ratings. In reality all it does is to encourage minors to experiment at a very early age. What happened to adults being role models for the world? How can society justify this? In the end, it is all about the money. Looked at what happened to our country. They sold our landmarks and sky scrapers to foreigners, and then they began leasing our roads to foreigners. Now, they are so overpriced that people avoid them. Travelers take the long way so they don't have to pay astronomical prices, and the same people have the nerve to call this a free nation. How so, when there are no freeways left and tolls are everywhere a person looks? This country has sold out the American public. The politicians line their pockets with our hard- earned money. The people need to find their way; God grows tired from our weaknesses. Fear! The wrath cometh! It will be so great as to wipe Mankind away. Change must come before it's too late. Finally, My Brethren, be strong in the Lord and in the power of His might. Put on the whole armor of God that ye may be able to stand against the wiles of the devil.

More people need to understand that it's not too late to welcome God. We can be saved just by asking and really trying to change. It's that simple. Saying thank you to the Lord for what we have been provided is a start. Giving thanks before we eat because many people are doing without, going to church and really listening to what is being said, and being a better neighbor are just a few of the changes that can be made to improve our life if only people take the initiative to do it. If only we ask for salvation, it will be provided. All we need is to ask. God does not ask for contracts for there are no expiration dates. He will take us up to His kingdom. If it weren't so, He would not have said it.

On the other hand, the devil is full of empty promises. First of all, his promises always end up short; they never benefit anyone but himself. Regarding his contracts, yes they do expire. Be sure to read the small print. Don't forget that. Go head. Be an idiot! He won't lie to you, Sucker. Look around. When people see you down, instead of giving you a hand, they will knock you down. That's where they want to keep you. Bad people want you to lose in life, for it makes them look better even though they're losers. It is sad but people fall into their traps, for we are so gullible we let the forces of evil win without a fight. If we stood up for what is right, the evil ones would disappear into the gutters or forevermore into the abyss.

Steven Long had regrets. He had lost his way for so long. If he could apologize to the people to whom he had caused pain, he would. He had been a lost soul for many years not because he had lost his parents when he was young but because God was not in his life. Then one day he got the wake up call. No kidding really. Someone had broken into his apartment and put a gun to his head. Luckily, it had misfired. That was it. He found God then and turned his life around. It's going on six years since that happened. He wouldn't have it any other way. Now, he doesn't have to look over his shoulder. Feeling useful now, he has self-esteem. He wakes with a purpose and gets to talk politics with the big shots that ride in his cab. People would be surprised how much he has learned from just listening. He gets so many insights on the market from playing dumb and pretending he didn't hear. After making some good investments, he now owns the cab and has a nice nest egg. Who would have thought Steven could have turned his life around to be a businessman? In high school all he did was drink and smoke pot because he wanted to blend in to fit like a shoe. He never made it out of tenth grade but here he was. When he stopped the drugs, he also stopped making excuses. He didn't drag his feet anymore, and he was surprised at how much he had accomplished.

His friends would say, "Wait for tomorrow; it's not going anywhere and neither are you."

He thought of the consequences. "My friends, don't put off what you can do today for tomorrow."

Arriving at the garage, he sees Dale. He's cool. He had known him for four years and never has to drag his cab in for inspection. Steven is pretty good at maintenance. It helps that he is mechanically inclined. Dale asks if there is any news about the bombings. There is no news and no one is claiming responsibility. Then, Dale says something that catches his attention. This morning Congress passed a new law that would require that all newborns have a chip inserted to track them in case they're separated from their parents. They had been talking about this for many years but now it's a reality; they're finally doing it. To think it started with dogs and cats and now it's moved up to humans. Did I mention all vehicles including commercial vehicles are equipped with black boxes and tracking devices? Uncle Sam did not waste any time to pass such laws making it mandatory. President Morgan pushed for the law when he was still governor. It's no surprise that it passed so swiftly with no objections. Now, the authorities know where you are 24/7.

"Dale, you know it's written in the *Bible* that the mark of the beast will be placed on most of the population. No man will be able to purchase or to sell unless he has the mark. At one time or another before the fall of Mankind, all will worship the beast. Their weaknesses will be their own demise. The followers of God will be tortured for His namesake. We must not give into the beast; we must fight!" Dale has turned pale and asks what they can do. Steven says he has a three o'clock meeting with Father John. "Do you want to join me, Dale? He might have some answers to our questions." Dale agrees and calls Lisa, his wife, to let her know that he will be running a little late. Finishing with the inspection, they talk a little more, and Steven says he will pick Dale up at two thirty. He needs to get going.

It's going on seven o'clock. Steven is running a little behind. His first fare is at Central Park, and he is going to the Chrysler Building. Traffic is about normal, and there is not too much talk in the cab. There is too much on Steven's mind. As he reaches the destination, the passenger gives him a two-dollar tip. He thanks him and leaves. As soon as he gets out of the cab, another person is waiting to board.

Steven looks in the mirror and asks, "Where to?" It's a big wig going to the United Nations and he is in a rush. As they make their way, his cell phone rings. He mumbles about the bombings. Listening intently, Steven hears him say something about Iraq. Trying not to seem interested, Steven doesn't look in the mirror so he can avoid eye contact. Then the passenger mentions Jordan. As they arrive, he gives Steven a long look but offers no tip. "Cheap ass," Steven mumbles to himself turning on the radio once again. Still nothing is said about the bombings. Are they keeping a lid on it? The rest of the morning is quiet. After lunch he picks up some weirdos going to Central Park. He's just not into it today. He doesn't want to make conversation for his mind is somewhere else. He needs to call Father John after this stop to let him know that Dale and he will be there at three o'clock. When he picks up Dale at two thirty, Dale mentions that Lisa wants Bruce to join them for dinner. She is a wonderful person. Dale and Lisa make such a good couple, and he enjoys their company to the max. They have two kids. Dale Jr. is seven years old and Jessica is five. They are very well disciplined and they help their mom. It reminds him of the old days. They arrived at three o'clock. Father John was waiting for them. He led them to his study where he asked them to have a seat. He told Steven to bring Dale up to speed when they left.

Rasime

Father John picks up where he left off by explaining what transpired upon Bruce's arrival in London. Lyle is waiting at the airport. He is happy to see his friend but his friend seems troubled. It looks as if Bruce has aged over night. What's odd is that they just got together four months ago, and he didn't look this way. What could be so wrong? Lyle would wait to inquire until they get home. He feared he might need to be sitting down. Bruce is quiet on the ride home. When they arrive, the staff is there to greet them and is happy to see Bruce.

Lyle tells Bruce to go and get settled. They'll meet in his study in one hour. Lily is talking to Bruce about Elsa and Robert saying how much they are missed, and she will be glad to see them for Christmas. Lily has been employed by Lyle for twenty years. She is a very dear person. Lyle is fortunate to have such a caring staff. Lily closes the door, and Bruce sits on the bed just staring at the ceiling. He is thinking about what he is going to tell Lyle and what Lyle's reaction will be. Suddenly, his eyes seem heavy, and he closes them to sleep. The next thing he knows there is a knock at the door. He doesn't realize that he has slept so long. It's Lyle asking if he is okay. Bruce replies that he is fine and will be right down after washing up to help clear away the cobwebs in his mind. Shortly, he gets the envelope and makes his way to his study. Lyle is waiting and offers him a drink, which he accepts. Lyle then calls Lily and asks not to be disturbed. Lyle takes a seat next to Bruce and says that he is ready to listen.

Bruce starts from the beginning. "Do you remember after we buried little Bruce how devastated Elsa was, and I was in no better condition. We lost not only our son but also our light. Lyle, I was coming apart. Had it not been for you, I can't imagine what would have become of us. You have been more than a friend. You are more like the brother I never had. Over the years I've mentioned to Elsa that I love you as a brother and she understands. She feels the same about Nora. She loves her like a sister. They are so close. Well, I became desperate after awhile not being able to have a son. It's not like we didn't try, but at the end the doctor told Elsa that when she was ill something had happened to her ovaries. There was a possibility of her not having any more children. Her health took a plunge because it felt like someone was sucking the life right out of her. Lyle, I could not bear to watch for part of me was dying along with her. You had gone home. I suppose I figured that Elsa was the next to be buried. You know how much Elsa means to me. I love her very much.

"About that time I started drinking; I mean **really** drinking to forget. That is when I met a man here in London. We got to talking and drinking. I had so much pain that I wanted it to go away. I later told Elsa it was a business trip, but it really was that I needed to get away. It had been eight months and Elsa would not make an effort to get out of bed. I met the man a couple of times. He told me that his name was Rasime, and he was in London on business. I asked him what kind of business, and he replied that it included happiness. Looking at him, I said, 'Are you for real?' He said again that it included happiness for he's in the market of selling incense, a potent extract, and that it has good marketing potential. Reaching inside the pocket of his coat, he produced a small vile and gave it to me. It smelled like jasmine. Then, he told me that this is just one of many more flavors. I asked him again what this nonsense is about happiness.

" 'Bruce, you have a lot of pain inside,' said Rasime. 'What if I knew a way to help you? I mean really help you make the pain go away. What is the price for happiness?'

" 'Rasime, I think I had better go for I'm drunk, and you're not making sense. There is no price for being happy.'

" 'That's where you're wrong. Everything has a price; some things are just more costly than others. Go home, Bruce, and think about what makes you happy. I will be here one more day.'

"I returned to my country the following day. As I was leaving, I thought back to this little man. He is of Indian descent. Could there be some truth to what he had said? Making my way back to my room, I was thinking that I needed to sleep. Dreaming of little Bruce, I awakened crying. I knew my son was not coming back. It had been eight months. I wondered if the pain would ever stop. Then, I thought about Rasime again.

He did ask what would make me happy, and it would be to have a son, an heir. I decided I would find him the next day and would ask him about it again. I thought that he'd better not be playing with my feelings, or he will feel the brunt of it. These days I don't have a sense of humor, not that I ever had one. The next evening I was back at the same pub at six o'clock waiting on Rasime to show up. I was concerned that he might not show because yesterday he had been here by five o'clock. Just as I was ordering another drink, I saw him making his way to my table. I motioned to the waitress to make it two instead of one. He sat down and waited for his drink.

"After the waitress left, he asked, 'Do you desire something, Bruce?'

" 'Rasime, I will tell you but if you think I'm playing, I will hurt you like never before. Do you understand me?'

" 'Yes, I understand.'

"I told him I had lost my son and to have another son would give me happiness. He said there might be a way. Then, he asked how strongly I desired it.

" 'Anything you need, just ask; you hear me?'

" 'You know, Bruce, you ask for something that ordinarily would be impossible.' Then, he asked if my wife can conceive, and I said that she had been sick, and the doctor had said there would be no more children.

" 'That's why I'm here so can you help me find happiness?' Then, I got up to leave. He reached for my hand and said to sit because he was not finished.

" 'Bruce, this is a bit of a challenge but like I said before, it's not impossible. Where can I reach you? It will take a couple of days, to say the least, to have an answer for you,' Rasime responded.

"I replied, 'I can stay here for as long as it takes you.'

" 'Fine, I will have an answer for you on Friday. This being Monday, meet me here at the same time. Bruce, I will need a recent picture of your wife.'

"Rasime then got up, and I asked him what it would cost me because he had said nothing about payment." He smiled and said, 'First, let's see what's involved; then it will be decided.'

"As he left, I looked at my shaking hands. It took both of them to hold my drink. I stayed a little longer to have a couple of doubles to calm my nerves.

"I made my way back to my room to call Elsa and tell her that it would be a few more days. I asked how she had been feeling. She responded that she was okay, for the most part, but I could hear the pain in her voice. The pain was not just physical anymore, but the situation was starting to work on her mind. I needed to help her. I tried to cheer her up. She's a good sport for she plays along, but I don't know who needs it more, her or me. We talked awhile longer. Then, I wished her a good night and hung up.

"The next couple of days painfully dragged by. I was consuming more alcohol just to be able to sleep. I went for walks to make the day go by because I was tired of being in my room. I decided to go to a movie and ended up seeing *The French Connection.* That turned out to be a good movie. I ended up going to the warehouse on Thursday to make my monthly orders. Under normal circumstances I called Bryon because I have been dealing with him for many years. All are surprised to see me. It's rare for me to stop. I told them it was convenient for me because I was in town for a couple of days. Bryon, the manager, took me out for lunch. Bryon is a pleasant fellow. I have been dealing with him for some time, but we had never met until now. He invites me over for dinner after calling his wife Hilda. She is happy that she is going to finally meet me. Bryon says he will pick me up at four o'clock. I tell him that I will be waiting here at the front door. When I get to my room, I call Elsa and tell her the news. She's happy that I have finally met Bryon. She sounds better than when we last spoke. We talked for awhile, and I mentioned to her that I would call back tomorrow. I told her I miss her and love her. Afterwards, I called the front desk and asked for a three o'clock wake up call.

"The phone rings. It's the front desk wake-up call. I thanked them for the call, and then I showered to get ready for my visit. I am reminded of my father's emphasis on first impressions. People treat you the way they see you. Father put it to the test literally to prove a point one day. He dressed as a bum, walked into the bank to apply for a loan, and shortly was escorted out the building. All along, I was watching observing his actions for I would be quizzed afterwards. Then, he change clothes and returned to the bank. What a difference! They even offered him coffee while he was waiting. Afterwards, he asked me what I had learned, and I said that it is important to dress properly for people do indeed judge you by appearance. Father went so far as to say that a person can be poor, but he doesn't have to be dirty. If he has only one outfit of clothes, then he should take them off and wash them for the next day. It's that simple. People do understand but they don't do it because of laziness, which should not be tolerated.

"Bryon is waiting for me at the door. Looking at my watch, I see I am a few minutes early. He smiles and says that Hilda is waiting for us. I asked him if there's a place to buy a bottle of wine. I don't believe in going anywhere empty-handed, especially visiting for the first time. We stopped at a little wine establishment for the varieties there are endless.

"I turned to Byron and asked, 'What's for dinner' and chose an appropriate wine for the meal. We arrived and Hilda was waiting with a big smile. I saw their two cute little rugrats. Hilda shook my hand saying seeing me has been a long time coming and looks forward to meeting the misses. They introduced the kids; Byron Jr. is nine and Jake is five. Byron insists on having a toast before dinner. We toasted to friendship and having the fear of God in our lives. Thinking that's a new twist, they began eating. Hilda explained that she had awakened that morning and decided to make a roast, which is odd for they would normally have had roast on the weekend. The kids were well-behaved and excused themselves after dinner. We made our way to the cozy sitting room. I told them that the next time I would bring Elsa, and I would like it if they stopped by our house the next time they are going to Manchester. If they just let me know in advance, we can plan something for we welcome their company. As I'm leaving, the kids say their good- byes. Hilda shakes my hand and says she was pleased to meet me. I thanked her for dinner and complimented her cooking. Driving back to my motel, Byron says that he has had a wonderful time. I shook his hand when we stopped and said I felt the same. I reminded him not to be a stranger. When I got to my room, I soon fell asleep because I wanted this day to end. Tomorrow is Friday.

"I was restless and didn't sleep well but that's okay because today is the day for which I have been waiting. I will get my answer this evening. When I was going to have breakfast, I remembered to buy something for Elsa, as I always do. She still gets a kick out of it. Just to see her face and hear her say that I shouldn't spend my money on her makes it all worth it. Stopping at a little shop, I found an amazing broach made of porcelain and black onyx. It's a woman face. I know she will like this for the bust is white on a black background. Elsa likes the high collars and she looks good, for she has a long, slim neck. By the time I return to my room, it's just before noon. Once again I call the front desk and ask for a three o'clock wake-up. Before I lie down, I get my things ready not just for today but also for tomorrow because I'm leaving at ten in the morning, and I don't have a clue what to expect tonight.

"The front desk calls at three, and I thank them once more. I get ready and then call Elsa telling her I will be home tomorrow evening. She says for me to be careful on the way home. I tell her I will take my time like always enjoying the ride. A good, long ride relaxes me. Hanging up, I take Elsa's picture out of my wallet. Rasime did say that he needed her picture.

"Arriving at the pub at four o'clock, I realized that I still had plenty of time because he wouldn't be there until five so I ordered a drink and waited. It's not crowded. The Beatles are playing one of my favorite songs 'Penny Lane' on the juke box. My mind wanders dreaming of a son. I was thinking what we would be playing, how I would be helping with his studies, and how I would be raising him with morals and respect. I wanted him to have the best schooling that I could afford. Yes, it will be good. Ordering another drink, I heard 'Electric Light Orchestra' in the background. It's close to five. I was beginning to wonder if this man is going to show up. Couples are coming in for it's the beginning of the weekend. I can hear the patrons' laughter making this place come alive. I went to the men's room, and on the way back I ran into him.

" ' Rasime, I already have a table; see the waitress,' I told him. As we make our way to the table, I order our drinks. I'm excited but I don't want to show it. I have to stay calm. We sit and he asks how I've been doing. I told him that I was fine, had taken care of all of my business, and now I was ready to begin.

" 'Did you bring a picture of your wife?' he asked.

" 'Yes,' I said reaching into my vest pocket and giving him the picture. He commented that she is beautiful and I thanked him. I asked him what we were doing here today, and he said that it could be done providing that I return at a certain time.

" 'First, there is a fee; then arrangements will follow. Bruce, we'll need to keep the picture, and the fee will have to be paid in full. The fee is ten thousand American dollars.' I told him it's too late for today, but I will give him the money in the morning. We agree to meet at the motel at ten in the morning. Then, I asked what's involved. He says that he can't reveal too much until payment is received. We drink some more. I figure if I keep him here long enough he will spill the beans, but I was wrong for this man can drink with the best of them. I leave the pub at eleven, make my way to the room, stop at the front desk, and ask for a wake up call at eight in the morning.

"Going to the bank in the morning, I began to wonder if this is a good idea. Ten thousand is a lot of money. American currency is worth more than the pound. I had agreed and would have to live with it. Robert, my banker, asks if everything is okay.

" 'Bruce, this is a lot of money. Are you in some kind of trouble?' I reassured him that I was not in trouble. I've known Robert for many years. I told him I'm buying some equipment and the chap is from America and only deals in American currency. Robert buys it. I leave and return to the motel. It's only nine o'clock so I prepare for Rasime.

"At ten o'clock he's knocking at the door. I motion him to have a seat. He asks if I have the money. I assure him that I do, but before giving him the money,

I ask him to tell me how this will play out. He tells me that one month from now I'm to return to the same pub at five o'clock, and then I will follow him to an establishment. Rasime guarantees that he will be there.

" 'I give you my word as a gentleman.'

" 'But I'm giving **you** ten thousand dollars!'

" Smiling, he says, 'Bruce, you can back out right now. If you don't trust me, it's not too late but you'll never have an heir. You will never be happy. Is that what you want because I will leave right now? Do understand me? I'm not here to negotiate so I ask for the last time what it's going to be? I don't have the patience.'

Giving in, I agree. Then, I give him the envelope repeating to him that the time is five o'clock one month from today. He nods in agreement.

" ' Yes, Bruce you're correct, and you are not to speak to anyone about this conversation. Are we are clear?'

" ' Yes, Rasime, I understand. Do I need to bring anything?'

" ' No, Bruce, just see that you're not late, for there is much riding on this. Remember, tell no one.' After he leaves, I gather my things and depart."

To Save a Child

Looking at Lyle, I wonder what he is thinking. He asks if I would like a refill, and I nod. Then, he asks me what happened next. I told him about my encounter with Sabula.

"How could you do something so despicable to Elsa? Was it worth it, Bruce?"

"You don't understand, Lyle. We lost little Bruce. You saw how Elsa was. I remember saying to you that I was scared and desperate. Lyle, I can't change what I've done. I need to save Robert. Will you help me? I'm here to end this. I have to. Robert is fifteen years old. He has less than one year. They will take him at the age of sixteen. Please understand, Lyle. I know what I did, and I can t change it. Do I need to beg? Is that what you want to hear? I don't have any shame left, but I do have a plan. That's all I have. Can I count on you?"

"What do you purpose, Bruce?" That's when I took out the envelope and handed it to him. "It's all the information I have on Sabula over the years I've been tracking it." Lyle gives me a strange look.

"Bruce, what did you mean by **it**?"

"Well, Lyle, it is not a woman or a man. It's the devil's second in command, and I'm not exaggerating either. I told you that I lay with a woman, but I was deceived. I had this dream after we spoke on Saturday, and it was revealed to me. It's the devil's second in command shape shifter. That's what it represents. Call me crazy, but if you join me in tracking it down, you will see for yourself. Can I count on your help? I don't know where else to turn. Tell me we can save Robert. I don't want to lose my son to it. My life is not important. Before I left, I made arrangements just in case I don't make it back."

Lyle sets the paper work down. We drink, talk, and drink some more until the early morning. Then, we make a decision to go after it. Lyle says that we well need some more help if we are to take a stand. He will call on the illuminate. He picks up the phone, calls someone, talks for a few minutes, and hangs up. Then, he says, "It is done. Bruce, go to sleep for they will be here in the evening. Sleep, my friend, for I believe it will be another long night."

I go to my room, lie down, and fall into a real deep sleep. The hours race by and I barely hear the knocking on the door. It is four in the evening. Opening the door, I see Lily who is saying the guests will be arriving soon, and that Lyle wants us to eat something before they get here. I tell her that I will take a fast shower and be right down. She smiles and leaves. I hurry and shower. Making my way downstairs, I see Lyle is waiting. We sit and eat, not saying much. After dinner, we go to the study and wait for our guests. He tells Lily to bring our guests to the study when they arrive. Once again, he asks not to be disturbed, and then we talk about the illuminate. It's been many years since the word has even been mentioned. I ask if it is possible that they can help. Lyle says that they have been fighting evil since the beginning. It's one of the main reasons it was formed, and to this day behind closed doors, they are still hard at work. Evil takes no days off.

At six o'clock, they arrive and are lead to the study. Lily knows it is something important. She knocks on the door and leaves. The first to enter are Earl, Max, and Tom. Lyle asks them to have a seat. Then, he offers them a drink and introduces me. They ask about my troubles and what is involved. While I'm talking, Lyle passes the envelope around bringing them up to speed as I speak. When I finish, they look at each other and ask, "What do you want?"

"I need help to save my son for his time is at hand," I replied. I tell them that over the years I've been tracking Rasime, and that he is now more involved in imports and exports than ever before. He has a warehouse in London. His main hub is in Bombay. My resources are following up on an address, for he still resides in New Delhi. Sources also state that he is branching out in the United States opening a warehouse in New York City.

"Once he is established," I continued, "I will be notified of his whereabouts in the states. At this moment he is in London and will be here for the next two days. I will have round-the-clock surveillance. If we are to track Sabula, we will need Rasime. He will take us to her den, for I know that they remain in contact. I show them pictures of the two in New Delhi. It's four years old, but Sabula is not one to take many pictures in this day and time.

"Sabula, unlike Rasime, is another matter for the place where I met it is long gone. It burned to the ground about one year after I was there. She has been very difficult to track but she resurfaces in Karachi. My sources were tracking her and then they disappeared. I sent another group who were able to pick up her trail, but the men that went missing were not heard from again."

Tom notices the pictures and remarks that the demon didn't age at all. They are compared with pictures that were twenty years old, and there is no difference. I went on to tell him that Sabula then moved on to Qatar and was last seen in Yemen about two years ago. Rumor has it that she was spotted in Mecca one month ago.

"I'm still waiting on conformation. Once all the data is reviewed, we can move swiftly. I don't believe that she has forgotten the pledge and time is running out. My informants will be contacting me in the next few days to confirm her status. Are there any questions?"

Tom asks why I waited until now to pursue this matter. "If you had any doubts, you should've taken care of this matter a long time ago," he commented. "How do you plan on eliminating this Sabula? Does she have any weakness that you know of?"

"No, but good always overcomes evil, and if we work together we stand a chance."

Next, Earl is asking how Bruce knows that she won't come after the illuminate once she realizes that they are behind the scenes.

"Isn't it obvious that she is also keeping track of you and your family? What safeguards have you put in place for your family? Once we move forward, there's no turning back. There will be casualties and the numbers could be great. Bruce, is this what you want, to start a war?"

Max asks, "Is she the antichrist?

"No, she's second in command.

"How do we fight it? What weapons are at hand? Is there a chance to win?

They say it will have super human strength, as far as I know. No mention of it having any weakness. I need to review the *Bible* finding out how to expose it and how to fight it. I will contact the clergy because we will need more help. Bruce, are you sure what you say is true?"

"Yes, I wish I were wrong."

"Then it's agreed that we fight to the death. We will save this child in the name of our Lord. God will be our shield from this day forth. We make a stand!" They sit and pray, for they will need the Lord's guidance if they are to succeed.

"What we decide to do will also have unforeseen repercussions. If this is the fall of Mankind, we'd better make the right choice. The choice is God, for if I die today it is for God," said Bruce.

They stay up planning until the early hours of the morning. They all have their duties to perform and agree to meet in two days. With all the intelligence that is gathered, they will decide what steps to take. Lyle offers them breakfast before they leave. Agreeing to stay, he lets Lily know, and when breakfast is ready they make their way to the dining room. They give thanks to God before eating and ask for His guidance and vigilance over Bruce's family. They finally let their guard down for awhile and relax taking potshots about how they met each other. It was nice to see them laugh even if it was only for a short time. Lyle told them how he had met Bruce and about the bidding and who had made off like a bandit in the long run. Lyle told of scrapping the tractor after six months of sinking additional time and money into it.

Max looked at us and said, "Bruce, you're the lucky one losing out on the bid." We laughed, finished our breakfast, and our friends departed. Lyle and Bruce spoke for a few minutes before Bruce excused himself and went to sleep.

The next two days they searched London for clues. Lyle was very resourceful. They tracked Rasime to his warehouse. They waited watching who came and went. They kept track of the individuals and got a break when Lyle spotted a friend. They followed him until they were sure he was out of reach. Then, Lyle got his attention. Lyle asked him to wait until he talked to him first. Lyle got into his car, and they talked for awhile before he motioned to join them. We ended up driving to a nearby park. There we went walking and sat on a bench and talked. Lyle introduced him to Ned Roberts. He is a little older than them, but he still seems fit for his age. Lyle explains their dilemma to him, and he acknowledges by saying he will help in any way he can. Ned says that the building is not only a warehouse but also a slave trade market, a revolving door for women and children who are sent to different parts of the world. That's what he was doing there.

"Lyle, I'm not for slave trade but times have gotten hard, especially since Wilma took ill. I don't have the funds or resources to cover her treatments. I'm ashamed of what I've become. I love Wilma so much. I'd be lost without her." Ned started to cry like a child. Bruce felt so sorry for him because it reminded him of Elsa when she was ill. Lyle calmed Ned down and told him that they would help with her expenses. He would not have to endure this any longer. Lyle asked Ned why he hadn't just asked for help, and he replied that he was too embarrassed and felt useless. When Rasime offered him some extra income, he accepted. Ned sympathized with people unlike himself who didn't have any hope. He would make them as comfortable as he could. He went so far as to tell Rasime that they were human beings. Rasime laughed and said if his conscience bothered him that much, he should just leave. It was easy for Rasime to say because his wife was not suffering. The past nine months he had dealt with it and was thankful that he would not have to return after those involved gave him the word.

A large shipment of Chinese has been sent to work the sweatshops in New York City. Rasime is making massive profits in the slave market. His next shipment is for San Francisco in a couple of days. Bruce looks at Lyle and says that Rasime needs to be taken down before he leaves the country. Lyle asks Ned to keep him informed but not to get the smugglers' attention. Ned says he is to return tonight to schedule the shipment. Rasime will be there. Ned tells us that Rasime does not travel by himself anymore. He has bodyguards around the clock who are well armed.

Lyle says, "We will arrange to care for Wilma. Ned, do you have any records of the activities that go on in the warehouse?"

"Yes, Lyle, I have manifests of the ships and of the people and their destinations for Rasime answers to a woman named Sabula."

"Have you met this woman?"

"No, but I know what she looks like because Rasime pointed out that she was his boss, and I made sure I didn't screw up for she doesn't have a sense of humor. Rasime said there is no tolerance for mistakes. Mistakes are usually fatal."

"When was the last time that you saw Sabula?"

" About two weeks ago but she is returning in the next two days to see this new client that has greatly increased their volume by thirty percent."

"Ned, you need to be very careful. All we need from you is a phone call when Sabula returns. That's it. Don't take any unnecessary chances, understand? If you are able, call from a pay phone. Try not to make the call from the warehouse because it could put you in danger." We walked back to the car and agreed we would wait two days for Sabula.

"One last thing," Lyle said, "Ned, as soon as we get your call, don't go back." They shake hands and leave. They had opened a trust fund and made all of the necessary arrangements for Wilma's care. They would be taken care of for the rest of their lives.

When they got back to Lyle's house, they called Max and the rest of the team. Lyle got in touch with the illuminati, and they started working on a plan to set the trap for Sabula. After Earl and Tom arrived, they made their way to the cellar. To their surprise it's like an arsenal of plastic explosives, mines, and guns of all types. That's not all; there was surveillance equipment.

"Lyle, are you planning on going to war or what?"

He smiles and says," You can never have too much."

When Max arrived, he was brought him up to speed on the layout of the vicinity and utilities for that might work to their advantage. Sabula needed to be caught off guard. If they lose here, it won't end here. The battle will work its way back to America and Bruce's son will die. Sabula cannot get her hands on Robert. If Sabula is right, then this is the beginning of the annihilation of Mankind. If Bruce fails, Lyle is to finish it.

Turning his attention back to his comrades, Bruce says, "We have two days. We have served Her Majesty. We have made our country proud over the years. Now we do this for God; may He guide and enlighten us. God is our only salvation. We need to put on His whole armor. We take a stand against a demon that's been here since the beginning of time."

Betrayal

Ned calls around noon and seems nervous. Bruce answers the phone and tells Ned to go home because there is someone waiting to take Wilma and him to the airport.

"Do not stop for anyone. Do you hear me?" Bruce tells Ned before he hangs up. Bruce then tells his men that at four o'clock they will strike. By that time it should be getting dark. Max and Earl were put on alert. They will call if Sabula is spotted. They wait at home until one o'clock. It is a two-hour drive. Upon arriving, they get into position. The warehouse is already surrounded. It's dark by now. Bruce asks Max if there's been any movement but he says there hasn't. Bruce tells the men to wait for his signal. Lyle looks at Bruce, shakes his head, and asks if this is a good idea for all of them to be together. He wonders maybe they should send in a scout like they did in Africa. They agreed to send Max and Earl. They would go and report. They both had served in Africa. Max specialized in recon and demolition and was not afraid to improvise. He was ruthless when it came to survival. The man will just not die. He has numerous medals for going above the call of duty. Earl is lethal at close range; furthermore, he is a resourceful communication expert. He spends his time in the field from Normandy to across the continent into Africa. He is a good soldier. Earl and Max make a good pair because they both have the killer instinct. Earl calls in and says they are waiting for the package to arrive. Lyle says not to worry. He knows Ned is very reliable. Their plan is to get as many of the refugees to safety as they can. On the layout print, Ned pointed to show us where they would have the Chinese. Max has confirmed their location. Once they go in, some of the group will free the people. Ned counted twenty-four. There are at least one dozen bad guys and Rasime and Sabula. The warehouse is coming down, literally. Max saw to it by setting plastic explosives around the main beams, and then placing wire charges throughout the building as per the plan. He knew how much time they had, not much but enough to save Earl and him. Out here, they were forty strong. That should be more than enough. They have large amounts of firepower at their disposal. The good thing about this is that they're in the country so it will take the police awhile to get there. By that time they will be out of there if all goes well. They wait patiently across the street in the abandoned building. There is no smoking or talking. Tom is on the rooftop doing recon. He was a sniper in the war and is still very sharp. So far, there is no movement. With all the time available, they planted land mines where they would be useful and marked them well. When it gets hot, and it will, no life will be lost on their account because they have taken measures to ensure everyone's safety.

Ten thirty and still they were waiting. The men were getting antsy so two men went to pick up something to eat. They had been here all day, and it was wearing them down. The men took two-hour naps. When they are needed, they will have to be sharp and alert. Food arrived and they took turns eating. Lyle and Bruce ate last feeling badly for Max and Earl. They had not eaten yet and had to be getting hungry. As they eat their food, Lyle tells him that the illuminate dispatched some men to keep an eye on the woman and Robert in the states.

"Lyle, I don't have a clue as to what I would do without your help. I have been blessed to have a friend like you, for even after all these years here we are."

"Bruce, if you had won the bid do you think that it would have turned out like this?"

"Lyle, if it had not turned out this way, it certainly would be a shame for I would never have had the pleasure of meeting you. On the other hand, it's much more than just meeting you. I have come to call you friend or brother. That's what you are to me. I've come to depend on you. Over the years, I know that it's mutual, for I would give my life for my brother. The main reason that I'm here today is you. Lyle, I am not connected as you are. Living in the states has changed me. I've become too comfortable and soft, not the hard man I once knew. Promise me, Lyle, that if I die this day you will keep your promise to watch over Robert. I know he's your godson; that's why I asked you."

" Bruce, I will honor my pledge to you, for I love Robert as if he were my son," Lyle commented sincerely.

The radio comes to life. It's Earl. "We have movement."

Bruce looks at his watch. It's eleven forty-five. Rasime is walking with Sabula. Everyone is alerted.

"We go in two minutes. Is that clear?" the team responds that they are ready. I look at Lyle and tell him to remember our pledge. He nods his head.

"Let's move out. Everyone into position." I call Tom on the radio and ask whether there is any movement outside, for I don't hear any. He says no one came in or out. That's odd. All along he has been in the building, and he was not spotted earlier. Well, how did they enter the building? There must be some secret entrance, and Bruce's group needs to find it fast.

"Max, do you copy?"

"Bruce, go ahead. I copy you."

"I need for you and Earl to find how Rasime got into the building. Backtrack before we can proceed. Copy?"

"I'm on it. I will get back to you just as soon as we find out. Everyone hold your position until I give the word. Copy?" Finally, Max calls back. We found an underground stairway where we were setting up explosives. Earl, what is Sabula's position?"

"They are making their way to the holding cells. We'll need to surprise them with gas. We will be using night vision." Max left someone in charge to kill the power.

"Kill the power in five, four, three, two, one," said the man in charge. Max and Earl, meanwhile, returned to their position awaiting the signal.

The building comes to life with all the noise. The men move forward and it starts out well. Bruce's men caught the human traffickers off guard. The men moved so fast taking them out just like they had planned. Some managed to free some of the refugees and were escorting them to a safe zone. Then, Bruce heard the screams. It's Rasime. He had deserted Sabula. He had three men running from behind and two in front. One of his bodyguards leading the way hit the first wire. That took out the two men in the rear. I know that Rasime didn't expect it. Just in that second he thought it was odd that they we were not following him. The number two wire is tripped as they make their way to the last bend before the trap door. Rasime is taken out along with another guard. The screams are indicative of the carnage in the air. The two guards in front make it to the trap door. Then the cries of agony and death are heard. As they reach to open the door, it comes to life. Death takes them without a care for these men are meeting their maker and now must answer to God. Max and Bruce were so happy that they had rigged it up because the dead will not hurt another human being. Earl says that he has the package in his sights and his men are surrounding her. They make their way towards her, and after the smoke has cleared, Bruce is able to see her for the first time in fifteen years.

"Bruce, I thought it was you. You know that you could have just knocked, and you didn't have to go to all this trouble just for me. What services are needed this time, another heir…perhaps a daughter? Tell me what do you need, Bruce."

The men looked at me and Max asked, "What's going on? Do you two know each other?"

Bruce tells Max and the rest of the men, "Keep your weapons on her. She is trying to distract us." Lyle calls for everyone to surround the men guarding the refugees. The rest have left to a safe house like we planned so it's just us twenty- eight men versus Sabula and her seven men. Her men were moved to another room with fours guards before they even walked in. They were following orders to the letter. There would be no contact whatsoever, and, yes, at the end there will be no prisoners. They all have their orders. By now the guards are returning from their task, and now they are thirty-two strong. Bruce acknowledges Sabula for the first time.

"I do not know if those visions of New York City were real or if that is what's in store for humanity but it ends now. Rasime is out of the picture and you're next to follow in his footsteps."

"Bruce, have you also forgotten our arraignment?" Sabula asks.

Max butts in again, "What arrangements do you have with this woman? Bruce, what are you not saying?"

Sabula looks at Max and says, "You ask too many questions." Then Max is shot in the forehead from above. Bruce is watching as this man loses the back of his head. He has this look on his face that makes him wonder if maybe he should have never asked that question. It's too dark from above to see who is shooting. "You know, Bruce, it didn't have to come to this. Didn't I say to walk away? You're an idiot because you still had time to enjoy eleven months to be exact but here you are with your commandos. So this is where I'm supposed to beg for my life? Come now, Bruce. You can do better than that."

"Sabula, you're going down you and whoever is up in the rafters will be joining you."

"Bruce, did you wait long? I mean we had to make this look real not just for you but also for someone like old Max, poor bastard. Isn't that right, Earl? You have to be on the winning team."

Bruce was too dumbfounded to reply but Earl was eager to say, "Yes, Bruce, you've got to get the benefits. We tried to get Ned to play ball. No matter, for he joins poor Wilma but not in the air, in the ground, if you know what I mean."

Sabula says, "By the way, Bruce you know that your men were given orders to terminate my guards. The gunfire you heard were your men that wouldn't join us. They were killed instead. One more thing, Elsa won't be attending the wedding and neither will Nora, the bride-to-be. Bruce, I've saved you a lot of expenses. Aren't you going to thank me? Weddings are so expensive. I've never cared for that uppity bitch. Nora thought her shit didn't stink. Well, guess what? It did stink. I was there and she even pissed on herself." Sabula laughs out loud and the men laugh with her. Tears roll down her face. "You had to be there. They never saw it coming."

Tears rolls down Bruce's face. He sees the truth in her eyes.

Bruce yells, "No, you're not leaving alive."

"Bruce, neither are you. Elsa, poor soul, we don't want to forget her. You'll be joining her in Hell with the rest of your kind. Hear me everyone and hear me well. This is your modern day Judas who sold out Mankind for an heir that's to be the ruler of this world. Mankind will fall and it will not stand until I say so, for I'm the new judgment. There is no God but me!

Bruce took his browning out of his jacket and took aim, but he never even got the shot off. From behind as he was falling he made himself twist just to see his face. It's Lyle with a smile. The last thing he feels is the kick to his side and Lyle laughing as the rest of the team is massacred. When it's over Sabula is horny and wants Lyle. He orders the men out of the building, and Lyle and Sabula stay and screw and fuck; for there is no love here but death, blood, and violence, the perfect ingredients for evil. Sabula promises Lyle anything that he wants. To hear Sabula is happy was so simple. It was a little promise she had made Lyle so long ago and here they are. Lyle jumped ranks moving up the ladder just like Sabula had promised. Lyle was on the right side; it was Sabula's turn to win. All that was Rasime's now belonged to Lyle, and the stock in Bruce's business, forty-nine percent, now belongs to Lyle. Now he would be awarded custody of Robert and would be the caretaker of Robert's estate.

"Poor Bruce, you worked hard all your life, and now it's time for me to reap your rewards. Whoever said crime doesn't pay, I call him a liar," Lyle gloated.

"To think it was all possible because of a little problem I had with Rasime so many years ago. It's still fresh in my mind like it happened just yesterday. I told that freak it was not over until I said so. You don't push Lyle unless you want to push up daisies; just ask Rasime, or what's left of him."

To think had it not been for that asshole he would never have met Sabula. He had complained to her, and she had told him that she would do him right. Actually, that's when she expressed interest in him. Lyle is handsome, and he will use it just like a woman uses her beauty to manipulate men. She asked if he would like to take Rasime's place and have even more wealth than he could ever imagine.

"Yes, what do I have to do?" Lyle asks.

She explained her dilemma. "All you have to do is follow this guy and keep me informed." It was no coincidence when they met at the auction or, for that matter, the bidding on the tractor. It was all arranged. On the other hand, his meeting at the pub was fate. Sabula asked if it was hard to betray Bruce.

"Not really, when I thought of all the benefits," Lyle responds. He looked over at Bruce who was facing down. You could see where the bullet had penetrated the back of his head and exited the front taking most of his face. He looked down and Sabula saw his erection. She wasted no time because she was ready for seconds. He thrusts into her for he feels so powerful. Their sweat mixes with the blood and flesh and he screws her even harder. He can't remember when he's had such a better time. As he gets close to coming, she can feel it and tells him to do it even harder. When he is spent, she lies next to him and caresses him to calm the animal in him.

"Sabula, is it true about Elsa and Nora?" Lyle asks.

"Yes, Elsa is joining Bruce in Hell for my people made sure of it when they shot her in the back of the head just like you did Bruce. Nora was not so lucky for they split her open like a banana and showed her the baby before they shot her. My people are ruthless sometimes. They do go overboard, but what a show they put on! Imagine watching **that** on the news! I guess Robert's reign will start early. Could it be a blessing?" They both laugh.

"You know, Sabula, I didn't think that it would be so easy to be so powerful. It makes me feel drunk."

"Good, Lyle. Enjoy the moment for it's just the beginning of what's to come. We have a lot to plan, for you are going to the states to bring Robert back here, and I will meet him. He has a lot to learn."

Father John asks again for Steven and Dale to return tomorrow because he is tired. As they are leaving, Steven asks him if they should return at the same time and he nods. Dale is flabbergasted so during the ride home he says nothing. They stop at the market and pick up a bottle of wine for dinner. While walking back to the car, Dale asks Steven if Father John is serious.

"Can this be true? When will it end? Steven, how do we fight it? Do we have the capabilities to defeat this monster? I don't know if I want to go back. What will I tell Lisa?"

"Let's face it, Dale, if we all feel the way that you do, then let's just wait for it to happen and die because that's how it going to be. We lose; he wins. That's it. On the other hand, we can ask God for his guidance and defeat this monster. It's possible that we can win. Dale, I'd rather die fighting than to just wait for it to happen." As we arrive he asks me not to bring up the subject in front of Lisa. I ask him if he will join me tomorrow at the same time.

"Will you let me know during the day? Call me. Dale, this is not going away, understand me? This is the real thing. Weren't you listening to Father John? He was being sincere with us."

"Steven, it's going to take more than just a handful of us, understand?"

"I hear you. We will recruit more men for the cause, but we will wait for Father John to tells us when."

Lisa is at the door with a big smile saying, "I was starting to wonder about you boys. Hurry; wash up for dinner." Steven went to the bathroom and washed up. Dale used the kitchen sink. Then they were seated and gave thanks to God for the meal. After awhile, it's like back to normal, and they are cutting up with Lisa. She is a wonderful person and a great cook. They finished eating and drinking the rest of the wine. Lisa was asked about the rugrats. She said they're spending the night at Mom's, for she has plans for Dale and gives him a big smile. Taking that as a clue to leave, Steven thanked them for having him over. He kissed Lisa goodbye and hugged Dale and told him he's a lucky guy. He smiles and says that Lisa has a sister that is available and is a good cook. Lisa says she will call her. She has mentioned his name over the years, and it's time they meet. She knows that her sister is also interested in meeting Steven because she has mentioned it before. For once, Steven didn't try to talk her out of it.

"Okay, Lisa, I well meet her but what is her name?"

"It's Penny."

"Do you have a picture of her?"

"Here, Steve, what do think?

"She does resemble Lisa. Her body style is the same and her smile is incredible."

"Make the date, matchmaker," Dale tells Lisa. Lisa responds that she will call Penny tomorrow so he should expect to hear from her.

"Steven, you will be coming back for dinner and Dale will tell you when, okay?"

"I am looking forward to meeting Penny. If she is anything like you, no problem," Steve says to Lisa.

"It doesn't get any better than this. I've met her and over the years she has a good sense of humor, and she fears God and loves her parents. She has been waiting for the right man. She is a firecracker. She has never been married. I asked Lisa why, and she says until she is ready she will not take that step because when it happens it will be for life. She will carry that cross to her death. She doesn't believe in divorce and neither do I," Lisa responds.

"Steven, my mom made it clear to us that we don't give up. We find solutions and continue to move forward. Ask Dale how many times over the years he wanted to give up, but we sat down, talked, and worked out our problems and here we are living by God's rules. If you are ready to take the next step, she is the one. Where you are weak she will help you, and the same goes for you. Do the same for my sister, and you will make a good team."

Rebecca

Driving home, Steven was wondering if this is fair to Penny. Should he be getting involved? She does look nice, and he had not been involved in a long time. He lost his honey Rebecca just before he cleaned up his act. He remembered getting home and finding her in bed with a syringe in her arm thinking that could be him. Looking into her eyes, he saw that they appeared empty, and she looked so cold that a shiver ran up his spine. He had wiped the foam from her mouth and closed her eyes. He wanted to clean her up, but then if he did they might have thought that he had a part in it. She was soiled and the stench was overwhelming. It took every bit of him to pick up the phone and call the police. He got rid of all the drugs and paraphernalia. He would always tell Becky that it was going to catch up to her, but she was in denial. She always responded that she had it under control saying that she could stop anytime. While Steven waited for the police to arrive, he remembered how they had met and that she was full of life and beauty.

They met at a lounge. She was twenty-three; he was twenty-five. They got into rock and roll. She made him feel invincible. He guesses the drugs didn't hurt. They dated for a few months, and they took the plunge and moved in together. She wasn't a good cook when they met, but she did improve. He helped her anyway he could. Becky was an orphan who never met her parents. Overall, she was a good person, but she didn't want anyone to touch her stuff unless she agreed because she would go on a rampage. She fought all her early life to keep her things, and so many times she ended up with a bloody mouth or nose to hold onto them. Mind you, she didn't seem the violent type, but over time in some close calls she saved his bacon. She would bite or grab whatever was close to her hands, be it a bottle or a glass, and use it with no remorse as a weapon. Steven had learned very quickly not to piss her off, but they got along well and rarely argued. Over time she did the same, allowing him to cool down, when he was pissed. One learns fast in a relationship what he can get away with and what he cannot. Steven guesses it's always better to ask and not to take the person for granted, which we often do by not having any consideration for the other person. For a couple of years they had gone out with friends to party. Their income amounted to Steven stealing and breaking into people's apartments. They had some close calls. When the alarms went off, and they often did because of the sophisticated alarm systems people had installed due to the rising crime rate, he was often barely able to get away. She never went into the building with him, for he feared something could happen to her especially when they were zoned out of their minds. The drugs, be it cocaine or pills, gave them the courage to do the deed. They were lucky to be alive.

Then over time, she started doing the needle. Steven didn't find out for a while because she was shooting up in her feet and would cover them up complaining about them being cold in the summer. Then, when they got to the point where they weren't showering together, he knew something was up and confronted her. She spilled the beans and said she had been turned on by this acquaintance they had who didn't turn out to be a friend. Steven then went to his house, beat the hell out of him, and told him that coming back to the area would not be beneficial to him. That was not the end of it. Becky was hooked and didn't want to go get clean even though Steven explained that it was having an effect on their relationship. She started to lose weight and gradually lost her hair. Recently, she had been complaining about her teeth hurting. He remembers her looking in the mirror and asking her if she liked what she saw. After awhile he knew when she needed her fix. The apartment would be upside down with broken dishes and dirty clothes everywhere, and she would be saying she wanted to die. He finally talked her into going into rehab. After many months she agreed. He told her that he would visit and bring whatever she needed when the staff allowed it.

She was all pumped up, seemed quite happy. He hadn't seen her this way for awhile. He thought maybe she was coming around. Steven had stopped getting high around her because he worried about her weight and health. He remembered the stroganoff dinner she made from scratch, her specialty, and how good it tasted. Since then, he had never really had a taste for it. They had major good sex that evening. He felt like she was back. She was even laughing. Over time her sex drive hit bottom. She was not interested anymore. She would say that she loved him but wasn't into the sex. She was only back to normal when she was under the influence and wanted to play. He didn't think that he would ever put up with this nonsense, but here he was taking it all in. When people are in love, they do stupid things and sometimes overlook negatives. At the end that's how it was with them. Steven did miss Becky but didn't miss the needle or the crap that followed. Yes, some called him chicken shit, but he was still there even after all these years. That wouldn't bring Becky back, but he did love her and would always have a soft spot for her. She never made it to rehab for the next day is when she overdosed. It sucked because he had been gone only for an hour fencing some things to get some money to hold them over. He had come home to find a needle stuck in her arm. Then the panic hit about how he could explain this to the cops. There would be questions, and they would want answers. He had lost his honey so close to getting her to rehab. That's the only thing that saved him from going to jail because it was he who had made the arrangements. When inquiries were made, they knew it was he who had been trying to help her and no charges were filed. They did, however, say they would keep an eye on him.

When Steven buried Becky, he promised he would quit doing drugs and had for many years with no regrets. "Thank you, Rebecca, for the time I had to live with you and the good times we had for we had more good than bad," he mumbled to himself. It has been sixteen years and he has not forgotten her birthday or the day she left this world. He has been with other woman over time but has not felt that special feeling. He guessed it was time to finally move on and close this chapter in his life. "I will not forget you," Steven said to the thin air. "Understand that I'm lonely and I need that comfort that I've been missing since you were here." Wiping the tears from his face, he arrived home. He didn't want to start a relationship feeling guilty but he needed to move on. Unlocking the door he suddenly felt this drain and just wanted to sleep until the following day when he would start a new life no matter what.

When Steven awakened in the morning, the news reporter was talking about the president taking steps to insure the public's well being. The vice president would fly to the Middle East to insure safety to the diplomats and to calm the people that were being affected by all the unrest. Meanwhile, the military was scrambling more drones to patrol the skies, for in my time it's rare to see a pilot. They are almost a thing of the past. The government has ratified that once the aircraft becomes obsolete, it will be mothballed and no further aircraft that are flown by man will be put into service. It's a different world that we live in and technology has evolved to the point where it's cheaper to build drones than to put human lives at risk. The American public is all for it because no longer are we losing lives to missiles that would lock in and go for the kill. Other countries still fight the old fashioned way and they pay the price. With today's technology it's hard to beat a drone versus a fighter pilot. It's no match. Drones are equipped with intelachips they pretty much fly on their own unlike when they were first introduced in the Gulf war. The intelachip was introduced in the campaign in Iran in 2015 and since then it's also evolved to the point where it's no longer necessary to have monitors. Just feed it the coordinates and it's off. It's that simple. It's so modern it can distinguish between enemy or friend in a matters of seconds. The majority of military aircraft have been mothballed for the last two years. Some will say that the only reason that Iran was beaten so badly and so quickly was because of the drone. That's when it was decided it was in the best interest of the American people to build on that technology. Now we are building unmanned vehicles and that's not all. They are being equipped with the intelachips from tanks to tankers to hummers. They say it's only the tip of the iceberg.

The military are contemplating submarines that will no longer need a crew. They will be able to stay under water for indefinite periods. Shipping lines are being looked into. They will be the next to implement the intelachip. We are relying too much on technology The people are buying all this crap. They justify it by saying they are saving human lives. Over the years there have been so many movies made about machines taking over. Wasn't anyone listening? It can happen even if it's not the machines waking up like in the movies. Nevertheless, one person or persons having too much power at their disposal can make a difference between life and death. The country is saving so much money that we can't see any further than the truth. Yes indeed, we become so blinded, so gullible, and so pathetic that we can't see the truth. Other countries still use humans to fight their battles but not us. We are saving human lives so we don't get the training that we once did. If we were to get invaded, what do you think would happen? It is like having a gun with no bullets. " Wait, let me load it"...like that's going to happen. That's my point. War is not good for anyone but it's a good policy to be ready at a moment's notice. The guy with the bigger stick usually wins, especially when he knows how to utilize it. That's why they practice. I hope that they find out who is responsible for the bombings. We have advanced so much since God created us, but we still can't live in peace. Steven needed to get ready to go to work, but it still bothers him that citizens accept anything that the government tells them without ever questioning it.

Having a typical day running up and down Manhattan and Central Park in his cab, Steven has a quiet morning. He called and reminded Dale that he would pick him up at two thirty. At noon he stopped and had a sandwich at Central Park. It's a nice July summer day where it's not too hot and there is a gentle breeze. It reminds him of how people take things for granted. With the sun charging our inner batteries, we are able to cope with the stress that we live in giving us hope for a better tomorrow. Think of what Father John will be telling us today. "Please, God, don't let the evil in this world. Win. This world still has a lot to offer. There are still good people that believe in you."

Steven was excited about meeting Penny for it's been some time since he'd been in a relationship. Now he was ready to start fresh. He finished eating and proceeded to his next fare to pick up a lady going to the Bronx. That should make for my last fare of the day. He was hearing on the radio that next year vehicles will start to be manufactured with batteries instead of gas engines. These engines finally have the technology to run all day without needing a charge. Batteries are affordable and the life span will be five years. Wow, it only took twenty years to make this a reality so next year he would probably be trading his cab in for one with a battery engine. He dropped the lady off and lucked out because his last fare was going back to Central Park where the garage is. He would call Dale and let him know that he would be there shortly.

Meanwhile, Steven talked to his fare about stocks and bonds. The man tells him there is a possibility that GE will merge with Boeing in the next couple of months. The merge will make the company the biggest military contractor in the western hemisphere. He needs to get on board but again must not mention it to anyone. Dean is a regular of his for many years. He tips well, and he knows that Steven is reliable. It was all because Steven waited for him a couple of hours to take care of some business. He was so appreciative that whenever he needed something out of the ordinary he would call Steven directly. That's how it is with people; one hand washes the other and both wash the face. It all comes back repeatedly. Arriving at Central Park, he thanked Dean and asked him to tell his honey hello. Dean says they need to go out for a drink sometime. It's been too long. His honey asks about Steven. They hit it off. Steven told him that they will go out soon and that he will call to let him know when. Driving to the garage, Steven was thinking what a nice guy Dean is. He didn't have to tell him because Steven already knew that Dean could get into trouble for letting him know. Steven decides to check into it. He'll tells Dale afterwards and tells him to keep it under wraps.

Dale is waiting for him when Steven arrives. Hopping in, they take off.

"Dale, are you ready to hear what Father John has to say today? He will tell us about Robert. Dale nods his head and asks if there is any way that he could be wrong. "I wish he were, but my heart believes it to be true."

"Why now? Wasn't this supposed to happen in the early twentieth century and it didn't. People prepared themselves. All the fanatics in the streets were preaching the end of times. Steven, they even had the year 2012 but it came and went. What makes you think that it's happening now?" Dale asked.

"Look around. See what's happening to the government: corruption, scams, scandals and all the unnecessary killings. Dale, we even clone people. We're playing God. It is not isolated anymore; it's worldwide. One extremist is killed and his clone appears. Then, he says it was his clone that was killed so who knows the truth anymore? A long time ago, they would say that we all had a twin. Now, it is not a twin but a clone.

"All of the hungry people here in our country are starving and nothing is being done to help them. Yet, look at all the aid that is being provided elsewhere. Dale, I do understand that they need help but how about the people here? Doesn't it make sense to help the people here first? One last thing, the news is all negative, nothing positive. When was the last time you heard something positive? Well, this is my point exactly. God is probably tired of us thinking we know more than Him. I fear that this is a wake up call. I'm worried but we can't run. Dale, I don't want to die."

Steven and Dale arrive. Father John is waiting at the door. He smiles and leads them into his study and asks not to be disturbed.

Education

Father John asks if they need anything before they start. He proceeds to tell them about Roberts's education and his training in the black arts. If there was ever a good person in Robert's body, it has been replaced with a ruthless, no-conscience individual. He will be taught to read people's minds and to manipulate them to the extreme. He will not have any remorse whatsoever, for evil is at hand. Humanity has been waiting for him for a long time. It's odd how people welcome evil. They think that they will benefit from it but no one does. People are disposed of when they are no longer needed, discarded like garbage, but what did you expect?

Lyle flies to the states to arrange to bring Elsa home to be buried with Bruce. Robert meets him at the airport. He is crying, and Lyle tells him that they are in a better place. Robert tells him that he is glad that he came, and he wants him to go to Nora's funeral for she was killed in such a bad way. Lyle understands telling him that arrangements are being made as they speak. He tells Robert how fond of Nora he was.

"She will be missed like your parents. We loved them. Robert, after the funeral we will stay here for a few days while they ship your mother. Then, we will join them in England and put them to rest."

"Uncle Lyle, who could have done such a thing to my mother and Aunt Nora? The police don't have any clues. They say the assailants even picked up the shell casings and so far there are no eyewitnesses."

"Do not worry, Robert. I will go to the station and inquire about the case and how it is proceeding. We will see justice. I promise you. Let's get started," urges Lyle.

They leave the airport and stop to get a bite to eat. After they go to the funeral home and Lyle talks to the director, he explains that he wants a special service for she was family. Lyle arranges to have Elsa transported to England, and the director tells him when she will arrive at the funeral home where Bruce is. Robert looks at him and thanks him. He doesn't have anyone else. He feels so alone having lost his parents.

"Don't worry, Robert," Lyle repeats. "I will take care of you. I will love you as my own son."

"Uncle Lyle, what happened to my dad? How did he die? Is it true he died in the fire and that the building collapsed on him and no one was able to rescue him? Is it also true that the funeral will be closed casket because he was burned so badly? Mother had said that he was to visit you. What was he doing in that building and where were you? They also said that the building was abandoned so how did it catch fire?"

"Robert, the gas in the building apparently was never turned off. Your father always enjoyed smoking. He didn't realize that there were fumes in the closed building. He was looking to acquire and to refurbish it before putting it on the market so that he could turn a good profit. I feel so bad because I was there and wasn't able to save my dear friend Bruce. I heard your father screaming and my hands were tied. The fire was so intense even after the fire department arrived that they had to let the fire burn itself out. There were small explosions from propane bottles that came alive with the fire. The commander would not risk another life even though I pleaded with him." Robert looks at his uncle and sees the tears. He hugs him hard and says that he understands.

"Robert, I've never had a better friend than your father. I loved him as a brother that I never had." By this time Lyle is all chocked up. It's hard to tell if he did feel guilt or remorse for what he had done. Hugging Robert, for an instance, he did feel bad for what he had done. He liked Bruce and Elsa. They had treated him like family. Sabula had told him to get close but not to get involved, but did he listen? Now, he is having second thoughts. He promises that he will take responsibility and that no harm will come to Robert. From this day forth Sabula will be in the picture, and he will be there watching for the first sign of trouble. He will take Robert and disappear because, after all, he is responsible for him. "I can't change what I've done, but maybe I can still save him. I'm truly sorry," he said to himself. They walk back to the car and Lyle tells Robert that when they go to England they will close the house and have someone watch it until they return.

On the way to the house Robert says that he wants to see Juan for he is worried about him. He has not heard from him since the killing. Lyle says that he will call him when they get home. He leaves a message for him to call back. Meanwhile, Lyle asks the staff to all gather in the study and regrets to inform them that their services are no longer needed, and the only ones that will stay on the payroll are the grounds keeper and one other person to keep up with the inside until they return or the house is sold. The women started to cry. He understands and tells them that they will get paid for three months' work. He will give all of them letters of recommendation, and if the situation were to ever change, he would call them back.

Robert goes to his room and calls Roger to tell him to come by. Roger says that he will be over in awhile. As Robert is waiting, he looks over his photo album and cries, for he's lost. Life will never be the same. This is the time in his life that his parents are needed the most to help with his decision-making. Why would any body in their right mind harm his mom or aunt? It's hard to believe that it was random. Is it just a coincidence that it happened on the same day his father died? Now he is packing and leaving all his friends behind. He is thinking that he is grateful to have his uncle, for he needs him more than ever before. He knew that his father would want him to go with Uncle Lyle, and that's what he was going to do. He decides that one day he will return and live in this house and will remember the love that his family had. If he is blessed with children, he will be a good parent and won't forget the way he was raised.

Roger arrives with tears in his eyes. They go back to his room, and Robert tells him that in the next few days he is leaving. He plans to stay in touch with Roger. Roger explains that his parents called and will be coming over in the evening to offer their condolences. They have already spoken to his uncle. They will be here at six o'clock to discuss Nora's funeral, for she didn't have any living family. Robert thinks again about Juan. He has not returned his calls. He worries about him explaining to Roger that since the killing no one has seen him. He hopes they will see him Wednesday at the funeral because Robert doesn't think that Juan will miss it, especially after not just losing Aunt Nora but also the baby.

"Lyle and I are leaving after the funeral. Please, Roger, tell everyone that I will miss them and that one day I will return to my home and start over," Robert instructs him.

Robert and Roger stay talking even after Roger's parents arrived, and they had stayed for a good while to talk. Mrs. Gant can be heard crying while the men comfort her saying that the Morgan's and Nora are in a better place.

"The baby, who could do that to a child? What is this world coming too when savages have no regard for life?" Mrs. Gant asks Lyle. "Have you any news about the killings, any leads?"

"No leads. They only left blood and everything else but no shell casings, no motive, not even a description of the vehicle that was used," Lyle replies.

The Gants leave at nine o'clock. We are exhausted. By the time they leave Uncle Lyle tells them that the funeral director called that evening before they arrived and said that they could put Nora to rest the day after tomorrow. The funeral would be in the morning after the mass. There would be no showing because of the condition of the body. The baby would be buried next to Nora.

It is a cold December morning when they arrive at the church and the Gnats are waiting for them. As they take a seat Robert looks around and there is Juan, who doesn't see him because they are behind him. Roberts tells Uncle Lyle that after the mass he wants to talk to Juan. There are only a few people but that's understandable because Aunt Nora was a private person. As soon as the mass and funeral ended, Robert walks over to Juan, and he can see the pain. This man is all broken up. Robert can tell he has shaved but his eyes lack sleep, and he looks so run down. Looking at him, Robert smiles and sees the tears in his eyes as they start to run down the side of his face. Robert loses it too crying with him and hugging him hard. They both stood there and just cried. No one approached. They let them be and when it was over, they felt the weight coming off their chests and breathed a sigh of relief. Now Robert felt that he could tell Juan that he needed to stay in touch. He says that he will be returning to South America, leaving in the next few days. He is selling his house and is not planning on returning, for not only did he lose his honey but also his son. Nora had just found out the day before that she was two months pregnant.

"Robert, I need to leave this place because there are too many bad memories. I will miss you. I will leave you my number. If you ever need anything, call me. I will be there for you, understand?" Juan asked. Robert introduced him to Uncle Lyle and told him how sorry he was for his loss. They talked for awhile and then said their goodbyes to the people. Robert told Roger to stay in touch and hugged Juan one last time. Robert and Lyle then left.

Driving to the airport, Robert felt better but now they had to go bury his parents, and he hoped to have the strength to do it. Uncle Lyle was quiet and distant. After they boarded and took off, Robert slept. He slept off and on dreaming of his parents at home eating dinner and having his father asking how his day had gone. In the dream his mother was looking at them and smiling but not talking. He told his father that he loved them and then woke due to turbulence. Uncle Lyle told him they would be arriving in about an hour. He read some magazines until their arrival. After they got their luggage, they went for a bite to eat and then went home.

"Robert, this is your home now so get used to the surroundings and staff, for they will provide you with whatever you need," Lyle tells him. Lyle tells his staff that whatever Robert needs should be made available to him. His staff is happy to see Robert. They feel so bad about his parents and about Nora. They knew Nora because she had visited with the Morgans over the years, and they all had liked her. Lyle tells him to get settled in that they will talk when he is done unpacking. Lily helps Robert unpack and tells him that anything that he needs will be provided so just let her know. Lily feels bad and Robert senses that he will ask her if he does indeed need something. She smiles and reminds him that Lyle is waiting for him in the study. Robert goes to the study. Lyle asks him to take a seat. They talk about house rules, and then Lyle tells him that tomorrow they well take a drive to the country to meet a woman. Robert never even asks why. He figures that Lyle has his reasons so he agrees. Lyle tells him the funeral will be Wednesday morning.

"Meanwhile, Robert, I will get you enrolled in school immediately the day after the funeral so that way you can start on Monday. We don't need you to get behind in your studies I promised your father that I would take care of you. I need to keep you busy. That should help you from becoming depressed. We cannot dwell on the past and we cannot change it. I don't mean to sound so cold, but one day you will understand. It's better this way for all of us to forget all the bad memories. We will make new ones, and you will be happy here, I promise you." Lily announces that the staff is ready to serve dinner. Lyle leads them to the dining area. They eat but Robert is not really hungry. Lyle senses that and says to eat what he can. Afterwards, Robert excuses himself and retires to his room.

Robert falls asleep and dreams about a beautiful woman. They are walking and she tells him that one day the world will fear him for who he is. Robert is trying to speak but cannot so he just listens, and she continues by saying that the good in the world will be a thing of the past. Evil has been waiting patiently but will be unleashed for all to see its true colors. No man or woman will be saved from this brute force. She says they will own the whole world, and God won't be able to save it this time. She tells him it is his time to lead; the destruction is nearing. She says she will prepare him in everyway for he is her seed; she is his mother. As they continue to walk, he notices that the colors and the beauty of the building behind them begin fading as they walk. The more they walk; the more it fades. Then he remembers the dream. He knows her and realizes who she is. She looks down at him, smiles, and confirms his suspicions.

"Yes, it's me, Sabula. I serve only one, and we both know him, don't we? Are you surprised that we are both created out of evil? It's in your blood. Have you forgotten why your dad had you help in the nursing homes and volunteer for several other church activities? They wanted to change you into something that you will never be, My Son, because that's not who you are. You are pure evil. Make no mistake that once the world finds out of your existence, some will try to destroy you.

"Therefore, I gather my troops and my pawns for the day draws near to battle. Forget the past for the future is yours, My Son, and when the time is right he will join us to rid the good finally for the last time. We shall rule for a thousand years, and no stone will be left unturned for all the good will be terminated. You won't forget this dream and in the near future, I will tell you something of most value to you concerning your father. Listen to Lyle for he will help and teach you things that you need to know concerning the government and how it's run. All the rest of your education will be me teaching you the art of evil and the art of retrieving souls to feed your needs. We have time now that you are here to polish your abilities to the maximum. You will not ever be afraid again. Remember, Robert, that a lot rides on your shoulders. Do not fail me for even you will pay the price. Like me, you have to answer to the dark one."

Robert and Sabula walk out to the terrace and see total destruction. She laughs and cries out loud that she has made this possible. New York City is in total chaos. Bodies are being burnt, and some are being dragged across the pavement until their limbs literally fall off. Buildings are on fire, and animals don't look like anything Robert has ever seen. The sky is a brown color, for there is no beauty here. Sabula says that evil needs no color for it feeds on flesh to survive, and the blood is all the color that is needed.

She says, "Look! New arrivals!" Robert sees white smoke, at first. Then the arrivals are turned into flesh. The men are branded with the beasts' mark. More troops arrive. The armies continue to grow as they speak. The men that refuse the mark are sacrificed, burned alive. The crowd that gathers applauds, dances, and asks for more bodies. They want bigger fires. Some are eating the burned flesh and laughing as they do. The smoke turns into women. It is a site to see. The women are then raped and eaten alive. What is left the animals consume. The women who manage to survive are turned into cannibals desiring flesh and bones. They drink the blood, fornicate, and scream for more. There is not one good thing in this place. Sabula calls this paradise. Robert feels sick to his stomach. She looks at him and tells him to get used to it, for this is evil at its best.

Hearing vehicles from a distance, Sabula smiles and says, "Aha! more troops. Robert, you made this possible, I mean, in the future. You had this idea that you got from watching a movie called *The Transformers,* and you made it into a reality. See how they change into different machines or how they connect to form a most valuable asset, for there is no escaping them?" She raises her hand. They connect and kill without mercy or remorse and continue to kill even more.

"Don't worry about the people. There are more where they came from. Some change to giant push movers like they had back in the day, and they chase the people down. As they run over them, the rear spits out the remains, and the blood turns the sky red.

Sabula laughs and says, "**There** is your color, Robert." He wants to turn away but can't. In some depraved way it's exciting and gives him a hard on. He looks at her, and she gets it saying, "This, My Son, is just the beginning. Enjoy for there is more to come. You will have it all. You will bathe in blood and from all the souls consumed, you will grow. You will thirst no more. Your hunger for women will be filled; no woman is able to resist you, including me. Welcome home!"

Waking from this dream, Roberts thinks it seemed so real. Never in his life had he experienced such a dream. It still was so vivid he could smell her perfume and was not scared anymore. He felt so confident and strong that he was hoping to dream of her again. He decided he would not mention it to Lyle from this day forth. He would remain Lyle's equal until he saw fit. Overnight, he had become a man with desires, and this would allow him to get what he wanted when he wanted it. No one would refuse him. He was thinking that he would learn all he could from Lyle, and then Lyle would serve him until he had no further use for him. Then Robert would discard him and take all that he has including his staff and proprieties. He wakes with hunger for knowledge will make Sabula proud and any good that was in him has been lost forevermore. Desire, power, wealth, and women, all that he can get my hands on, will be his. Then, he feels the burn from his hand. The sign is glowing. It makes him feel invincible. He remembers the way he felt running track and not feeling tired or playing basketball and not missing except when he chose to. Playing football and carrying the ball to the end zone, yes that's how he felt. Robert knew he would grow inside and out. People would not recognize him when he returned to the states, for he would rule mankind. If they chose to follow, fine. If they didn't, he would watch them die. He would create those vehicles from his dreams. He had a lot of planning to do and time to do it in.

Lily knocks on the door and tells Robert that breakfast will be served in one hour and he should get ready, for Lyle has the day already planned for them. After he showered, he joined Lyle for breakfast and little was said. Lyle told Robert to meet him in the car, for they are to meet a woman that he had spoken about. It's about a two-hour drive. He asks why Robert is so quiet. Robert answers that he has the funeral on his mind and says that he will be glad when it's over because then maybe he will be able to sleep better and move on. He jumped in the back seat and took a nap but he didn't dream. Lyle wakes him when they were nearing the woman's house. It's a big colonial home with iron gates, with four pillars, and flower arrangements at the bottom that complement the home. The lawn is well manicured. The home is painted white with black trim; it's nice. As they approach the front door, they smell sage but it's strange because there is none in sight. Lyle rings the doorbell and an old fellow, probably around seventy years of age, greets them. Robert wonders why he is still working at his age. The man looks at him with cold eyes. They are lead to Sabula's study and are asked if they need a drink. Lyle requests scotch and water and a cola for Robert. After he returns with the drinks a short time later, Sabula appears.

She looks elegant wearing a fire red dress that complements her flaming red hair, green eyes, olive skin, and full lips. She is beautiful. Robert feels a rise in his pants. Embarrassed, he tries not to seem overwhelmed for he's bewitched. He remembers what she said in his dream about them. He stands to shake her hand, and she senses that he's nervous. She smiles and says that she has that affect on men and women. Lyle looks at Robert and Robert sees a little jealousy in his eyes. It's odd, but Robert is not worrying about Lyle even though he is bigger than Robert, for Robert knows that he can put the hurt on him. Sabula takes Robert's hand and tells Lyle to leave them. He should return tomorrow in the early morning with a change of clothes for the funeral. He is not happy at all and when he approaches her, she backs away saying that he had his turn and that it's over. If he ever tries different, he will feel her wrath. She tells Lyle that it will be Robert sharing her bed.

"Get used to it. Do as I say for the rules have changed. You do as I say. You know better than anyone else what happens when I'm pissed. Now go!" As he is leaving, she reaches, grabs Robert's cock, and tells Lyle that no harm is to come to Robert, understand? He sees her stroking Robert who smiles at him as he turns and leaves.

Sabula knows what Robert wants. She takes him to her room and then he smells the sage again. She asks if he has ever been with another woman, and he tells her no. She giggles and says that she will have to make it extra special. She instructs him to undress and to lie down and wait for her to return. Robert does have an idea about sex but he's not quite sure. He has read the books, seen the pictures, and talked with friends but until a person has actually done it… well. Lying down he waits. She returns in a red, see-through gown. He can see her big aloes and hard nipples and hairy pussy. She is hot and so is he. She does a dance before she climbs into bed. She gets under the covers and tells him to relax and let her do the work, for they have all day and night to get it right. She is so soft and as she goes down on him. She doesn't stop until he comes in her mouth. She smiles as she swallows. He never had the faintest idea that sex could feel so good. Now, he wanted her even more. She told him to rest for today was for him, but later she would teach him how to please her in everyway. She told him that she requires a lot of attention; her body needs a lot of care. From the way that she moved and cried when he rode her, Robert understood. Therefore, he screwed her even harder and she begged him not to stop. When she did come, her juices overflowed and her body was shaking with spasms. At first, he thought he had broken her. After he realized what had happened, he understood. For the rest of the evening, that's all they did, and he loved it. Now, he knew why Lyle was jealous.

Sabula afterwards explained that one day Robert would be president of the United States. Then their pawns would set the gears in motion, and they would begin the end of mankind as people now knew it. She told him to learn all that he could from Lyle, for one day his services would no longer be needed. Lyle would be disposed of like the rest of them.

"Robert, we will promise them whatever they want to hear, understand? Then once we obtain what we need, you know how it is. We don't keep promises. Who do they think we are? When can anyone honesty say that we have kept a promise? They are not dealing with God. We do a contract, and people had better read the small print for their own sake. Robert, in all the time I've been around, people don't ever really 'get it your way' like the McDonald's phrase. We don't work that way. People are so gullible they believe anything anyone says. Remember the dream, the souls that you saw? Well, that's what I mean. They buy what I'm selling, and then I take their souls and they belong to me. Over the years I've had my share of complaints from pharaohs to assholes. It's all the same to me, but they signed, and it's all over but the crying. Catching one right after the other and this is nothing, for in your day the numbers are going to be astronomical. Robert, by the time you're president hope will almost be nonexistent. You might have a few stragglers, but it won't make a difference for the majority will be easy pickings. Robert, do you prefer to stay here with me and have Lyle come here to teach you?"

"Yes, I want to stay, but I had my eye on Lily. Have Lyle bring her to me after the funeral. Then, we can share her until she breaks." They both laugh and she tells him that he is a fast learner. He hugs her, turns her over, and takes her from the rear. She loves it. She cries as he is coming in her ass and says that they will do Lily even better for both will have their way with her. They lie side by side. She says that Lyle won't be happy with the news, especially about losing poor Lily. They laugh again.

Sabula looks at Robert and says, "You are evil."

He replies, "Get used to it for the apple doesn't fall too far from the tree." Tears run down the side of their faces as they laugh. She tells him that he will be fun to have around. He smacks her ass and says to order something to eat for he is famished. Afterwards, they sleep in each other's arms, and for the first time in many months, he sleeps well. They both do because the plan has begun and there's no stopping them.

Lyle leaves. He is so pissed that he would kill that kid if it were up to him, and he would take his time just to make him suffer. All the way home he thinks of different ways of killing Robert. Then right before the end, he would tell him about his father… how he met his death, how he screwed Sabula over his dead body after he shot him in the back of the head, and how he had even kicked him when he was down, literally. If he ever even looked at him the wrong way, he could have an accident that could not be helped. If Lyle ever had the notion to save him, he could just forget that because that would not ever happen after what he had done. How dare Robert interfere! Lyle figured that since he was there Sabula would make some time for him like in the past. That little bastard was taking what's his and Lyle didn't like it. Had he known, he would've never left the states alive. Lyle vows that he will have the last laugh, for they will pay in due time. Lyle arrives home and asks not to be disturbed. He goes to his study, pours himself a drink, and continues until the phone rings. Lily says it's Sabula so Lyle takes the call. By the time he hung up the phone, he was furious. He called Lily to his study and asked her to prepare his and Robert's clothes for the funeral, for he will have to leave early to pick up Robert and Sabula. Then once again he asks not to be disturbed, and he drinks himself to sleep.

Lily wakes Lyle at four in the morning, and he is not happy, but he must obey for he has his reasons. Lily brings him some coffee and sets it on the night stand and leaves. While he is showering, she prepares him an English muffin and a egg. She times it just right. He smiles and tells her that he wouldn't know what to do without her, for he has grown very fond of her lately. She seems extra special not just in looks but the way she handles herself. She is a very positive woman. It does surprise him that she has no fellow that he knows of. The brat won't be living here so maybe he should reconsider having a relationship with Lily, for she does understand him like no other woman that he has met. He thanks Lily and even gives her a hug that catches her off guard. For the first time she sees him not as a boss but as a mate. He tells her that when he returns they will talk and not about shop. She is so excited for deep down she has been waiting to hear these words for a very long time.

Lily came to work at the age of eighteen just as soon as she was able to leave the orphanage. She had spent most of her life there. After she was abandoned at the age of seven, she grew up fast and spent most of her free time reading. It was her escape. The other kids would tease her. It didn't matter, for she continued to read and fantasize about living in a home that was hers where she no longer had to share her bedroom or bathroom. One day she would be the one setting the rules. Then, she would dress the way she wanted and not have a dress code, not that she was complaining. There were a lot of people that were worse off. She understood that. She lucked out when she came to work here. All Lyle had asked was that she didn't steal from him, and if given a task to do, do it to the best of her knowledge. If unsure about the task, she was just to ask Lyle always. He said that it was cheaper than to waste money and time. Over the years this house became her responsibility. Lyle enjoyed that she took her time and did what was needed even before he asked. Now, she didn't have to worry about sharing a room. There was plenty of space with five bedrooms. This house is big at seven thousand square feet. Most important is that over the years she has moved up the ladder. With his older staff retiring now, she gives the orders and is nice about it. One cannot forget the past but can improve the future, and she's proof that it can be done.

Lily has been employed there since 1970 and now it is 1988. She's thirty- six years old and has no kids. This had been her choice after living in the orphanage. She figured that she wasn't cut out for kids because it would not be fair to them. Kids require a lot of attention and patience, something that she doesn't have. She loved them but having none was her choice. She was happy to work for Lyle, and now her dream might become a reality if that is what Lyle has in mind. She would tell the staff to make an extra special meal, a candle-light dinner with all the works. She planned to dress up and apply just a little makeup, for it's rare when she uses make-up. Lily is not used to wearing tight clothes. She hides her body even though she works out and does have a nice body. She has a nice derriere to complement her long legs. She is five feet eight and weighs one hundred twenty-five pounds. She has nice firm breasts, thirty-four B-cup. If Lyle wants her, she will make him a good mate for she has eyes only for him. Over the years Lily has had her share of admirers, but no one she considered pursuing. Now, finally, her dream is coming true. For the rest of the morning she is in heaven.

Lyle leaves to pick up Sabula and Robert. On the way down, he remembers what he said to Lily. He smiles to himself and thinks, "Wow, I not only caught **her** off guard but also **myself** for it just happened. It was not planned but now I'm happy I did it. I'll stop and buy her some flowers and a box of chocolates. She will like that and then we will talk about the future. If Lily agrees, we can leave this place with the wealth that I've amassed over the years. It will be sufficient to last us a lifetime. We will disappear, for I have grown tired of all this. We'll get new identities and passports; then we can surely disappear."

Lyle sees the house from a distance and his mood changes. He vows that he will get through the day and will not let them get to him. He has his agenda and they have theirs. He parks and takes Robert's suit with him. It's a black suit with black shoes, black tie, and white shirt. He rings the doorbell and the old man opens the door and leads him to the room where Robert is waiting. Robert has a big grin and tells him to lay the suit on the bed, for he will be out shortly after he showers. Lyle goes to the parlor and waits. Sabula appears dressed in black looking as beautiful as ever. She asks him how things are going.

"Fine, here I am to take you to the funeral. Afterwards, I've made plans and won't be available for a couple of days. Sorry, but something came up that requires my undivided attention. I won't be able to start Robert's schooling but as soon as I return I will take care of it," Lyle responds.

"Don't worry. We have time. By the way, Robert has requested that you bring Lily here. Since we have time, we will use her as our playmate. Robert has an interest in her. We can't deny him. I also find her interesting. I want to explore her body with Robert. Just last night he was saying that we could possibly break her, but that really doesn't matter. She can be replaced. You don't mind do you, Lyle? It's all new for the boy. Robert's hunger is almost overwhelming. She touches her pussy and says it's sore." She goes on to explain that Robert wouldn't let her sleep last night and this morning she woke with his cock working in her mouth, and she still could taste him. "Lyle, you were good but Robert is fantastic. I need some help. Now that he's been introduced to the opposite sex, he desires even more. I'm afraid that for awhile he will be this way until he quenches his thirst for pussy and ass. After the funeral let's pick up Lily and bring her here. We will do the rest." She smiles, "That well keep us busy until you return."

Lyle is dumbfounded. What should he do or say? Should he admit that he has in interest in her? Will they understand? Could he suggest someone else for there are many women that he could bring here under false pretense? Lyle takes a chance and says that there is a woman that is ideal for them. They can break her. Then he would be more than happy to get rid of her.

"Sabula, I will call her right now. That way she will be ready for you and Robert. In the meantime I can find a replacement for Lily. You know how important she is to me. Please, I need a couple of days to replace her." Sabula agrees to it and says the woman he calls better be good, for Robert will not be happy as he had his heart set on Lily. Sabula comments that she doesn't want to disappoint him, for one day in the near future he will be their master. She reminds him that he only has a week so don't let her down.

Robert enters the room, and Lyle says that he will be waiting in the car. Sabula explains to Robert about Lily, and Robert is pissed. She tells him that in a week they will have their way. Lyle is bringing a replacement they can play with. They will have to make her last a week if he agrees. "Don't look so blue," Sabula says, "I did say that you would learn to please me, and now with her help she can teach you how to please a woman. Practice, Robert, that's what we will do. Lyle did say that she is a fox." Robert smiles as they walk to the car to go to the church and then to the funeral. The priest notices that of the relatives that were there, not one shed a tear for the departed, not even her son. If anything, he could not understand why the giggles of all places. The priest was happy when it was over. He was the first to leave. He had never experienced anything like this before in his thirty years of service. Right after the service, Lyle, Robert, and Sabula went to get a bite to eat. They asked Lyle to call the woman, for all this had made them horny. Lyle ordered them a drink before he made the call.

Lyle excused himself and called Cindy. She was about thirty years old and was a blond. She enjoyed fucking and sucking but she liked her drink first to loosen up. He told her to get ready for they were going to party like no tomorrow. She was surprised to hear from him because the last time she sensed that she had pissed him off but could not remember how. She had been a little wasted. It had been three months ago. Maybe he had forgotten by now. Either way, she was happy to hear from him. He did know how to wine and dine a woman. Lyle told her to put on her dancing shoes and that black dress he bought her. He would pick her up at five in the evening so she should be ready because they would be having some friends joining them. Cindy was thinking that's not how it normally goes. He usually just says to be ready at five and he hangs up. Now she would have to do her hair, for she likes to make a good impression. Lyle is a unique individual. This time she wouldn't make a fool out of herself. That way Lyle would keep calling her. This time Lyle could do whatever he wants including her ass. "I'm going to make it special and won't screw it up this time. I miss Lyle and miss the way he makes me feel," she thought to herself. She still had plenty of time to get ready.

Lyle went back to the table and told them that it was set for five. They will like her. She will be happy to meet them, and she's a lot of fun. Robert asked if she is good in bed.

"Yes, she is good for the whole night and is not afraid to try different things," Lyle comments. Robert says that he cannot wait to meet her, and they both agree. Lyle looks at his watch. It's only noon; they have five hours.

"Maybe I can use this to my advantage," Lyle thinks as he orders a bottle of their best champagne, and they start to drink. I know that Robert is not used to drinking, but Sabula is another story. She can hold her own. Lyle suggests that while they wait, they play a game that involves shots. "Are you up to it?" he asks them.

"What's the game, Lyle?"

"It's trivia, a little history, a little science. They are excited. They begin the game and for the next couple of hours they play. Sabula gets stumped a couple of times and they laugh. Robert is not too far behind. Lyle looks at his watch. It's three o'clock, and they are pretty wasted. Then he makes his move.

"Robert, you drink like a pro," Lyle begins. Robert looks at him with his blood shot eyes and says that he can get used to this in no time. "Robert, I sense that in no time you will be teaching me. " I'm an old man and don't want to slow you down in any way."

"Yes, Lyle, you are old indeed, but you are useful to the cause. I will learn all that you teach me, for Sabula says that you are the best when it comes to finances, even better than my father."

"Sabula knows that we've never been in a better position than we are now. We have the means. When it's time, we will have even more. I ask that you grant me a favor, for I grow tired and have been thinking of the future. I've never been married, don't have any heirs, and am asking if it would be possible for me to take Lily as my wife. We have been seeing each other in secret for some time. I love her and would not ask for anything else but your blessing," Lyle says.

Sabula is the first to answer. "You sly fox, I have never taken you as the marrying type. Why now, Lyle?"

"We've been waiting for the right moment. We would like it if Robert were the best man. We would feel privileged if you would be the maid of honor. We thought of just having a small wedding. I ask for your blessing."

Robert says that he would be honored to be Lyle's best man. Sabula agrees and asks when they plan to marry.

"Soon, very soon. That's why I need to go to London to buy a wedding ring. Would you care to accompany me? It would make it even more special if both of you were to join me?" Sabula orders another bottle of champagne. They drink and Lyle feels relieved for now. He needs to break the news to Lily. Robert says that Cindy better be good now that Lily is out of the picture. She will have to do until they find a replacement for Lily. They finish the champagne and leave to pick up Cindy.

Cindy is ready and waiting when they arrive. Lyle introduces them to her and they leave to go to a club. She is happy to see him and tells him that they have some history. It's been awhile since they were out, but she's been looking forward to it. At the club, they drink and dance and have a good time. Lyle feels sorry because he knows what awaits her. Maybe it won't be so bad. Robert seems to be having a good time. Sabula is not complaining either. They both dance with her and when they sit, they have her in the middle. Cindy looks at Lyle and says that she was supposed to be his date. Lyle replies that it's all good because they are all friend here so not to worry. There is always next time. Tonight is special because Robert just arrived from the states and this is his first time out. Lyle told her that he would really appreciate if she understands. Robert calms her down, and then shortly afterwards they start to work on her. Robert is horny and Sabula is not far behind.

Once they make their move, hands start to disappear and Lyle suggests that maybe they would be more comfortable at home. Smiling, they agree. On the way to the house they work on her in the back seat. The moans can be heard. Then they undress her. She looks at Lyle in the mirror and he pretends not to see. Robert has her go down on him while Sabula is right next to her joining her at taking turns on Robert. Sabula's fingers disappear between Cindy's legs, and she moans with delight. Meanwhile, she is working on Robert until you hear as he comes in her mouth. Then Sabula goes down on her, and she tells Robert to pay attention. He will be joining Cindy after she comes in her mouth. Cindy explodes, shaking with uncontrolled spasms. Sweating, Sabula kisses her. Then Sabula hikes up her dress and tells them that it's feeding time. Cindy's never been with another woman; however, is eager to please. Robert joins Cindy. They both go to work on Sabula's legs which are spread as wide as possible. Cindy goes first and is amazed at how soon she had Sabula coming. Robert is watching and playing with Sabula's breast. Then it's Robert's turn. As he goes down, Cindy and Sabula kiss. Sabula keeps Robert's mouth busy and every time he tries to change with Cindy, she says no for he will get his first feeding. After awhile, Sabula starts to shake. She is close. She gets Robert by the hair, guides him to her sweet spot, and then shakes even more. As she is coming, she moans with pleasure and tells him not to stop for she is feeding him, and Robert is trying to keep up with her. Understanding now what he is doing, he feeds with pleasure until she tells him to stop for she is so sensitive. Now he doesn't want too. He wants to see what more he can do to her. Then he slips a finger up her ass. She explodes again and then they sleep for the rest of the ride home.

Looking at the rear view mirror, Lyle see that Cindy will fit right in and he doesn't feel so bad. He wakes them as they near the home. They are still naked. Lyle is glad he has tinted windows. These people are so bad they say the hell with the clothes. They walk naked straight to the bedroom of the house. Lyle tells them not to worry about tomorrow, and they understand.

He tells Cindy that Robert and Sabula will provide transportation, and she asks, "Are you not joining us? What happened to our date?" Lyle tells her that he has some pending obligations and must leave but she is in good hands. He assures her that they will take good care of her. Sabula's gives him a kiss tells him good-bye and not to worry about Cindy because they will take care of her in many ways. Lyle tells Sabula that he will be back in a week, and as soon as he returns, they will begin Robert's education.

On the drive home he thinks of Lily. Even if they get married will she be safe? Lyle decided he would make plans for the near future because once he's no longer needed, Robert and Sabula will get rid of him just like they did Rasime. His death was no accident. They knew where the munitions were being placed. Sabula called it collateral damage; Lyle called it getting even. He feels that he does have time to help Robert. Robert still is young but needs to prepare for the future, just in case. The world is evil and they will try to eat him up. Robert seems so sincere about Lyle getting married and that's good. Lyle will keep them happy for as long as possible. He will transfer his funds to Cayman Islands and get new passports and all that he thinks they will need for their disappearing act when the time comes. He will talk Lily into getting plastic surgery when the time is right. He realizes that they will have to be careful burning all the paperwork to eliminate the paper trail as they move along. He doesn't think it should be too hard since that they don't really have relatives. If Lily loves him the way he thinks she does, they will make the best of it. What counts is being together and getting away from all this madness, for I fear it will get worse for humanity. They don't have a clue at what's in store for them. It feels good to be getting home. He will put his plans into motion tomorrow but for now he wants to see Lily.

He opens the door and there she is with a big smile asking if there is anything that he needs. He can't believe her. It's three in the morning and she is fresh as a daisy. He smiles at her and then she hugs him. Lily asks if he's hungry.

"Yes I am, but would like to take a quick shower. Lily tells him that's no problem because the food will be ready by the time he's done. She also tells him that she will have his clothes ready. He thanks her and goes to shower thinking that he should have done this so long ago instead of taking her for granted and not seeing her for who she really is. Lyle vows he will make it up to her by being a good husband. After finishing his shower, he approaches the table to find a cup of coffee. Sipping his coffee as he dresses, he then makes his way to the kitchen where she is waiting. There are eggs, bacon, and toast on the table. For one of the few times she joins him. It's still early so they have the kitchen to themselves.

After awhile, he asks her about the two of them. She says that she enjoys working here even after eighteen years. He looks into her eyes and asks if she has any feelings towards him and she says, "Yes." He takes her hands and says that he has never been married. Then he asks if she would do him the honor of marrying him. A tear rolls down her face and she says that she would love to marry him any day of the week. They stand and he kisses her for the very first time. It feels so natural. It's odd, but then he thinks how good it feels to have her in his arms. She tells him that she had planned a special evening but was a little disappointed when he called saying he would be in late. She told the staff that there was always tomorrow. Now, Lyle gets the surprise of his life.

"Lyle, I have loved you for a very long time. My dream has come true. I will make you happy in all aspects of life. You will not want or need from this day forth," Lily tells him.

"Lily, I feel the same for you. Today I buy you a ring, and while I'm gone, start planning on a small wedding for the best will be our honeymoon," he told her.

"Lyle, would you enjoy having a Valentine's Day wedding? Tell me what you think."

"Excellent," he responds. After kissing her, he leaves for town.

Lyle went to the bank to make arrangements dividing his fortune between an account in the Cayman Islands and one in the Swiss bank. Then he went to his connection for passports and credentials, for he has all of Lily's information. His connection assured him that he will have all that has been requested in a couple of days. Lyle is to pay half upfront and the rest when he returns in three days, according to his connection. Lyle then goes to the jewelry store. The owners are happy to see him for he has been a regular costumer for many years. Then Lyle sees the ring that will represent his love, and sizes it the same as the ring that he had borrowed from Lily. He stops to buy some flowers and chocolates.

Returning home, he feels hope for their future. Lily is surprised when she sees the flowers and chocolates. She hugs him. The staff is happy for them saying that they make such a nice couple. She tells Lyle that she has started to make calls concerning their wedding. The church has agreed to squeeze them in. Lyle has made large contributions over the years. He has helped pay for the wing when they ran out of money so they were able to open on time. They were also very grateful because the children who were being relocated would have beds and a roof over their heads. Lyle never having kids still had a soft spot for them. He remembers growing up and wanting, but not being able to have, even the basics for most of his childhood. Feeling alienated from the rest of the kids, he made himself a promise that if he were ever able to help he would, and he was blessed to be able to give to the needy and the less fortunate. He explaines to her that Robert will be the best man and Sabula will be the bridesmaid. Lily agrees for she has met Sabula over the years, and she got along with her. Lyle tells her that he mentioned to Robert and Sabula that Lily and he had been seeing each other for awhile. He tells her he has his reasons, and if they were to ever ask her, please support what he was telling them. The only reason he gave Lily was that he didn't want it to seem like he was desperate. He asked her to please just say that it's been about three months. Lyle just decided it was the right time to make the first move, which he did. Lily says that it's no problem for she really doesn't care, and what matters is that she loves him and that it's mutual. The rest of the day is spent planning the wedding. She has some women on the staff helping her. That gives Lyle a chance to take care of some loose ends. He enrolls Robert in school telling them that he will start in two weeks. He asks the school to be understanding of Robert because he has just lost both of his parents. It's been really hard on him. The school personnel understand and feel so bad. They say they will make him feel comfortable. Lyle suggests that they don't bring up the subject and they agree. After paying his tuition for the rest of the year, Lyle buys all his supplies. Lyle is even given a tour of the school and he thinks it's unreal how big it is.

Saturday Lyle picks up the passports. Paying the man, he checks to make sure they're in order before leaving.

The man mildly protests, "What, you don't trust me?"

Lyle looks at him and smiles, "Just keeping you honest," and when he returns home, he'll put the paperwork away in his safe. Lyle also includes a letter to Lily with instructions in case something were to happen to him she would be able to get out with a moment's notice. Lyle realizes that he will have to cover all bases because the future is not set, and the day can come along when he wishes he had taken the necessary steps to insure Lily's safety. He hoped that day would never happen, but just in case, Lily can survive and move forward even if it means that he doesn't make it out alive.

He closes the safe and stares at it. Then it hits him about what he had done to Bruce and how he had betrayed his brother. Now, he must deal with the consequences. He will indeed pay because one day it will all come out, and Sabula will make sure that Robert is told only what benefits **her.** That's how it works. He was a fool to believe her. Look what happened to Rasime, taken out without remorse. Lyle knows he's more valuable, but by the same token, he knows he can and will be replaced. For now he follows orders and watches and listens for the first sign of trouble.

"Bruce, please forgive me. Greed has its own reasoning. Money makes you do things that you would normally not do. Promises were made. Mine in particular was made long before I met you. I never thought we would be so close. It was not to happen like this," Lyle thought to himself as the tears ran down his face. He cried like a child, and the tears didn't stop. He continued, "Why didn't I warn you? I had the time to do so, but I didn't," and he cried harder then. "How about Elsa and Nora and the baby? It is despicable the way they were killed in broad daylight, the way they butchered Nora, and the agony that she must have felt knowing that it was not only she who was being killed but also her baby who had no sins. She was only an innocent mother with child who wanted to provide a future and a loving home for her family. She never had the chance. I will never be able to forget the look on Juan's face, the emptiness. I took all that away from him, his future happiness. Please forgive me for I was blinded. I promise not to ever let that happen again. God, I ask you to forgive me I know that in the end I will have to answer to you about what I did, and what I failed to do. Please don't let them hurt Lily or take their revenge on her. I know when I die I will be going to join the rest of the evil doers, but I deserve it, all of it. For now, I will be the best person that I can from being a good husband to advising Robert about doing the right thing. Maybe I can make a difference in his life. I will try to have patience with him. The effort will be made. I owe that much to Bruce and Elsa."

The week flew by and Lyle returned to Sabula's home on Wednesday where they were waiting for him. Lyle asks Robert where Cindy is. He smiles and says that she is taking a shower. She has been taking a beating from both of them. Sabula is happy with her and they plan to move her in. She is a keeper, very resourceful, and they like that.

"Tell Robert that I enrolled him in the high school, and he starts in two weeks."

Robert is pleased and asks what changed Lyle's mind about his taking a break. Lyle tells him that he deserves it. Then, Sabula asks about Lily. Lyle tells her that she is fine and that he has asked her to marry him. They are planning a Valentine's wedding and asks if he still can count on them.

"Lily will need you to join her in getting sized for the dresses, and Robert will join me to do the same with the tuxedos. Plan on going this Saturday morning. We can meet with the tailor; from there the women can go to the seamstress." Sabula asks if they can include Cindy as a bridesmaid.

"Sure, why not?" he hastily responds.

"You know, Lyle, I think that Cindy has a thing for you," Sabula comments.

Lyle responds, "They all do." Everybody laughs and it is settled that they will meet at ten in the morning so not to be late.

That's when Cindy appears. She looks good, even better than the last time he saw her. Even her bottom looks good. It has more of a shape to it, a nice curve. Wow! He tries not to stare because he doesn't know what they did, but it's clearly an improvement. She gives him a big hug and kiss, and Robert tells her that Lyle is spoken for and she asks if it's true.

"Yes, but I will always care for you regardless," he assures her. She says that she is happy for him and asks who the lucky girl is. He tells her that it's Lily.

She is surprised. "Lyle, she is a nobody. Isn't she your maid?"

"Well no, she has been my assistant for many years. She is not the maid but the person in charge when I'm not there. "

"When I was at your place, isn't she the one that took my wrap and told us that dinner was ready? Cindy asked.

"Cindy, she did that because she wanted to, not because she had too. The important thing is that we are getting married. I'm asking if you would like to join us." She looks at Robert and Sabula and asks them if they are going. They answer yes.

"Ok, but I still can't believe that you are marrying the maid. You know in my eyes that's all that she will ever be, but I guess that's your choice. Wasn't she adopted or raised in an orphanage? How you manage to degrade yourself by not marrying someone of your stature is beyond me," Cindy concluded.

Lyle felt like slapping the shit out of her. What made her so special? Had it not been for him, she would still be in her apartment hoping that the phone would ring. Talk about being ungrateful, but that's fine. "When they're tired of you, they will cash you in. I hope that you're still alive," Lyle thought. Cindy walks to Robert, sits by him, rubs his manhood, and says that Robert is her man and Sabula is her woman. Thanks to me she has the best of both worlds which she plans to keep, which is good for her. Lyle is thinking that she just better not be fucking with him because she'll never be in the same category as Lily. "You will always be trash. That's where I found you, and that's where you will return in the end," he thought.

Sabula gave him that smile. Lyle knew the look. He told them not to forget about Saturday at ten and not to be late. As he leaves, Sabula walks him to the door and says that she will have to teach Cindy some manners. She regrets to inform Lyle that Cindy won't be making it to the wedding. He didn't even try to defend her after what she had said. Her mouth got her back into trouble once more, so be it. Sabula gives Lyle a kiss and squeezes his butt. As he is walking away, she says he still has a nice butt for an old man and Lyle smiles. Robert tells Lyle that he won't be late. Lyle says thanks and reminds him not to forget about school starting in two weeks. The supplies are on the table. With that final comment Lyle leaves.

Sabula turns to Robert and says they have a problem. Robert asks what it is. "It's not you, my love, but the tramp that is here. I've never been so embarrassed in my life. You come into my house, and then you are disrespectful to my guest and you think it's okay. Bitch, I will teach you to be respectful of my quests. Robert take her downstairs. Sabula calls the old man to prepare her table, for we have need of it. She pours herself a strong drink before she joins them. As they make their way downstairs, Cindy pleads with Robert to let her go. Robert has not been in this part of the house. As he turns on the light switch, he is amazed at what he sees. Sabula has cages of snakes, spiders, and things that he has never seen before. She struggles to get loose but Robert will not have any of it. Now, he is intrigued as to what Sabula has in store for her. He lays her down on a table and straps her in. By this time Cindy is hysterical, pleading with him. She says again that she is sorry that her mouth got her into trouble. When will she learn?

"Robert, I didn't mean anything. I was just jealous. I was kidding, no pun intended. I was caught off guard. I thought it would be me marrying Lyle. He always seemed so interested in me so I was surprised when he left me here, but then it turned out for the best. Please talk to Sabula. I will do whatever you ask of me, just don't let her hurt me. I love you both. I will change. You will see. I will not ever do that again. Please, Robert, help me convince her. You can if you desire. I will take care of you. Don't you want me? I will stay here for as long as you want. There is nothing that I won't do for either of you. Please give me a chance," she pleaded.

Then they hear Sabula making her way down the stairs. She asks Robert if she is tied to the table. Then the old man appears with a silly grin. Robert moves away from the table, and the old man rips her blouse open, then her skirt. Her panties are next and her bra. The old man even pinches her nipples, and then moves away from the table.

Sabula says," You don't have manners but that is the least of your troubles for you will feel pain like you have never experienced it before." Then she takes out her tools and tells Robert to pay attention for he is to help her to induce pain. "Take this and brace her head to the table." Cindy will no longer be pretty. Once she is strapped, Sabula unleashes hell on her. Sabula spares no pain. Her pets are also used. Sabula is very creative when it comes to pain, for she as been around for many years. As she strips her flesh from her thighs with her scalpel, she feeds it to her pets, and Cindy cries in agony. Then she cuts off one of her breasts and shows it to her before feeding it to her pets. Then, she removes an eyeball. The blood gushes from her eye socket and the screams that follow are deafening to the ear. Sabula spares no pain. It is like she is possessed. Her eyes grow dark and her hair glows blood red. The more she inflicts pain, the darker she becomes. Robert has never realized that evil was so intense, but at the same time it excites him. Sabula enjoys what she is doing. Robert can't understand why he wants to see more, and he asks her to inflict more pain for his pleasure. She looks at him and tells him that he will taste his first of many souls. It will help him to grow and once he has tasted it, he will crave for more and he will not be denied. She then spreads Cindy's legs as wide as she can and straps them to the table. She opens up her pussy with an instrument. Then her pet snake goes to work sliding into her. By this time, the old man stuffs her mouth with a ball to drown the cries. Poor Cindy, she will not be coming out of this in one piece. Not only does her body but also her soul belong to them. Robert remembers the white smoke.

"Watch as I take her soul and give you the taste of a dying life. Enjoy the moment for this is the first of many to come," Sabula tells Robert.

It's ironic that in all this time Cindy has never asked God for His forgiveness. Maybe then her soul would have been saved, but because she didn't ask, she would be joining the rest like herself that have no faith in God. It's sad that even in the end she refuses to accept the free choice that was given to Mankind: take my flesh but my soul belongs to God. In the end she was discarded like trash. Someday maybe people will wake up to the truth that evil is evil and that won't ever change. Remember it's all empty promises, for once they get what they want they will also be joining the trash. As Cindy takes her last breath, Sabula tells Robert to get close to her mouth and feel the sensation. Absorb her soul. Take it all. As the soul enters his body, Robert feels the need to puke and Sabula tells him that it will pass so don't stop taking it in. As the last of her soul is ingested, Robert stands up straight. For the first time in his life, his eyes are turned blood red, and he feels how they burn, not with pain but with power. He turns to Sabula and says that he understands now for evil is great and powerful, and he looks forward to more feedings. They tell the old man to leave them, and Sabula goes to work on Robert with the blood mixing with the sweat. They stay there for most of the day. Then while they drink her blood and kiss, the blood runs down their cheeks. They laugh and marvel at the body at how in so little time it was changed to the point that nobody could tell it had been Cindy.

All the while Roberts's eyes were still burning, but it's ironic that he is still able to see and even better than before. The sign on his left hand also burns to the point where he can touch the flame, but it doesn't bother him in any way.

"Sabula, I like what I'm becoming. My dreams will come true. With your help, they will manifest into reality, and you will serve me. Mankind will fear me. People will worship me in the end, and I will unite all the people for the good of evil. God will lose this time, and he won't get another chance to get it back because I will be stronger than he will ever be. Once we are done here, we move to the top, and we don't stop until He is no more and everything will be all ours," Robert said determinedly.

"Robert, there is one thing. The dark one is your master, and he will be taking charge once you defeat the good. You need to know that we will answer to him so don't get ahead of yourself," she warned.

"Screw him. I won't bow to him or to anyone. He is lucky if I let him take a portion of what I accumulate. I do all the work and then he reaps the rewards. I don't think so. You tell him is he out of his mind."

"Robert, please think about this for a moment. We have been planning this for millenniums, and then you think that in one stroke you can change what has been in the books since the beginning of time. Robert, you were created to be a tool just like me. That's all, no more no less. You'd better understand that not even you have the strength to do battle with him. You will perish if you try. Let's not let this spoil our day. Please let it go. I need you, Robert. Take me. I'm yours. We have much planning and plenty of time. Now are you going to take me, or will I have to call the old man?"

They both burst out laughing. Robert takes her and for the rest of the day they enjoy the moment.

Lyle leaves and thinks of Cindy. She left him no choice. He was pissed but not to the point to kill her. He would not mention her again, for he knows Sabula and her temper. How many have fallen to her trap? She gives you some line and hopes that you get tangled up. That's why she still lives because she knows when to shut up. Robert must be with her. She would insist on it. She'd be educating him in the fine arts. His schooling has started. He will never be the same. Sabula will have him drink her blood to add more poison. They will have to be very careful around Robert, for he has tasted blood and he will hunger for more.

Father John explains that there is more. This is just the beginning of Roberts's transformation. Father John is tired. Please come back tomorrow at the same time, three o'clock. Before Dale and Steve leave, they sit and pray asking God for guidance and his protection. We are starting to see the real world, and it's frightening. Father John says that the more they learn the more in danger they will be for evil hates good. It's getting to the point that it can even smell you. Father John blessed them with holy water and they left.

On the ride home, Steve asks Dale if he wants to stop and have a nightcap because he says he could sure use one.

"Fine, but after that I need to get home. Lisa will be waiting," Dale replied. They stopped and had a couple of drinks. Dale ends up calling Lisa to tell her that they are on their way. Tonight Steve doesn't stop in. He drops Dale off as he is getting ready to leave Dale tells Steve that Penny will be over on Friday. He tells him not to make plans. Lisa will call him tomorrow. He is just to act surprised because he is not supposed to know.

"Dale, I will pick you up at two thirty. You are going back."

"Yes, Steve, I will be waiting for you but it's getting creepy. I don't know how much more I can take. I have to think about Lisa and the kids. Do you believe all that he says?" Dale asked.

"Yes, every word. I am scared too, but I'm glad that you are there with me,"

Steve commented.

"Thanks."

On the drive home Steve thinks about what he just said about believing everything that he does. It makes him sad how the world is crumbling in front of his very eyes. Is everyone else so blind that they don't see what is happening? Please, God, help us to overcome evil. Open our eyes so we can see the truth before it's too late. Steve parked the car, walked in, and did not even remember when he fell asleep.

Hearing the alarm, Steve told himself that today he is staying home. He called in to work, and they asked if he is sick. He lies and says yes but he will be in the next day. Before hanging up, he has them transfer him to Dale. Steve tells him that he will pick him up at the market. That way he doesn't have to stop at the shop. The rest of the morning he just slept. Then, in the afternoon he showered and watched the news before he left. There were no leads so far. They seemed to have everyone out there looking for extremists but again no one was claiming responsibility. It's peculiar that no one is coming forward like in the past. They couldn't wait to post it on the internet. They would have a field day saying jihad or Muhammad was their motivator. "This act was intended to put fear in the hearts of the infidels and to let them know that the fight was not over. You hurt Iraq and Iran, but we are still here. You lost the Afghan war so you pulled out like the Russians. You cowards go and hide. We will find you and bring much pain to your doorsteps." These were the usual rants on the internet. For many years that's all people heard, but lately the Muslim extremists have been quiet. Steve was thinking that it's as if they've been asleep. Is it a good sign, or are they waiting to grow in numbers to execute a massive assault? Now, with what Father John is telling them will the extremists unite with the antichrist and will Mankind battle both, or will they stand for what is right, the survival of Mankind. They also believe in what is right. Not every race or creed is right or wrong, but they have different opinions. That's what makes us human. In the end we know that God will unite us all like in the beginning. Until that day there will be factions that believe differently for their own benefit or for their own greedy sakes. People will suffer and die. These are some of the points going around in Steve's head. He was wondering in the end who would be fighting on the right side because so many would be deceived. Will it get to the point where people are fighting their own brothers and sisters like in the past as it was in World War II with Germany? How many families were torn apart from Hitler's brainwashing? "I ask you, God, for that not to happen. Please intervene before it gets to that point in time," he prays.

On his way out of Steve's apartment, he notices that it's a beautiful day and decides to walk to absorb some sun and charge his inner batteries. He is thankful that at the current time he can still enjoy the outdoors, for pollution is almost nonexistence since almost all vehicles run on batteries or propane. Even factories have cut emissions. Some things have gotten better over time while others have not. There are more people living on the streets, including kids. People help as many as they can but it's a shame that they can't feed them all. They are able to feed the elderly and the handicapped and help as many of the kids as possible. Many of Steve's friends help in shelters and provide nourishment for unwed mothers. More help is needed but they also encourage the healthy to find employment, to get back on their feet, and to remember that others are also in need and not to forget. Man is selfish many times. We forget so easily once we are on our feet. Some came from the streets or were close to being in the streets had it not been for having faith in God and trusting in Him. We were given a second chance. Steve knows that he is proof that God does exist. He doesn't forget his past but remembers what it took to get out of the gutter. Now, here he is enjoying the moment all thanks to his Father. "Thank you, God," he utters wholeheartedly.

President Morgan says that it will get better but it all takes time. He is addressing a summit about the homeless in the next few days. He is also trying to jump start the economy. He has done a lot in the short time that he's been in office to get this country back on the track; however, in the end he needs to be stopped because he is the antichrist. The *Bible* states that he will perform miracles and people will be deceived. The decline begins with the country having high unemployment, schools closing in record numbers, and insurance being so expensive it will take a miracle to straighten everything out. Then when the mark of the beast is branded on the people, they will build idols to worship him as a god. Fear will blind people, hope will be lost, and their fate will be like sheep losing their direction without their shepherd. Others will follow him of their own free will for the benefit of what's in it for them. "How much do I profit and who do I replace moving up the ladder?" these vain greedy, materialistic people ask themselves. Steve's body shivers as he thinks of the future. It scares him because so much has been accomplished in the last twenty-five years, people still can't get their priorities right. Steve remembers reading the Commandments. They weren't only written for the old but also the young. We are still able to apply them even in today's world. It's not too late to believe in them. Steve guesses it's easier for people to be bad than to be good, but in the end they don't only lose their body but also their soul in the pits of Hell, joining the rest of the non believers.

Steve stops and gets an ice cream cone. He continues walking and remembers what Dale said about Penny. He looks forward to meeting her.

He will take some flowers, some desert, and will even iron some clothes to make a good impression. It's been awhile since he has dated, but he knows Penny from pictures even though they are not recent. Lisa has spoken about her over the years, but he still needs to be on his toes. Maybe something good can come from all this. Then if God wants them to be together, it's fine by him. Being older now, he thinks with his brains, not with his pants coming off.

At two-thirty Steve picks up Dale who is waiting for him. "That's a new one. It's me who always is waiting for **him**," Steve thinks to himself. His phone rings. It's Lisa who is all excited saying she called him at home, but there was no answer so she called his work.

"They said you were sick. Are you okay?" she asked.

"Fine. I just picked up Dale. We are on our way to Father John's. You want to talk to him?" Steve asked.

"No, it's **you** I need to speak to," she said. "Do you have any plans for Friday?"

"Well, let me see. You know how it is being a businessman. I need to check my schedule," he joked.

"Stop kidding around. I have some good news for you. Penny will be here Friday. Dinner is at six o'clock. Don't be late, please. Shave and look your best for it's important," she informed him.

"Okay, I will take a bath even though it's not Saturday."

"You know if you were here right now I'd pop you in the head. Don't let me down, Steven."

Now Lisa wants to talk to her man so Steve hands the phone to Dale, and for the next few minutes all you hear is "Yea, yea won't forget to tell him." He hangs up saying "Isn't love wonderful? Oh! She said for you to iron your clothes because you need to make a good impression. That way Penny won't think that you're still a bum."

"Why would she think that?"

"I'll never tell. You know women and how they gossip."

"You mean more than men? She will call you Friday to remind you not to be late. I think that she really enjoys playing matchmaker."

"By the way, Dale, why does she call me Steven when she knows that I don't care for that name?"

"She does that to get your attention. Believe me, if she could change **my** name when she is serious, she would." They both laugh.

Payback

They arrive. Father John, who is waiting for them, again asks if they need anything before he begins. Robert is now enrolled in Cambridge. He is well-liked and excels in sports, receiving scholarships and grants. There is no stopping this incredible man. He is at the top of the dean's list. His classmates envy him for in business he is like no other. He can take a worse-case scenario and make it work for him. His professors are amazed at his accomplishments in business. Robert is ruthless. He is the same way in economics using brute force to accomplish his goals. He has a knack for turning things around. He doesn't take no for an answer. They marvel at his ingenuity for there is no problem too big or too small. Lyle has taught him well and now he reaps his rewards and looks forward to graduating. He told Lyle that he would be moving back to the states. He has sent his transcripts to Hartford College, for he is going home. He is also calling back the staff they had, for they were like family. It will help the transition of moving back home.

Robert runs into Lyle at the market, gives him a hug, and tells him that he misses him and Lily. Lyle is happy for him and invites him over for dinner. Lily will be happy to hear the news because they have been married for ten years and, by choice, have no kids. Lyle calls Lily and tells her that Robert will be joining them. She is happy to hear it. Now that Robert is in college he seldom stops to visit. It will be a special night. She will make apple pie, his favorite dessert. All the staff is happy to hear that Robert will be joining them because they have seen him grow up and now he is a man. They all cater to him, including Lily, and spoil him rotten. She goes overboard and Robert eats it all up. They have his room ready in case he decides to spend the night, mind you his own room. Robert is also very polite and he is a ladies' man. He uses it to his advantage but Lily misses him too. After all the years that have passed, she has grown fond of him. They had had their differences over the years but had managed to get past them and here they are.

Lyle asks him about Sabula, and he says that she is in the Middle East conducting business as usual. Robert tells Lyle that over the years she has finally started cutting him some slack by letting him live his life. They still get together to perform rituals. They even still have orgies but now Sabula tends to get a little jealous, for they pay more attention to him and she is not happy. She has been gone for almost four months. She called and got pissed when he told her that he was leaving right after graduation. She told him that she would be back before he left.

"You know, Lyle, even though she still tries to treat me like a child, I try not to let it bother me. It's a no-win situation. I hate to disappoint her, but I must live my life even though I'm supposed to be this bad ass. Sorry for dumping on you. I don't really have anyone else to turn to," Robert confided to him.

"Don't worry. You can always count on me, for I'm on your side. Do you want me to talk to her when she comes back? Maybe she will listen to me. It's been awhile since I've spoken to her, but I will give it a shot," Lyle said. Robert gave him a hug, thanking him and telling him that he won't be late for dinner. "We eat at five; that's how it's been since we got married."

"Lyle, I have not forgotten. There are some things that you remember because they mean something special and that's one of the many memories that I cherish," Robert told him.

On the way home Lyle reminds himself to buy some flowers for Lily and notices that it's April 12.1998. This year is moving so fast. Where did it go? He remembers that they need to renew their passports. He will call his connection tomorrow. He always has to be ready because Sabula has changed and not for the better. He never has discussed this with Lily, and he hopes that day never comes. He needs to contact the banks to let them know that he's still alive. He has gotten too comfortable since he got married. "What's wrong with me?" he wonders. "Never in the past would I be caught off guard. I need to be more careful. Since getting married it's like, they left me off the hook and all these years Sabula has not asked for anything. Robert is the same, never asking for anything, including Lily. He's been over to the house and in all these years he's never hit on Lily. If anything, he has been very respectful. Lily loves him as a son and treats him like one. She spoils him and not one holiday or birthday is missed. Robert knows it. Over the years he has told me that he looks forward to holidays, for Lily makes it extra special for him. We will miss Robert when he leaves. Maybe we can visit. We'll see what happens with Sabula. Hopefully, she will get with the program. If Robert is to reign in the states, then one day he will be president and that means his days are numbered here in England."

Lily is waiting for him as he pulls up the driveway. He sees that she is wearing her apron. She's been busy in the kitchen. Lily has always enjoyed cooking for him. Even after they married she continued to cook for him. She is a good cook and bakes even better. Since they've been married, Lyle has gained fifteen pounds. It's three o'clock. Robert would be there at five so Lyle needed to finish getting all the paperwork for tomorrow because he will see his connection to renew their passports. Meanwhile, Lily is all smiles, for they are having a special guest for dinner. After she is done in the kitchen, she goes to shower. You can hear her singing. She does have a nice voice. He feels so lucky to have her. When she comes down after her shower, she looks beautiful, so soft, and smells like strawberries. "Lily, you are the kind of person that the more you age the more elegant you get," he tells her.

"Oh, Lyle, I bet you tell that to all the girls, you softy."

"I mean it truly. I love you. Have you ever had any regrets about us?"

"Dear, why don't you make us a drink while we wait, for it's still early and we have time to chat? Lyle, for vacation I would love to go to Barbados. It's a little island. Forgive me, Lyle, because I ask them to send some brochures without asking you," Lily apologized.

Lyle takes Lily in his arms and pats her on the rear and says, "Next time, ask me for my opinion. You might find me very agreeable." She laughs and says it's a deal. He fixes her another drink. They talk about his work and about Robert going home to the states. She asks him about Sabula, for she has not seen her for a very long time. Lyle tells her that Sabula is in the Middle East on business but will be there before Robert graduates. Sabula will not miss it for the world because her dream will be in motion and a little closer to attainting. Then it's only a matter of time for Robert to take his place in history. "Lily, we need to make plans for Robert's graduation. We need to make him a party, invite his friends, some of his professors, and make it special," Lyle suggests. Lily says that she will start planning immediately.

"We still have time to make a party that he won't forget. Lyle, I'll start tomorrow. That is a great idea and with him going to the states, I don't know when we will be able to do this again. In the fall, I would still like to go to the island, okay?"

"Lily, you arrange for the party and our vacation. I trust you to make the right decisions. In the end just tell me what you did so I know what to expect," Lyle instructed her.

At four forty-five their guest was at the door with a bottle of champagne. After the hugs, they went into the dining area and had supper. It was pot roast with all the works. Dessert was apple pie with vanilla ice cream on top. Afterwards, they went to the sitting room, and Robert did the honors opening the champagne. The rest of the evening they laughed and talked about him going to the states. They told him that he would be missed, but they planned to visit. He was happy to hear that. Tears ran down his face, and Lily hugged him and told him not to worry because he would always have the two of them. They told him just to pick up the phone and call because it's not like he can't afford it. They laughed. Robert is well off over the years. Lyle has doubled his father's earnings and has Robert paying close attention as to how it was accomplished. Also, that's how he taught him about finances in real world situations. Lyle showed him from the beginning not only to be ruthless but also to be smart. After Robert learns how to manage his finances, Lyle cuts him loose but still is in the background. He is there to answer any questions that Robert might have. That's how confident Robert is to do it on his own. Lyle is proud of him. He would mention it over time. It was important for Robert to hear that he was on the right track with his decision-making. His parents would be proud.

Over the years Lyle had become compassionate even though he never asked God to be forgiven. He knew what he had done. Being sorry can't change what a person has done. He has to deal with all the lives that were affected from his decisions. Lyle knows where he is going so he will enjoy life to the fullest. In the end it will be Hell for eternity. He will be joining Bruce, Cindy, and Rasime there too. One thing that makes him feel good is that Robert was taught to be on his toes and his finances reflect that.

"Robert, remember if you ever want to come home just say so," Lyle tells him and Lily agrees. They drink some more. Robert leaves at about ten at night and is sorry that he kept them up so long. As he leaves, they hug him good bye. Lily tells him not to make any plans for his graduation. They are having a little something there at the house. Robert explains that it's not necessary. Lyle tells him not to argue with Lily, for it's a lost cause. Robert tells them to promise him that they won't go all out. He says he's not really into parties. He will be there and so will Sabula. She promised to be there, and Robert knows that she won't let him down.

"Fine. Bring her here, the more the merrier. It will be nice to get together and reminisce. Robert, you're not supposed to know so act surprised. We just didn't want you to make other plans elsewhere," Lily explains.

"Okay, Lily, I will pretend to be surprised. I love you guys," Robert promises as he leaves. As they watch him drive off, Lyle asked Lily why she told him because now it's not a surprise.

"Lyle, what would happen if we made plans, and then he didn't show up because he was invited elsewhere?"

Lyle looked at her, gave her a kiss, and said, "Now I know why I married you."

The next morning Lyle goes to town to take care of the passports and the rest of the paperwork. His connection tells him it takes three days. Today is Wednesday, and everything will be here Saturday morning. While he is in town, he shops for supplies and arranges to pick them up Saturday around noon. The next couple of days fly by. Saturday morning he picks up the passports and the rest of the paperwork. Then, he picks up his supplies. Returning home again he decides it's time for Lily to know about the passports and the codes for the bank accounts before he places them in his safe. Lyle calls Lily to his office and asks her to take a seat. He tells her that if ever anything were to happen she should flee as fast as possible. She must leave the country and tell no one where she is going for her life could depend on it. He shows her the passports and new credentials and tells her about the accounts in the Cayman Islands and the Swiss account. He goes so far as to tell her about the doctor that has been paid in advance for the plastic surgery if the situation warrants it.

"Make no mistake. This is no joke, for it's time for you to know. I love you. Lily, I don't want to lose you, for you're all I have so please take me seriously. Instructions are in the safe. Don't worry about the things here because they can be replaced," he advises her.

"Lyle, you're scaring me. Tell me it's just a joke, for in the time that we have been together, never have I seen or heard that you have any enemies. In addition, are you not planning to join me, for you speak only of me? What is going on? Tell me. I'm your wife. I need to know because I love you and want to grow old with you. The last ten years have been incredible. You owe me," she pleads. She shakes him and shakes him some more. Now, she is crying and telling him that she will not leave his side. Whatever is the problem, they will face it together. If they need to leave, it will be both of them. "Do you understand, Lyle? I'm here for the duration. Over the years you have said never to run from your problems. Why are you starting now? You'd better practice what you preach. Now tell me, when is all this supposed to happen? Give me a time frame so I can prepare for the worse. I'm not leaving here by myself so get used to it. 'For better or worse,' that's what the preacher said. What is this about plastic surgery? Why would we need it?" Lily asks.

"Okay, you want to know the trouble I'm in? It stretches far. These people have connections all over the world. There is a possibility that even with plastic surgery we won't be safe. If the time comes and we run, we run for the rest of our lives. Can you live like that? What I'm trying to do is save you from all that. I have lived a long life and with you by my side. These last ten years it has been worth it, making it special. I don't want to ruin it. I prefer to face the music myself and give you a chance to live. It's not like you're leaving me, Lily. We've done things in life that sometimes we can't change back, no matter how hard we try. I'd rather not involve you for you are still young. Over time, you can meet someone and start over. If it turns out for the worst, I know that it will end with me, and then you could live in peace. Think about what I say to you. I could live through you, for we have many memories so I won't be forgotten," Lyle explains.

"Lyle, I won't leave you. We will face this together. Just tell me what to do when we run. We will stay together no matter what. I will start to prepare by getting my papers in order and packing my clothes with all that we might need. Lyle, I will be ready in a moment's notice. I will not fail you, and I promise not to say anything to anyone, agree?"

"Lily, that also includes Robert and Sabula, not one word," he admonishes her.

"I guess there is no talking you out of this, so fine," she assures him.

"Get ready. Be prepared, for I fear the day draws near," he makes his final plea. They hug and kiss each other and speak no more of it.

The weeks fly by so fast and now it's June. Sabula has just arrived in town and is furious with Robert because she doesn't want him to go to the states. Telling him it's not time, she worries that he will ruin all the careful planning. He must listen to her because she knows better and what is good for him. She is so pissed that she won't lie in bed with him even though she wants him but refuses to give in until he listens. She makes a mistake telling him that she is in control. Then Robert explodes. They can be heard from one end of the house to the other.

"Bitch, I can kill you right know for you're no longer needed. I'm not a child any longer," he reminds her.

"You will do as I say and if you ever raise your voice at me, I will rip your throat out. Then, I will shove it up your ass. Do I make myself clear? Then, he pulls out his cock, and she goes to work on him until she swallows. For the rest of the day he screws her hard and ass fucks her, but he doesn't go down on her. She does not even try to ask, for she knows that he enjoys going down on her but is not pushing it because there is always tomorrow. Over the years, Robert's powers have grown strong in the black arts. Sometimes he is not aware of how strong he is, for he is a lot stronger than she realizes. She needs to get him under control. She will ask Lyle for help. He is not ready to venture off, and she's not ready to lose him. Robert is sleeping. She thinks about the future. He is a grown man but his training is not finished.

After all the careful planning, she will not let him ruin it. This has taken a lifetime to plan. Robert is more important than he knows. I have to answer to the dark one, and he will not be happy, especially with Robert wanting to go to the states because now is not the right time. Failing is not an option. He will have my head. Sabula needed to come up with a plan. She has just returned from the Middle East where so much money and effort is being placed in the future. My armies are needed to strike at a moment's notice. All the extremists that wait for the day are being assembled and dispatched throughout the United States, for the day nears. Robert has to do what he was born to do. It is his destiny. My pawns have been buying stores as fronts. They have been busy setting up shops and storing munitions. Politicians are being bought, for the day will come and their services will be needed to take control. Real estate is being purchased to train troops throughout the states. When they strike, it will be all at once. They need to be caught off guard. Canada will be providing launching areas to attack from the north, and Mexico will assault from the south. With the combining forces that are in place in the states, it will only be a matter of time before chaos is unleashed. With the pawns in place we will be able to attack the United States from both sides, and in no time, she will surrender. Robert has no idea of this contingency plan. It's on a need-to-know basis. Utilities and waterworks plants will also fail, for we have pawns running them. So much planning is involved, but in the end, this is where Mankind falls. The dark one has taken measures to ensure victory. He is aware of Robert's behavior and is planning accordingly.

"Too many years of planning have been involved for some schmuck to think that it's for him. Not on my watch, Robert. Soon, you will feel pain like you've never experienced before," Sabula reflects. "I have to report, and I'm more scared of the dark one, but in the end, who knows to whom I will be loyal? There is still time left and so many things can change. It's better to prepare for the worst. That's how I have managed to survive all these years. In the end I can tell Robert that I did it for him and that it was supposed to be a surprise. Men are easy to figure out. They think with their cock and their ego is never far away. It's how you work it that makes them come for more," and she laughs.

"From here we will take over the rest of the world. We will move into Mexico waking our sleeper cells. Our troops will spread. They will make their way to South America. Then, we strike Canada. It will fall next, and we will then continue north taking Alaska and working our way to Greenland until it's all ours. Troops in the Middle East will launch attacks on Israel and spread death and chaos throughout the continent. The Soviet Union falls first and once we have their nukes, China will follow the same fate. We will spread like wild fire. No place will be safe after we conquer the rest of the world placing our pawns. Then, my master will join us. Then, and only then, will we challenge Him, their God, for the final battle and this time we will win. It makes me horny just thinking of the day," Sabula reflects. Now, she needs Robert again so she wakes him and gives herself to him. She burns inside in anticipation of the day to see it all come crashing down burning and knowing that Mankind participated in his own downfall. His weaknesses for pursuing false hopes, vanity, and greed were his demise. By selling out his fellow man and by worshiping false idols, these were all the necessary ingredients to make this happen. Yes, all this will come to pass. I need Robert to listen and the dark one to be convinced that all is going as planned," Sabula concludes.

When Sabula and Robert are done, they fall asleep. In the morning, she wakes Robert with his cock in her mouth. She will do anything to please him. She needs him to reason with her. When Robert is done, they talk and she explains to him that he cannot jeopardize all that she has planned; therefore, he agrees to a compromise and will stay here until the fall. After that, he leaves for the states. She will introduce him to some people that have influence in the states, and if that is his choice to leave, then she will work with him from afar. Now, she feels better thinking she still has control over him.

Robert asks her if she is joining him for the party that Lyle and Lily are planning for him. "Yes, Robert, I will join you. I would not miss it for the world. It has been too long since I have seen the happy couple," Sabula explains.

"The party is tomorrow after I graduate. I'm supposed to act surprised," Robert comments.

"You too?"

"Don't worry. We will leave with plenty of time to get to the party. Remember, it's a special day. You are all grown up, Robert. You know I have a surprise for you," Sabula told him.

"Sabula, you don't have to get me anything. I have you; that's enough. I don't need anything else. I just want us to get along. I'm sorry about what I said yesterday, but you do know how to push my buttons. Will you forgive me?" he asked.

Sabula went to the other room and returned with a very expensive suit and all the works. "Go try it on and see if it fits. Don't forget to try on the shoes," she reminds him. Robert goes to the other room to change and returns. "Wow, all the women will be after him including myself," she thought. "He is so handsome." Robert is now a man standing six feet five and weighing two hundred and twenty pounds, all muscle. She takes pictures of him, for this is a special occasion. Then, he goes and changes back. He returns with a big grin and thanks her. He gives her a hug and a kiss. Next, she takes him to town to have a manicure and a haircut. Afterwards, they have a fancy dinner. For the first time since he can remember, they retire early, for tomorrow is the big day. Robert will have a full night's sleep. That night he does not dream and doesn't wake until he hears the alarm clock.

In the morning he eats breakfast, and they leave for graduation. They meet up with Lyle and Lily. They all tell him how handsome he looks, hugging him, and then they take their seats and wait for his name to be called. When his name is announced, Sabula and Lily get busy taking pictures. Robert grins when he accepts his diploma. All his fellow students cheer, and some of his professors join in. It's a sight to see. When it's over, they go to the house, and the party begins. Robert acts surprised and he thanks them. They have live music. The band Asia is playing and the people are enjoying the music. Everyone is dancing, including Sabula with some young man.

Lily says, "Let's join in," so they hit the dance floor. The rest of the evening they had the time of their lives. There was plenty to eat and drink, for there had to be at least three hundred people on their lawn. It was good that Lily had planned for the extra people by hiring extra help for the evening. Robert was having the time of his life. They were surprised how popular he had become. Women just followed him. Not that he complained, but when he was at the house, he seemed so quiet.

Lyle remembered Cindy. All those years had passed, but he would never forget what he had done to that poor woman. Then, Lily came and saved the day by taking him back to the dance floor and helping him to forget. He loves Lily and is glad that she chooses to stay by his side. While he's holding her a little tighter, she looks at him and gives him a kiss. She then tells him that she loves him.

Robert afterwards dances with Lily, and Sabula uses the opportunity to tell Lyle about her problem with Robert. She is not showing her emotions, but he can hear it in her voice.

"Lyle, over the years I have not bothered you, but I need you to convince Robert to stay. He is making a big mistake by leaving. He will put my plans in jeopardy. He is not ready. He told me that he mentioned it to you, and you were happy for him. How dare you say that to him with all of my plans that are being put into motion? Do you realize that I just met with extremists in the Middle East promising them that in the future if we will work together, there will be victory, and they will have their share of the pie? Lyle, they are providing safe havens and training grounds for more of my troops. They are being left in charge until my return to care for the storage of weapons of mass destruction. They will bury more munitions and supplies every day until the storage bunkers are complete. Then, they will be transferred until the right time when we strike.

"Also, we have some very talented people arriving to help with the last of Robert's training, for Robert will die, and they will bring him back. Then, he will be invincible. At that point he will not have a piece of good left in his body. Lyle, I need you to buy me some time. I need at least one more year. I won't forget what you do for the cause," she promised.

"Okay, but in return, I ask you for a favor. After this, I'm through. Done. I want out! That includes Lily. We'll leave this place. You can keep the properties, but we're out of here no questions asked, agree?"

"Lyle, are you serious about leaving the organization, the one that over the years has filled your pockets? Don't forget the blood that's on your hands. Does Bruce ring a bell? What do you think Robert would say to that? Do you think he would forgive you?"

"Sabula, are you threatening me? Did you forget that we screwed over his dead body? Robert is not listening right now. What do you think will happen when he finds out? Sabula, you have far more to lose than I do. I die, but **you,** what do you think will happen to you? Don't fuck with me."

"Lyle, does it have to come to that? Come on. I'm kidding. Do this for me, and I will think about what you asked, really, but think for a second how much has been invested in you over the years. Hypothetically, if you were to leave, who is next? It could cause a chain reaction. We do not want that. Lyle, aren't you happy with your life? Look around. You have it all. Lyle, do this for me, and like I said, I will think about it. I promise you." She gives him a kiss on the cheek and tells him that Robert will stop by the next day.

After they finish, Sabula gets Robert's attention. Then, Sabula gives Robert his present. It is a Jaguar limited addition with all the bells and whistles. Robert is overwhelmed thanking her and saying that she should not have spent all that money. Sabula hugs him and says that he deserves even more. Robert thanks them and thanks the band Asia for playing at the party. The people are not forgetting that party for a long time. At the end of the evening, Robert left with a very attractive woman, and Sabula left with the young man she had been dancing with much of the night. Then as the people were leaving, the staff started to pick up and put away so the mess would not be so bad the following day. There is no telling what time they would wake up, for they were exhausted in more ways than one.

Now, Lyle knows that Sabula is not going to let him leave. This is where he starts to panic. It's only a matter of time before Robert knows the truth. Sabula did say that Robert needs to stay for another year so that means that he has about six months to disappear. He will convince Robert to stay by telling him to take a break for a year from school. Then, he can give it his all, but for now it not only benefits Robert but also them to buy some time. He will tell Lily to plan for the vacation in the next three months. She had her heart set on going in the winter. Now, they are going in the fall and won't return.

Robert arrives at four o'clock and has dinner with them saying that he had a wonderful time, that his honey loved his car, and that he did not get home until morning. After dinner they went into his study, and then

Lyle told him about taking a break from school. At first, he didn't want to. Then, Lyle told him that he owes it to himself. When he leaves, it's going to be all work and no play. Lyle tells Robert that even **he** needs a break so enjoy life while he can, for in the future he won't have this luxury. It will be all business. Lyle tells Robert to think about it. He can enjoy that car, take it out for a ride, and find some honeys to spend time with.

"Live, Robert, and then go back to business, for you have worked so hard over the years; you need a break. Robert, even Lily is planning our vacation as we speak, for life is too short not to enjoy the moment. When was the last time you did something for **Robert**? Think about it? I will not take no for an answer. One day you will thank me," Lyle tells him.

"But you've arranged already to have my records sent to the school in Hartford. They are looking forward to me being there in the fall," Robert responded.

"Don't worry, Robert. I will take care of you. I know the dean and will call him Monday to schedule you for the following fall, okay? Don't worry. Let me do this for you, and then promise me that you will enjoy your time off. I'll tell you what. I will reimburse you for the money," Lyle reassured him.

"No, Lyle, it's not the money. I was looking forward to going home to see my friends and to move back into the house that I call home."

"You have time. Trust me. You won't regret it. In addition, you will have more time to spend with us, and Sabula is looking forward to spending more time with you," Lyle added.

"Did Sabula speak to you about me because we had a similar conversation, and I told her that I wanted to leave but she wanted me to wait?"

"No, Robert, it is my idea. I'm telling Sabula that you are taking a break. You deserve it more than anyone I know. Maybe now we can go fishing like we used to. You still enjoy fishing. Now, you will also have the time to do all that you have not been able to do in a very long time," Lyle persuaded him.

"Okay. You've convinced me. I'll talk to the dean and also to Sabula. Then, next fall I will leave no matter what anyone says. For the rest of the time I'm off, I will enjoy myself. Now you will excuse me, for I need to get back and sleep. I will call Sabula and tell her the news so tomorrow call me, and I will let you know how it went," Robert told Lyle as they were walking to the front door. Lily was there waiting. They gave Robert hugs, and then he left.

Lyle told Lily that he needed to make a call, and then they needed to talk. Sabula answers on the second ring and is delighted to hear the news.

"Lyle, I knew that you would not let me down, for Robert still listens to you. Okay, Lyle, I will remember this. By the way, I still have not forgotten what you asked. You know that you will be hard to replace for you have that smooth tongue and that suave persona. You've saved my bacon once again. I will let you know my decision in a few days."

"Sabula, if Robert asks, tell him that it was my idea and that you never asked me to intervene. Unbelievably, he still trusts me, and I would like to keep it that way, understand?"

"Yes, Lyle, I will act surprised. Thank you, and you will hear from me," she hangs up.

Lyle goes to find Lily and tells her that when they leave it will be for good. There has been a change of plans, and they will go in three months. He reminds her to tell no one for their lives depend on it. He will finish getting all that they will need. They can never return but will be able to live and still enjoy their lives to the fullest. One day after they leave he will tell her all of it, but for now she will just have to trust him.

"Lyle, it involves Sabula, doesn't it? Tell me that much. I won't ask you anymore until you decide to tell me," Lily assures him.

"Yes, Sabula is the reason. That is all I can say for the moment. Do not ask any more questions. I can't answer anymore, understand? Your life is too important to me. We have three months. We will play along. Please don't ever let on that you have any idea. Sabula will be visiting us like she has always done in the past. We will welcome her and treat her the way we always do. It will be alright. You'll see, for we have our plans and that is what's important. Now please finish arranging our flight and our room. We will check in and pretend to stay but in reality, we are not staying. Find out their schedules but don't buy the tickets to South America. We can get lost over there for a long time. It's a big country. Also, the surgeon is located there just in case he is needed. You arrange to go to Bogotá, from there to Paraguay, and from there to Tierra del Fuego. You will go buy the tickets. Once we get our room in Barbados, be sure you get confirmation numbers. Also, when you purchase the tickets, make sure to make them under these names," he says handing over our new names. "From here we fly under our real names. After that, we use our new identities for South America. Before we board we will get rid of all traces of our past. Then, we start a new life. Don't forget to buy hair color, for you will be a brunet for awhile, and I will be light brown instead of black. I will also shave my beard. We will do all this before we board our flight.

"Lyle, we are in danger right now?"

"There is a possibility. I'm not sure, but just in case you will know what to do. I'm sorry for all the inconvenience that I'm putting you through. That's why I didn't want to involve you. Lily, if there is ever a time that the bottom falls out, leave and don't come back I will have an idea where to find you. Just stick to the plan," Lyle concluded.

Meanwhile, Sabula is making plans for Roberts's death in order for him to be reborn. She meets with the foreigners, and they plan when to execute their final ritual, for it is a delicate procedure. One mistake and all is lost. Sabula explains to them that if they screw up their whole country will pay with their lives. Now they look at each other. They know Sabula's wrath from the past. She has decided the fate of wars. They know that with Sabula there is no right war but only what's in it for her. Who is paying the most determines who wins in the end. They say they need a week to prepare. Thursday at midnight it will be done. She leaves them for Robert has returned. She is anxious to see him.

"Robert, did you enjoy yourself last night? It seems the party was a success. The music and food were very good. Lyle and Lily went all out for you. They really care about you. It's fortunate you have people that care so much about you. All your life you have been pampered, but now time is almost at hand, Robert. You will shine like no other before you. Hitler will look like a pussy next to you. The world will bow to you for you will do unimaginable things. You have one ritual left. Then, you will be ready, but it will take a lot out of you. It's important for you to recover fully. That's about three months' rest, no sex, booze or extracurricular activities."

Robert smirks and says, "That's bull. Don't you know who I am? Who do you think you're talking to some schmuck that just got off the banana boat? Sabula, maybe you need the rest but not me because my powers are off the charts," he stated emphatically.

"Please, Robert, I'm only thinking of you. Listen, why do you fight me? I've treated you well over the years. Have you forgotten?" she asked him.

"No, Sabula, you have your own agenda. I grow tied of all this. What would happen if I refused you? What is my worst-case scenario?" he enquired.

"Hmm, let me see. World domination fails, and you get booted back to Hell. That doesn't sound too bad, for that's where you came from, or is it that you've grown fond of this world and all that's included?"

"Tell me, Sabula, was it this good for you in Hell? I mean the parties, the food, the clothes, and the sex?"

"You bastard, how dare you speak to me in such a manner, for I'm not one of your whores. If you were not the chosen one right now, I would have you in chains and would rip your flesh right off your body and feed it to my pets. Do not ever confuse my generosity, for even you can feel my wrath. You will do as I say, or you will meet the dark one. He will put you in check. Is that what you need? I grow tired of all this so I ask you for the last time and will never speak of it again. Will you listen or do you prefer to hear it from him? He is not as kind as I. He doesn't have a sense a humor. Take your pick," Sabula demanded.

"Okay, Sabula, don't get your panties all wound up. I will do as you ask. When is the ritual? Thursday at midnight, but you will have to be here early for preparations. Fine. Let's go screw. Your backup boy toy didn't seem to satisfy you last night, did he?" Robert chides her.

"Stop pushing my buttons, Robert. I'm not in a good mood,"

"Now you know how it feels," he responds. They make their way to the bedroom. He tells her to get on her stomach, and he goes to work on her. Later that evening you could never tell that they had ever been arguing. They were back to kissing and hugging. Over time they each tested each other to see who would back down first, but lately Sabula had been catching hell to get him to agree to anything. For now it's all good, and she manages to get her way. Now she waits for Thursday for the final ritual. Then he will turn and there's no turning back. Then the last part of his training begins in the black arts, for he will be taught to look into the future to manipulate minds to make those incredible miracles. Yes, he will be ready for that day. The whole world will see! Sabula gets wet between the legs just thinking about it. She wants Robert some more.

The days fly by, and then it's Thursday. Sabula's henchmen tell Robert not to eat for the whole day. Water is fine but that's it. Then at about ten in the evening, they take him to another part of the house that he has not been in. That's odd for in the time that he has been living here, he thought he had seen it all. They walked into a chamber, and it's lit only by candle light. It's all in red and smells of sage. Sabula is dressed in red. Everyone else is dressed in black. Robert is led to a table where they lay him down. Then, he is strapped to the table. He remembers Cindy and the rest that have met the same fate over the years. It was not this table, but it was similar. How bad can this be and why the straps? Then, he remembers he never asked Sabula what was involved in this ritual. It can't be that bad.

She would have told him, right? Sabula walks up to him and says not to worry because today he will be reborn. Then, she starts to speak in foreign tongue, and he worries for "reborn" was the last word she said. How can he be reborn when he is alive? Now he is really worried but can't move and now Sabula's in a trance. Some of the men with cloaks join her speaking in foreign tongues. Then, they give him a drink that tastes bad, but they encourage him to drink it all. He sees a knife about eight inches long that Sabula takes with both hands. She begins to recite some words. Then she raises the knife over her head and strikes him squarely in the heart, and the pain that follows is excruciating! His life flashes before him, and in the meanwhile, he's freaking out and then he dies.

Then Robert meets the dark one. He is waiting to welcome Robert. "We meet at last. We don't have much time, but that will change in the future. A lot rides on your shoulders for the fall of Mankind. Sabula has been working on this venture for many years. Don't disappoint me; don't let it be in vain. Here repercussions last forever. You don't want to be joining your parents, do you Robert? See over there." Robert turns and sees his mother. The dark one's henchmen are peeling her flesh right off her body and eating it. She cries in agony asking him to make it stop.

He looks at Robert and laughs saying, "That can be you."

Robert asks him to please make it stop, and he asks the dark one why. "She is my mother. I beg you to stop. She was a kind, caring person," Robert pleads.

"Robert, that's what's makes her so special. She cries for your father's sins. He betrayed me. This is all his fault, not mine. All he had to do was to just walk away when the time came, but he chose to mess with the bull and got the horn. Oh! Did I mention that he is over there? Where are my manners?"

Robert turned and looked. Sure enough, Bruce is there but is fine. Robert doesn't understand. He does not have a scratch on him.

Bruce yells, "Robert, don't listen to him. It's all lies." Then Robert hears his mother in pain. Her right arm is being ripped off, and the maggots are now feasting on her.

She screams, "Tell him to kill me! Make it end, Robert, please. Have pity, I don't belong here. I was a good mother and wife. Make him stop!"

Then, a creature about ten feet tall and about four hundred fifty pounds with teeth like a shark grabs her from behind and tears at her flesh with its teeth. It has small ears and hands that could make a basketball disappear. The legs are as thick as pillars and the feet are three feet long and very wide. As he rapes Elsa from the rear, his eyes glow yellow like a lightning bug, and he moans with pleasure as he drives his two-foot long and about six-inch wide "tool" into Elsa as they watch. Elsa is being hammered. Her little body was not designed to handle this brute. Then, in front of Robert, he takes it out, shakes it, and grins. He looks over to Bruce, and for the first time, the creature speaks.

"Bruce, I've loosened her up a bit. Now, you might be able to find your keys. At this, the dark one and the creature laugh so loudly that it rattles everyone's brains. Elsa wants to pass out but can't. Then, the no-haired creature raises Elsa's ass and spits on it telling Bruce that this might hurt just a bit. Elsa turns and pleads for it to stop. It takes a bite from her right ear as she screams. He positions his cock to her ass and rams it all the way in. Robert looks at his mom's eyes as they bulge from their sockets. Her head drops and the thing looks at Robert.

"You could be next! It's not so bad," he concludes as he and the dark one begin again to laugh. All of this is definitely an attempt to drive a message home to Robert that this is Hell and no one is safe. Being forced to watch is Bruce's payback. When the creature is near to the end, he takes it out of her ass, and two henchmen release Elsa. They now position her so that the thing can come in her mouth. She refuses, at first. Then they punch and kick her. When she opens up, the penis doesn't even fit into her mouth, but the thing forces it in just far enough for her to catch all the discharge. All the while, he is laughing.

Robert's father struggles to free himself from the chair, but when he realizes that he is unable to, he cries for the suffering he has caused Elsa. "How can one live this way and not help?" he laments to himself. "I'm so sorry, God."

Robert asks the dark one, "What will make you stop?"

"Fulfill your destiny, and I will push her upstairs. You know what I mean."

"No! Right now, not later. You do this and I will serve you," no questions asked, but right now you let her go and get that thing off her and make her whole like she was and let my father join her."

"That's not possible. We had a contract that he failed to fulfill so he's a keeper. He will just take her place if you don't mind," and he laughs. My father looks at me and nods his head. Then I look over and my mother is whole again. Robert tells the dark one to let him say good-bye to his mother, and he agrees.

"But don't take too long," he warns Robert, and he laughs again.

"Mother, I love you." She hugs Robert and tells him that she misses him and that she will pray for him. She says she will ask God to forgive their sins. His mother was a very religious person. That is why the dark one enjoyed having her here. Her pain was music to his ears for evil loves pain. The dark one craves it.

Then the dark one says, "That's enough of that. You make me want to cry. Now go before I change my mind." Mother turns into a white mist and even here one sees the glory and hears the trumpets, and then Robert cries for he knows his mother is finally home where she belongs. Then, he looks at his father, for he has taken her place. There is nothing that he can do about that for now.

"Are you happy now? I gave you what you wanted. Now, you belonging to me and are without free will. Remember what happens when I'm disappointed. Don't make me mad, for I don't have a sense of humor. Just ask your daddy, for when you leave we get to start on him, goody."

"I want to tell father good-bye," Robert pleads. "You have my promise. I will keep it."

"All right, say your good byes and don't take all day," the dark one warns him.

Robert walks to his father and tears flow from his face. Bruce tells Robert that he loves him and not to worry, but he says that Lyle and Sabula betrayed him. All I wanted was to save you from all this. Sorry, Son, forgive me, but I trusted him, and he shot me in the back of the head. Then, he screwed Sabula over my dead body,"

"Dad, I'm sorry. I will give you satisfaction. You know he will be joining you. I will rape and kill his woman in front of him, and remind him of his past deed."

"No, Robert, please don't harm Lily. She is a fine woman like your dear mother. Promise me that no harm will come to her. Lily loves you like the son that she never had. Lyle never deserved her. She was too good for him. Let her live. That's all that I ask. Sabula will get hers, I promise you. It may take awhile, but I won't forget. Now, I must go. I love you."

Robert says hugging and giving him a kiss on the cheek, "I won't forget you, Father."

"Okay, you are ready to go back. You've been here way too long. Sabula must be freaking out by this time. Tell her I will be in touch. Oh! By the way, you have all of my powers. I mean most of them. Sabula can be a handful. Better you than me, for I could not wait to find something for her to do that would take awhile, the high maintenance bitch. Robert, don't let me down. Remember your daddy and what happens when you fail me," he concluded. Then, Robert feels himself being pulled back into his body.

Meanwhile Sabula is going nuts. It's been way too long, and Robert is not responding. She starts to panic. The closest person to her pays with his life, poor bastard. Never get too close to her especially if she has a knife in her hand. She yells at the rest of the men to do something, for they will face the same fate as their comrade. They struggle to bring him back. What should have taken a few minutes has taken twenty minutes. She tells them that if he wakes with brain damage, they had better start digging a grave. They are trying different ways to bring Robert back. Not knowing if they are the next to die, panic can be seen in their eyes. Then, finally, Robert coughs and she screams at the top of her lungs and starts pushing bodies away from Robert.

"Let him breathe, you fucking idiots! She places an air mask on him. Then slowly he starts coming around. She is crying. Robert doesn't know if it's because she worries for him. or if it's because she would have to answer to him, and he will not tolerate failure. Afterwards, they put Robert on a stretcher and take him to his room. He sleeps but thinks he hears screams. Yes, indeed, that is what happened. All had paid with their lives even though some pleaded that they indeed had brought him back.

Sabula would not hear it. "Off with their heads!" she commanded. She drank their blood as she killed them. Afterwards, she even bathed in their blood because it was done for the last time. There was to be no turning back. Robert is reborn even though he scares the shit out of her. Fucking assholes is what she has to deal with. Incompetent people, they are lucky that they still have a country so help me.

Robert is alive and that's what counts. She will baby him for a while. "Asshole had me worried. I could have killed him myself. If he ever pulls this kind of crap again, I will. That is the last ritual. Now we just have to finish his training, and he is done. Then, we wait for the right time. Now, I need to call my connections in the states to get the ball rolling, for he will need guidance in politics, the right influences to maneuver the proper channels, and procedures to move up the ladder. He will need the right professors so let's start from there. He will blossom in the right political environment, and with a little help, in no time he will be right where we need him. Once he becomes president, then it's only a matter of time. Please, let these years fly by," Sabula thinks to herself.

Robert sleeps for three days straight without a single dream. Then he wakes. He is starving. He remembers the knife and feels his chest and low and behold nothing, not even a scratch. Then he looks at his chest and is amazed that there are no scars, but he knows that it hurts like hell. Then, the rest is a blank. For the rest of the day all he does is eat. Then, he sleeps for another two days and wakes up starving. This goes on for two weeks. He didn't realize how weak he had become. His body was drained of water, and he needed plenty of nourishment. He felt like he couldn't quench his thirst. Now, he has an idea how vampires feel thirsting for blood, trying to quench the never-ending thirst, always needing more. Then, he slept once more. The next couple of weeks he didn't really leave the bed except to do his business. That was pretty much it. After two months of this, he finally came around. He had had enough sleep to last for a long time.

Sabula was happy to see him out of bed. "Come on, Robert. Let's get out of here. You have been cooped up too long. Let's go breathe some fresh air and get some sun by taking a drive," she encouraged him. Now, Robert is excited. They leave and for the next couple of days they just enjoy the moment, for summer is at its peak. Robert cannot remember when the last time was that he was able to just admire the scenery and take in the fresh air. Sabula is encouraging him to have fun, if one can believe that, and she seems to be enjoying herself. They end up staying out for three weeks.

Time flies and summer draws to an end. Now, Robert insists on staying out one more week, and Sabula says they must get back but he reminds her that it was **her** idea. He tells her that he will not ask her for anything else if she will please give him one more week. "Look at my tan. It's almost even." He smiles at her, and she gives in. Lately, she can't seem to resist him.

They have not been intimate since his ordeal even though they have only one month left. Sabula will not take any chances or let any women get close to Robert. She is going to screw him and not let him out the room until she says. Sabula has not been with anyone, not because she can't, but because she will wait for Robert. She is fond of him. Then she tells him that they will take a ride to Glasgow for the week. He is excited for it has been a good while since he was last there, and he had such a wonderful time. So many babes…but he understands no contact no harm in looking or flirting so for the next week he still manages to enjoy himself. When it comes time to return home now, he is really thanking Sabula. They take the scenic route and all they talk about is what a good idea it was to just leave. Then they laugh. Robert falls asleep while Sabula drives. She ends up having to wake him when they arrive home. It is late by the time they get home, and he retires to his room and sleeps for the drive was wonderful.

Sabula is also exhausted but is content for in the end it all works out. All that is left is his final training and that won't be a big deal, for Robert has the power now. All he needs is a little direction and it's done. Had she known how long this assignment was to last, she is not sure if she would have volunteered. Now it is different for she is fond of Robert even though he stands up to her. Maybe that's why. The rest are afraid of her, and she can smell fear. She lies down and sleeps, no dreams just peaceful sleep.

In the morning they have breakfast and Robert tells Sabula that he will take a ride and will visit Lyle and Lily. He tells Sabula that he will be back for dinner.

"Sabula, do you need anything from the market?"

"No, Robert, I'll be waiting for you to return. We will have some guests that I want you to meet. Don't be late." He gives her a hug and a pinch on her ass and asks, "How much time do we have left? Robert, we have three weeks and then you're mine, for I'm gonna eat you up and when I'm done with you, it will take you another week to recover." They both laugh as he leaves.

"Please, Robert, do not be late and send my regards to the happy couple," Sabula tells him.

Robert lately takes his time driving. He is not rushing anymore because he prefers to spend his time enjoying the moment. It's true he has been reborn. It's odd that Robert forgot that he died, and after waking up that morning, he never gave it a second thought. Then he feels his chest but there are no scars because he has healed completely; however, some things that are still fuzzy in his mind. They do not make sense, but he can't remember what happened when he died. It's all blank. Should it matter? Should he tell someone or wait for it to come back to him? He continues driving and thinks about some other things that are important to him like Sabula, Lyle, and Lily, for he will miss them once he moves to the states. He makes his way up the drive. They are outside working on the lawn, for they are still active even though they have staff to care for the lawn. Lily enjoys getting her hands in the dirt. She once told him that it reminded her of when she was growing up in the orphanage. That was her escape. She would pretend that she was Alice in Wonderland digging a tunnel to escape to a fantasy world. She would laugh saying that she was getting too old for fantasies. Looking in her eyes, he would still see the sparkle because the magic was still there. Robert envies her for in this sense she is still a child in a woman's body. When she laughs, it's genuine for not only does she laugh from her throat but also from her eyes. She is the real McCoy.

One day maybe he will meet **his** Lily, and he will make her happy, but until then Sabula will have to do.

Lyle gives Robert a big hug and tells him how much they've missed him. Lily follows and tells him that she was ready to send out the troops to find him, for the summer draws to an end, and he was nowhere to be found. She had hoped to see him before they left on vacation, which would start in just a few days. Robert explained to them that he too was on vacation, and that he had just returned. They have some of the staff prepare lunch; meanwhile, they tried to catch up on what had been going on in their lives. Robert thanked Lyle for calling the dean and arranging his classes for the following year. Then, he agreed that he indeed needed a break, for he was worn out and hadn't realized how much until just recently. After lunch, he stayed for a little longer and said that he needed to get back. Lyle asked him about fishing. How about tomorrow morning early? They could meet at the lake and fish until the fish stop biting.

"Are you game?" Lyle asked.

"What time, Lyle?"

"Four-thirty. Don't bring anything unless you have a favorite pole, for I have all that we need."

"It's a date, Lyle, but I will bring some crawlers that are guaranteed to get the fish to bite," Robert assured him.

"Fine. See you at the lake, Robert. As he leaves and gets into his car, he feels lucky to have them both.

He stops and buys flowers for Sabula, something that he has never done but is compelled to do. He gets home about four in the evening, and Sabula is happy to see him and is delighted to see the flowers. A tear runs down the side of her face.

He smiles at her and says, "You do have a heart."

"You wish," she retorts. "It's just that my allergies are bothering me. That's all. Men are always buying me flowers. It's no big deal."

Then Robert grabs her, looks her in the eyes, and says, "Yes, but they're not from me," and he kisses her and his hand goes to her sweet spot, and she's wet.

"Stop it; you know we can't, not for another three weeks. You have never brought me flowers before. Why now?" she asks.

"Maybe I care about you," Robert responds and then goes to his room to shower for their guests will be arriving shortly.

Sabula can't seem to understand him for when she thinks she has him figured out, bam! He surprises her again. Is that why she is attracted to him because she can't seem to read him? In all her life, she's never had this problem, for when she grew tired of people, she would just drop them. Easy come, easy go. That's all there is to it, but Robert enjoys pushing her buttons. This guy screws her up. She can't stay pissed at him, and now look. She needs to change her panties, and she smiles at herself.

The guests arrived and by this time Robert is with Sabula greeting them. They sit and have dinner. Afterwards, they make their way to the veranda and have drinks. Robert doesn't drink but is still fascinated at what these strangers are saying to him about his powers. They will help him unlock his true potential. They tell him that it will only be a matter of months. Then, he will be ready.

Robert asks them, "I won't need to die, will I?" They look at each other and answer no. Sabula squeezes his hand, for this is no time for jokes. "Okay, when do we start?"

They answer that they will begin right after Labor Day. It will be a full moon so they must wait for that day. They tell him that the same applies when they finish. It will be a full moon, and then it's done. They say that it falls on Friday so not to make any plans because it will take most of the night.

"I understand," Robert assures them. "I will be ready and will do what you ask of me. For the rest of the evening they read old books. They asked him to familiarize himself with these books that were to be used for his schooling. After they left, he continued reading for awhile. Then, he remembered his plans with Lyle and that he needed to wake up early so he went to sleep.

At two o'clock the alarm went off. Robert didn't have the energy to get up but managed to drag his body to the kitchen. Now he's glad that he asked them to set the alarm. After his first cup of coffee, he feels the life coming back to his body. Before he journeys back upstairs to get dressed, he remembers the crawlers. He takes them out of the fridge in the back room and sets them by the door with his keys. He washes and then fills his thermos to leave. On the way he thinks about the books that he has read and is amazed at all that is involved. He ponders where Sabula finds these people. That woman is very resourceful. She never stops surprising him. As Robert gets near the lake, he sees light. It's Lyle waiting for him. He looks at the clock on his radio, and it says 4:10 in the morning. Lyle asks if he needs a refill before they start. Lyle tops him off. Then, they launch off the pier and for the next four hours they fish and get caught up on what's going on in their lives. Robert asks Lyle where he and Lily plan to go on vacation. Lyle says that they are leaving Thursday to beat the weekend rush and are flying to Barbados.

"Wow! Lyle, it's only two days from now. I take it Lily has you packed already." Robert knows how organized she is because he has gone on vacation with them. A week before they left, Lily had everything in order. Over the years she would pull out her pad and start checking off her list. Lily never missed a beat, and she seemed to never forget anything. Honestly, she would take inventory.

"Robert, you know Lily. She is still the same." Then they laugh. Some things never change, but he likes that quality. She is the most organized person that he has ever met. That's what attracts him to her. Not only does she care about her finances, but also she cares about her health, and she is not afraid to get her hands dirty. He couldn't ask for more.

"You know something, Robert? I'm making this vacation special. We are going to renew our wedding vows," Lyle confides. "I have not told her, but I will tell you that I love her and would be lost without her. Robert, some things are more important even than money, for you can't buy love and that's the truth. Love starts from the heart, and then you push it throughout your body until it overwhelms you. Then, it takes control of your emotions to the point that you can't eat or sleep. All you do is think about this person, and what makes this grand is when it's mutual. That, my boy, is true love so if you ever feel that way about someone, then you are halfway there as long as the other person feels the same. Then, it's only a matter of time. Have patience for that is a requirement. When it does happen, keep her because equally committed relationships grow scarce. It is easy to find pussy, but it's hard to find a good, devoted woman. Robert, you should not even be thinking about this, for you are in your prime. Enjoy yourself. Venture out. Travel to meet women from different cultures. Explore. You will be surprised at what you encounter," Lyle concluded philosophically.

In the end they did not catch many fish, but they talked, laughed, and planned on doing this again. Lyle asked Robert if he would join them for dinner, but he said that he had plans. He would be happy, though, to drive them to the airport. He asked what time the flight was leaving. Lyle told him it leaves early, but that he really didn't have to get up extra early for them. Robert insisted so Lyle told him the flight departs at five in the morning.

"What time do you need me to be at the house, Lyle?" Robert asks.

"Be here at three in the morning if you don't mind," Lyle answers.

"Okay. I will see you at three. Send Lily my love. Thanks for a wonderful morning," Robert says.

"Thank you for joining me. I too enjoyed myself and thanks for offering to take us to the airport," Lyle said. They docked and took their belongings out of the boat. Robert told him to take the fish, for it would smell up his new car. He told Lyle that he wouldn't forget all that he had done for him over the years. As he left, Lyle watched him driving off, and he doesn't know what to think, for he is scared. He can't read Robert.

Sabula has never given him a straight answer. If anything, she's been avoiding the issue since the last time they talked. She has pretended to be busy not calling Lyle back for the last month. He stopped and told Lily that his fears are coming true, but that they need to stick to the plan. Now they have two days left and then they're gone. As he drives home, he still worries now that Robert insists on taking them to the airport. If they leave early, then it will look suspicious and if they wait for him, it could be a trap. Sabula promised to give him an answer. Should he stop by the house and confront her or play along and take his chances? Lyle decides to chance it and have Robert take them to the airport.

When he gets home, Lily asks him how his day went with Robert. He says that they caught some fish but Robert donated his. They didn't catch much, but they had a good time so it was worth it. Lily gives the fish to the cook and then Lily joins Lyle upstairs. He goes to take a shower and Lily decides to join him. They make love in the shower and afterwards take a nap. When they wake, they talk about what is going on but will leave the rest to fate. They will call the staff from the hotel and tell them that they are not coming back. They will leave instructions in the study with six months' pay. Lyle talks to the realtor to put the house on the market. They will have their possessions packed and put in storage. Staff members will supervise the packing. Once the house is empty, they will notify the realtor. Once they are settled in their new home, they will have the rest of their things shipped to their destination.

The next day they take care of those last-minute preparations and then wait. They try not to show their excitement. The staff has no clue, which is good. Lily says that she is ready. Robert calls to confirm that he will pick up coffee and donuts for the ride and be there promptly at three. Lily and Lyle take a good look at their home for the last time walking throughout the property. There are so many memories they wish it were different, but then they pay for their mistakes. Life does not forgive for this is Heaven and Hell.

Throughout life people have said that we do not leave this world until all matters are settled, be they good or bad. Mainly the bad is what keeps us here the longest. Look around. So many people think that they can screw their fellow man without any repercussions. They are actually just digging the hole a little bigger. In the end they wind up broke, alone, and in despair. One last point is that they don't make it to eternal glory. Lyle knows that he will be one of them for his sins are too great. It's just a matter of the time before his sins catch up to him; nevertheless, he hopes that Lily lives to be of old age and decides not to live alone. She has been an inspiration for him, and he is sorry for his sins.

Lyle and Lily have dinner and retire early in the evening because they want to be ready; they set their alarm clock for one thirty. Their staff has been excused early. They are delighted for it's a beautiful day, and there is still time to enjoy the evening. Now, they are able to start their holiday early, for they will have a long weekend especially due to Monday being Labor Day and the Cummins on vacation.

Meanwhile, Robert is into his studies, for Thursday at midnight starts his last schooling of the black arts. He hopes that it will only take a couple of months like the strangers said, for he is tired of all this business. He should not complain because it is very interesting so far. In the time since he started reading, he is able to lift objects and to hold them while he moves other objects. He has been reading on teleporting but will wait for the strangers to teach him, for he is a bit leary about trying it by himself. He continues to read an old book from the Dark Ages. It explains ways to develop his strength starting from the mind and working all the way through the body to the index finger. Then he learns how to take aim and release. It's easier said than done, for he's been working on this since Sabula's instructors gave him the book, but so far nothing. He feels his strength flowing from his mind but can't seem to concentrate enough to make it work throughout his body to his index finger. It sucks because that's just the finger. Then they illustrate the whole hand and then both hands and from the eyes. He thinks, "Imagine the power I will have once I develop my skills. There is no stopping me, for the world will tremble at my feet. I will be their God. They will worship me. Sabula is right; the evil grows in me and I like it."

Then he remembers when he was in Hell with his mother suffering. He recalls the pain that he felt, the flesh being ripped off her body, and the beast having his way with her. It was all coming back. Why couldn't he remember why until now? Then, he explodes with anger and out of nowhere he takes aim and disintegrates the wall in the room. The whole wall collapses to the point that it shakes the foundation of the house. Sabula comes running in with the strangers right behind her. They are stunned. They all look at her. She asks what he has done. Then, he unleashes another blast at the gazebo which is in view. It's destroyed. His anger grows, and he tells all of them to leave. His rage is mighty. He must remember all of it, not just his mother but also his father. He needs to calm down so he can remember.

"What was it that the dark one said?" Robert tried to recall to himself. He sits down and then tries to recall his mother being taken to the eternal glory, and his father, what did he say? He thinks back and then all at once it hits him. He was betrayed by Lyle. He shot him in the back of the head, and Sabula was there to witness the brutal killing. Then, he continued telling of the way they had screwed over his dead body. "Lyle, you killed both my parents. Now you will pay and you will pay dearly," he promises himself. Then, he remembers the promise he made to his father. He had promised not to harm Lily, and he would keep that promise. He looked at his watch. It's nine o'clock. He will call Lyle over, for tonight he dines in Hell.

Lily answers the phone and Robert asks to speak to Lyle. She wakes him and he asks Robert what he needs. Robert tells him that he needs to see him right now. He tells him not to run, for he knows what he did and if Lyle doesn't remember that's no problem, for Robert will remind him.

"Lyle, if you run she dies, understand? Your time has run out. How do you want to proceed? You come here, or I come to get you, for the longer you make me wait the more I will enjoy hurting you," Robert says determinedly.

"Robert, please can we talk about it? Let me explain. You need to know the truth. Sabula put me up to this. She planned it. I did not want to do it, but she forced me. My hands were tied. I loved your father. He was my friend. Don't believe what she tells you. It's all lies. I will not run. I will be there in one hour. I will tell you all of it in front of her. No need for me to lie, for I know the outcome, but you will know the truth," he concludes. He hangs up.

Lily is crying, and she tells Lyle, "Let's run. They won't find us."

"No, Lily, if we do, when they do find us they will kill you, and that is even worse. Stick to the plan, for they are not going to harm you. Leave this place and don't ever return. Forget me and start a new life. I've been living on borrowed time for a very long time now. It's time for me to put this to rest. I need to get ready. I do not want him to get angrier than he already is."

"Lyle, you told me it was Sabula that you were afraid of. What's going on? Tell me the truth. You lie to me. Why does Robert want to harm you? What haven't you told me?"

"Lily, I've told you too much already. Just get my clothes ready. I need to leave. Stop pushing me. I won't tell you. I love you very much. Thank you for all the memories, but now I must go and meet my maker for this is Heaven and Hell. A person can't leave until he pays for all that he has done. Over the years, I have done my share. I would tell him that I'm sorry, but that's not going to fly with Robert."

"Lyle, call the constable. Let him know that your life is in danger. He can protect you."

"No! They can't protect someone that is already dead. Lily, let me go for the clock is running. I don't have much time. Call a cab because I need to leave right now." He hugs and kisses his wife for the last time." Stick to the plan. If you love me, don't make it worse." He goes to load his gun taking extra clips for his Beretta. Then he leaves. As the cab is driving off, he looks back one final time at Lily and their home.

Meanwhile, Robert is planning his first of many kills. Once he tastes the fear, he will look forward to more. Robert over the years has seen his part of death but until tonight, he has never actually killed anyone. Sabula always included him in her victim's torture, for it fascinated him. It fed his need. He would get off on it, especially sucking up their soul. After the first time that he witnessed Cindy's demise, he has hungered for more. Now, he will experience first hand how it feels to take the life out of a person and to see the glow leaving the eyes as they grow dark like that of a shark. As the heat from the body is replaced with cold as it stiffens with death, he will be in command of his powers. He will have some fun, for Lyle will not die easily but a little at a time. In the end, he will welcome death, but it won't come for Lyle. He will make him pay dearly by keeping him alive as long as possible. Killing his father was a big mistake, but the pain that his mother had to endure, that is what sent him over the top. He also had the chance to kill Robert before he was reborn, but he did not.

"What did he think? I would forgive him? Lyle is smart in finances but not too bright in finishing the job, or is it that he didn't have the stomach for it? He killed the father and the mother, but his conscience wouldn't let him kill the son.

Sabula will pay but not tonight. Her days are numbered. She will be even more special than Lyle. Tonight, I concentrate only on Lyle. I will play Sabula's game.

She does not have a clue to my experience in Hell. I will take her and observe her actions. The day will come when she is no longer needed. Then, I will have my revenge. She will be even sorrier than Lyle because by then my powers will be even stronger than they are now. She will feel the whole wrath. I will remind her of every detail just like I did Lyle. Then, she will feel pain like never before. I will feast on her fear, and she will know that I will take it all in before I decide to let her die. I need to finish for the hour draws near. Lyle should be getting close. I will call Sabula and tell her to be by my side. The rest of the strangers are to stay away," he concludes to himself.

Sabula enters the torture chamber. He gives her instructions telling her it's going to be a long night, and they will be needing her tools.

"Make hast, Woman, for Lyle will be here soon, and I do not want to disappoint him," Robert commands. As he finishes preparing the table of death, the old man says that Lyle is approaching the house. Robert tells the house staff to please escort his guest to the chamber. There will be no turning back. Lyle keeps his word, which Robert knew he would. Sabula asks what Robert has in store for Lyle.

"The truth about my father is what is more important than anything else," Robert responds. Once I have the truth, then the pain will follow because I'm a patient man and I have all night."

"Robert, how sure are you that Lyle was involved with your father's death?"

"Sabula, I had a vision and over time I learned to read visions for they are not wrong," he commented.

"Robert, you never said what happened to you when you died? How come? I've asked you numerous times, but you evade the question. Why?" she inquired.

"Sabula, I do not remember to this day. What do you want to hear, a lie?"

The old man leads Lyle to the chamber before they descend. The old man locks the door behind them. Lyle knows that he has not long to live. He will go out fighting. He will not be tortured. He will save a bullet for himself. He won't give Robert or Sabula the satisfaction of killing him. His left hand is on his gun, and he has a tight grip on it. The old man will be the first to fall. Then Robert will follow. Now he's happy that he brought extra clips, for in the end he will probably need them. Lyle decides to get cocky because he figures what does he have to lose? Therefore, he smiles as they near Robert. Now, Robert doesn't know what to make of all this, for he figured that they would have to carry Lyle in and strap him to the table. It's odd.

"Lyle, you walk in with a grin, but that's not the way you are leaving. You killed my father, and now you get payback for the pain that you inflicted on my family. You're lucky that I let Lily live, for she could be joining your fate," Robert reminds him.

"Robert, for that I thank you. It's me that you want. Let's get on with it. The only thing that I want to say in my defense is that Sabula was behind it all. She made a deal with your father, and was there to collect. Your sixteenth birthday was the deadline that your parents had to hand you over to Sabula. However, your father was having second thoughts so he came to me for help," Lyle explains.

"That's why you betrayed him because he asked for help?"

"No! I had my own agenda, an agreement that was made with Sabula long ago before I met your parents. I was to keep an eye on your father, and that was it, but that all changed at the last moment. Sabula raised the stakes and offered me more. My greed blinded me so I accepted and here we are. Bruce was my friend and I'm sorry for the betrayal, but I can't change what has already taken place. Robert, you know that I love you as a son that I never had. Please forgive me. Again, Sabula is the one to blame. She had options that were not utilized and that could have prevented the death not just of your father but your mother and Nora too. Ask her who planned your mother's fate, for in that I didn't have any part. I admit your father's death was planned, and we knew what the outcome was going to be even before we went in. Nora didn't have to happen, but Sabula never liked her. She was a freebee tossed in. It is horrific how they butchered her and the baby and cut it out of its womb. The baby was still alive so they slashed its throat and discarded it like trash. Ask her to tell you who planned that, for my hands are clean. I've done bad things in my life, but that is something that I couldn't do. Sabula, you're so quiet that's not like you usually. You have so much to say. I'm done but you're left," Lyle concluded.

"I have this strong feeling that I will be seeing you in Hell, Lyle. That is all I have to say to you," Sabula responded.

They look at each other, and then Lyle shoots the old man in the back and keeps shooting until he has to reload. Robert is moving way too fast; however, Lyle wounds Sabula in the face. Lyle sees the bullet strike her right cheek and explode out the left side with teeth and blood following behind. She screams in pain and Lyle tells her to get used to the feeling for in Hell it will be worse, but then that's where she came from. Lyle is using hollow points. After striking Sabula, he manages to strike Robert in the right shoulder. The shot explodes, and Robert cries out. Then, Robert unleashes some kind of blast from his left hand, and it rips off Lyle's right arm. As he is turning right, Lyle is still shooting at him and his arm races passed him. Then, he feels the blast once more, and this time his left leg explodes. As Lyle is falling, he shoots Sabula in the left ankle. It explodes as she cries and hits the ground. She manages to see her ankle, and it's only being held by her tendons and blood is gushing out. She is trying to stop the bleeding. Once Lyle is on the ground, Robert kicks the gun out of his hand, and he goes to work on him. Then, the real pain starts, for he is merciless and his eyes are completely red. He gives Lyle another blast and half of his torso is annihilated. Lyle doesn't have a clue as to why he's still alive, but he is nowhere from being done. With his finger Robert starts carving Lyle shredding his skin. The pain is unbearable. Then, he pulls out his right eye and stomps it on the ground. Next, he rips out his tongue, and then finally the blow finishes Lyle off. With his bare hand, he pulls out his heart and while it's still pumping, he eats it.

"Lyle, I have avenged my father and mother," Robert proclaims. He looks over and sees Sabula. She is all screwed up bleeding from her face, and what's left of her ankle. She got some payback, but it's far from being over. He holds on to his right shoulder. It's bleeding pretty well but as he looks at it, the healing has already begun. As he works his way up the stairs and calls for help unlocking the door, the strangers come and carry Sabula upstairs.

They take her to the hospital. She is in critical condition because she has lost so much blood. They are surprised that she is still awake from the shock and not in a coma from the trauma. After they operate on her, they will induce a coma for her to recover. Sabula is going to require a lot of attention and treatments that will last for many months to come. After she recovers, then they will start to do reconstructive surgery building her a new jaw. They will also have to replace her teeth for most of them were shot out or damaged. Her face will never be the same. Once a very beautiful woman, now the beauty has left her for the remaining time she has left on this earth. They were not able to save her right ankle. They had to amputate right below the knee. Her stay in the hospital will be for months. She needs to learn to walk after they attach a prosthesis to replace her lower leg. She will not be happy when she wakes. Pity the person who gives her the bad news. Robert asked the doctor to let him be there when they give her the bad news because even though she is in bed, she will not take it lightly. Sabula is responsible his parent's death, but he does, for the most part, feel sorry for her. That will probably change in the future but for now he will be by her side.

Lyle was supposed to be by his side for a very long time and see what happened to him? Now he resides in Hell. All those years that he lied to Robert's face saying how much he loved them, and he was the one to pull the trigger. He was Robert's role model and now he's gone. Robert vows that from this day forth no one will be close to him unless he chooses him or her to be with in the end. Robert vows that it will be him against the world. The dark one will pay for what he has done to Robert's mother and for what he is doing to his father. He will not be forgiven; that Robert promises himself. He will suffer the most. "Everyday I will practice my book and in the end my warriors will battle for this world, and I will take all that is mine. After the collapse of the world ending in my victory and I'm done with him, the dark one and the beast, I will go after the God of this world. I will take my place in history, for they will worship me in the end," Robert vows.

Father John looks up at Steve and Dale and tells them that Lily is never seen or heard from again. "When you return, we will discuss what happened to Rita. Her death was no accident. Please come back Monday at the same time. Then we will talk more about her death." Again, they pray asking for guidance. Father John walks them out and comments on the beautiful evening. They wave to him as they drive off. Dale asks Steve for his thoughts about what Father John had told them.

"It's unreal but my heart tells me that the man is not lying. Think about it? What would he have to gain? Dale, do you think he is crazy?"

"Yes and no, but what are we supposed to do with all this information? How do we use it? Dale, I believe that Father John is preparing us for a conflict that is in the works, good versus evil like the *Bible* says. The only difference, however, is that it is in our own back yard and not overseas."

"Steve, do you really think that the conflict will begin here?"

"No, I believe that it will **end** here. Don't you remember the similar dreams that Robert and his father had? It is possible that over time the *Bible* was manipulated to make us all think that the end would be fought in foreign lands but in reality, it was changed for the end is here. The foreign lands are just a staging area. I truly believe with all the foreigners that reside in this country, especially the Arabs, Indians, Chinese, and Russians, some will be fanatics. The right ingredients will exist to overthrow this country. We will need to unite to fight for our freedom to exist not only from the hard liners but also the antichrist. We must wait for Our Savior to return.

"Look around at all the people who have lost their life's savings to brokers swindling them with no remorse. Even when they are caught, they make bail and walk away. That's it. They are not even required to make good on the bad that they did. The corruption that has become part of our daily lives is just part of it. Then, you have porno that is everywhere and the queers, rapists, and child molesters. Do I need to say more? Turn on the TV and what do you see but man on man and woman on woman in prime time. Kids see all that garbage and they imitate. Does anyone care? No, because if they did it would not be on the screen. Dale, I'm scared but I'm not ready to give up my country without a fight even with all its faults. If Father John asks me to join the fight to save our country by getting rid of this antichrist, then I must. If you think it's bad now, imagine how it would be with him in charge and to have his permanent mark on your forehead or your hand. Then, to have to worship him without any freedom of choice is despicable. When I die, that mark won't be on my body, for my soul belongs to God and that is it. Dale, we're doing this together because I know that you have more to lose but also you have more to save. When we go on Monday, we will ask how to begin to prepare and how many people are with us. We will need munitions, medical supplies, food, water, generators, gas, and fuel to start. We will need to relocate, probably to go west and establish a strong hold. We will leave our women and some men who will stay to protect them. We will take the fight to them leaving no trail behind. We will travel at night. Dale, I will cash in my stocks and bonds. I suggest that you do the same, for we will need a lot of resources to finance our fight," Steve concludes determinedly.

"Steve, can we take a break? Let's talk about something else, for I have a headache. Tell me that we're stopping for a drink. I will call Lisa. You know how she worries. Also, don't forget about tomorrow. Penny is looking forward to seeing you," Dale reminds him.

"Dale, can you see me dating Penny? I wonder if it will work out."

"Steve, are you having second thoughts? Don't start that crap. You've complained over the years that you grow tired of living by yourself. Now, you have the chance to change all that. You had better be there, or Lisa will come and drag you to the house. She can be very persuasive, and if you piss her off, you are on your own. I mean it. You don't want to see that side of her."

"Okay, I will be there for dinner. I was planning on bringing flowers and two boxes of candies for her and the kids so are you happy now?"

" Really, you're bringing flowers and candies? I don't remember when the last time was that I've done that for Lisa. I'll tell you what. Since you're going there; pick up some flowers for Lisa and a box of candies. I would really appreciate that and so would Lisa. Do not forget to get a nice card. Call me on the way here, and I will meet you at the door so I can fill out the card," he instructs Steve.

"Wow, Dale, you're such a romantic. I sense a little kiss butt."

"Steve, don't say a word for you will be doing the same in the future if we have one."

After two beers Dale calls home and tells Lisa that he has reminded Steve about tomorrow. He will be home in a little while. She thanks him for calling and tells him to be careful on the way home because she loves him. After a few more beers they make their way to Dale's house. As Dale is getting out the car, he tells Steve that dinner is at five.

Meanwhile, Robert is flying to Iran to meet the minster of operations. Sabula is with him, and she reminds him to tell those assholes that they'd better not screw this up. It has taken many years to plan and many, including Iran, have paid with their lives for their mistakes. That is why they lost the war in so little time. Their incompetence was their downfall. They were so arrogant at the time that they were blinded by their hatred toward the West. They did not plan their actions accordingly. That was their demise because their troops were scattered around the country and when Sabula's forces invaded catching them off guard, they were confused. When the dark one's force launched their drones that were equipped with the intelachip, the Iranians were easy pickings. The drones flew day and night and the weather was not even a factor. For the first time in the history of war, it was won by unmanned vehicles. Technology was at it best. That is when it was decided that future wars would be fought in this manner, and so it was decided that no further aircraft were to be built. The campaign in Iran lasted only a matter of weeks. The Iranians suffered many losses and their troops were annihilated. In the end they surrendered to the dark one's general and a treaty was signed. Then after the war, the victors dismantled the Iranian nuclear weapons destroying their capabilities for future use.

Now, Robert and Sabula go back to see how the troops are doing with their plans. They promise them their revenge. Most of the problems that the Middle East faces are partly their fault. They are instigating a fight to move people out of an area that is vital for their plans. Then, they cover-up what happens and move forward. The killer is that they also promise the rag heads that they would have a part in invading the United States so they really are trying to impress us. They cannot wait to get to American soil and cause destruction. They want it bad. Sabula and Robert figure the more help the better because they see this big picture of world domination. Those boys think small, but that's good because it helps Robert's cause and Sabula is not bitching about it either.

These days Sabula does not have the sense of humor that she once had, but understand that since the incident with Lyle, she has never really recuperated. Besides the limp, her face is covered with a veil. Even after extensive surgeries she has never regained the beauty that she once had.

"Now, when do I hit on her? It's always from behind. That's the only way I screw her. I feel sorry for the old bitch. I've never kissed her after the incident, but she still sucks me off. It has been years since I have eaten her cookie. I just can't get passed the knee," he laughs to himself remembering that day so long ago. "I did manage to get some pay back not just from Lyle but also from Sabula. Either way she still has her day coming, for the dark one and I have an agreement. She has no clue that I know what she did, and in the end I will be taking her out. One good thing is that she never really raises her voice to me or pushes my buttons anymore. Poor Sabula, how she changes from bad-ass to ass-kisser, isn't life wonderful?" he continues to chuckle to himself.

As they land, Robert needs to check on supplies: munitions, drones, and a new arsenal of transformers that are to be completed. They've just started production on the second generation. Those are going to be fun when they strike the United States, and when they move south and then north. Robert cannot wait to see what kind of destruction they create. He has a lot invested, and today he gets to see his rewards. The troops will be using live bait for the demonstration. It should be quite a show. It gives him a hard on.

"Sabula, come here before we depart, for I have a snack for you. Sabula sets on a chair, for it's hard for her to bend her knees. She goes to work on him and in no time it's snack time. After she licks him clean, they take a ride to the secret bunker where the troops wait for his arrival.

Bunker

When they enter the bunker, they descend about a half mile. Then, they come out to a big clearing and see the minister of operations with some of their other friends.

"Welcome, Mr. President, we have been expecting you. This is our most modern facility. It's completely undetected by satellites or by any other reconnaissance. It's been in production for the last ten years, and we are always upgrading. Would you care for a tour, for you paid for most of it?"

"Yes, we welcome a tour. Don't you think, Sabula?" She is not even noticed or acknowledged. It is sad because she is the one that planned this so long ago. Because of her condition, Robert asks before they start if any stairs are involved.

"Mr. President, not to worry for we have the means, and it involves no stairs, but we do have a wheel chair for her use," the minister assures him.

"Please, call me Robert. We don't have to be so formal here. We're all friends," Robert assures him.

"Yes, Robert. We will start from the bottom and work all the way up. Is that okay?"

"Fine. Let's get to it." They end up descending another mile, for they are deep into the earth.

"Robert, this is where we store our inventory from food to munitions to supplies for the drones and parts for the transformers," the minister continues informatively. Sabula decides to use the wheel chair. It's electric so it's convenient for her to use. Robert walks with the rest of the group amazed at the size of the area. There are hundreds of jets, vehicles, drones, missile launchers, tanks, and helicopters. They say that more are arriving everyday. Robert is tickled pink.

"You've done well. You will be rewarded. My money has been well spent," he tells the minister.

"Robert, let's go to the lab, which is in the next floor, and you will see technology at its best. We have invested in the best scientists in the world. They are building your army of transformers, the second generation. They are awesome and they pack a lot of punch. Yes indeed, they are a sight to see. They have different sizes from miniature to small for reconnaissance or middle-sized for ground assault to the massive for total destruction. They have demonstrations set up using real people so you get the true benefit." The minister waves his hand and the people are released. They are instructed to run and hide. The ones that are successful are promised that they will live. Then, the troops release the monsters of destruction, and in no time they find their prey. With no remorse they kill and mangle their bodies. They hear the screams and cries as Robert's machines perform with little effort.

"I'm impressed but how will they perform in the real world?" Robert asks.

"What you see is what you get," the minister responds.

It reminds Robert of his dreams, and it makes him happy to be bad. Sabula is able to witness this wonder. It's ironic that they end up spending most of the day experiencing different scenarios. At the end Robert asks where the troops were able to find all of the volunteers. The minister and Sabula smile and say that they were the survivors of the recent attacks.

It's true that in the attacks no survivors have ever been located. People thought it was odd to just find dead bodies. Robert learns that after the attacks, people that were alive were brought here and used as guinea pigs.

"It's an excellent idea," Robert said," because there is no sense in wasting people that are already dead. How many of these people do we have?"

"Not to worry for we have a couple hundred. The ones that you see here refused to join our cause. We are planning another attack in a small village in the next few days, for our numbers are increasing every day. Then, we stop. Tomorrow we will inspect the biology department. It's incredible in size. I know that you will enjoy it. So much has gone into its planning.

Nothing was spared to please you. Therefore, the rest of the day we wine and dine. Women are at your disposal or men are available for Sabula."

Sabula doesn't join in anymore. It's been years. She retires to her room and waits for her company. While she waits, she drinks. The women here are slaves for there is nothing they won't do to please. If they don't please for whatever the reason, they join the rest of the herd waiting to be slaughtered. At the end of the evening, two of their most beautiful women join Robert. They are not slaves but family members. Robert knows that he pisses people off, but he doesn't give a shit. He's the president. They join him in bed, and they don't hold anything back. That's Robert's type of woman. Afterwards they eat a snack, and then he proceeds to give them another screwing. Life is good and so are these women. They take their turns drinking his milk because they are so eager to please him. They even ask him to screw them in their ass. The next few days they will be sleeping in his bed. The one with dark hair is the minister's daughter. The minister had resisted at first, but in the end he could not deny Robert. The red head is the wife of the minister's brother. She had taken a liking to Robert the first time he saw her. He needed to remind the brother that he gets what he wants for not only is he the president but also his master. The brother was not pleased so he was escorted to the lab where tomorrow he will meet his fate. Screwing the wife made him even harder, for she was eager to please him in the end. She slept close to him asking if she could join him the next day. The dark haired one wants Robert to take her to the states to please him. She is beautiful, young, and full of life. Being a softy, Robert decides to take them both back with him. They are delighted to hear the news, and they are incredible in bed. It's odd that neither of them has ever spoken of their husband or of their father. That really didn't matter to Robert. He decided to send for both of them, set them up with visas, and provide a place for them to live nearby. He owns them. They are his property to do with as he pleases. They are excited to be going to the states. He tells them that they need to sleep because tomorrow he needs them to get up early as he would have another full day. Also, she will get to see her husband die in the lab. It's sad, but he needs to set an example for the rest of his comrades. They will think twice about refusing him. When he returns, he will screw the wife repeatedly. She will be his number one. She will accompany him to the functions and will keep the other one in check. It's all good. They will provide him company in the states, and when he grows tired of them, they will be replaced just like everything else.

Sabula cannot complain. She had her pick of two men to please her while she was getting drunk. They first bathed her. Then, one carried her to bed where they kissed her all over and made her come in their mouths. She had one licking her ass hole while the other licked and sucked her pussy. She got her fill. She used them. They both screwed her at the same time. She loved it, and she made them kiss her mouth. For the rest of the night she didn't let them sleep for she was horny. She knew that tomorrow she would not be joining Robert so tonight she would have the time of her life drinking and getting screwed. Lately, she felt as if Robert is getting to the point where she is no longer needed. He doesn't ask for her opinion like he once did.

The dark one would not grant her audience like he often used to do so she could not complain like before because no one listens ever since that dreadful day. Not only did she lose her beauty but also the clout that she once had. Men still fear her but it's different. Now, men turn their faces when she walks by. Before they would send her flowers and would wine and dine her. She's got to the point where she pays to get screwed, for the men and woman tell her that they love her because they want that bigger tip.

"Those bastards and bitches think I'm stupid, but I still have some powers," she analyzes for many of them have left her. She no longer is able to change or teleport or able to lift objects, but she still has a little power left. One day in the near future that can be the only thing to save her. All she does now is play along taking orders. Before, she was the one to give them. Now it's very different. She misses having the authority and power that she had in the past because Lyle screwed everything up. She watched him die but that was not enough.

When she finally left the hospital, she searched for Lily. She is able to track her down in South America using her resources. Then, she remembers the doctor and inquires if Lyle had contacted him.

"Yes, indeed, but what's in it for me?" the doctor wants to know.

"Well, first you get to keep your miserable life. Then, the reward that I'm offering you get to keep. Where is she? It doesn't take all day to answer, or you could be included because what is one more to add to the list? Tell me, Good Doctor, and don't leave anything out. The reward is very generous," Sabula informs him.

"Sabula, the woman called two days ago and arranged to be here tomorrow morning at nine o'clock. Because it's for you, I can have her sedated. Then, I will call you and you can take her out the back way. Would that please you?" he asked.

"Very good, Doctor, I knew that we could reach an agreement. My men will be standing by just making sure that she is completely out before you call. We don't want her waking up when we're taking her out," Sabula concludes hanging up. She is pleased she will get that bitch. Just thinking about it makes her wet. For six months she had been waiting. Now it comes together like a puzzle. Lily thought that she could run, and Sabula can't wait to see her expression. All the pain that Lyle caused her, including taking her beauty, will be avenged. Now, she walks around with a cane. "How humiliating," she sighs.

Meanwhile, Lily is happy. She called the doctor after the surgery. She will disappear for good to start her new life. She promises Lyle that she will stick to the plan. Her heart is heavy, for she left right after Lyle died. Lily's been living for the past six months in Tierra del Fuego but will need to go to Concepcion for the doctor has moved. Lily plans on leaving tonight. That way, tomorrow she can take in some sights. Then, the following morning she has her appointment at nine. Afterwards when she heals, she plans on flying to Ireland and from there wherever her heart desires, for she is very well off thanks to Lyle. She misses her husband and would prefer to have him instead of the money. He was her first love. Many nights she cries herself to sleep wishing she could join him. If she only knew that Lyle never made it to Heaven for his sins were too great.

Lyle only remembered God when it benefited him. God doesn't work that way, for if one truly loves God, the love must be constant. That's what is wrong with this world. People look for God when they need something. Other than that, they can't seem to even give him thanks for the food that they receive let alone the roof over their head. The only time they go to church is on Christmas or Good Friday and Easter. Then, they look around for someone to recognize them like they need a witness. Loving God is full time all the time. He is Our Savior, our salvation from damnation. He requires no contracts, just our love. Just because we donate, doesn't mean that we are forgiven for our sins. When we donate, we do it because we want to and not because we are looking for redemption, or anything else for the matter. One day we will all have to answer for our sins, but if we choose to change and really mean it, God will forgive us as long as it doesn't include killing or something that we did that was so awful.

Lily calls the doctor the next day to confirm her appointment. The doctor is pleased that she has called.

"Good, Lily. I'll see you at nine," he says hanging up. He thinks this is easy money because Lyle has already paid Lily's part. He has really paid for both, but Lyle is not with her now, and he is not going to ask about it for he will keep it all plus the reward. That's the best part. He didn't even have to get his hands dirty. Then, the greedy bastard wonders how much the reward is so he can use it for a vacation. Lyle paid him forty thousand. Whatever he gets from Sabula added to that makes this a pretty lucrative deal.

The next morning Lily is excited. These are her last days in this country, for as soon as she is healed, she will take the first flight out, never returning to this jungle. She can't stand it here with all the insects and screwed up cultures. She wants out. She arrives ten minutes early. The doctor is there waiting for her. Then, he walks her to the room and in no time she is out. Sabula walks in right after Lily is out cold and gives the good doctor ten thousand for his part. Looking at the chair while Lily is asleep, Sabula looks at her features and tells the doctor that she was more beautiful than her. He replies that he could do some more work on Sabula to correct some of her jaw imperfections and maybe he could help her with the limp. Sabula looks at the little man and tells him that she will be back so get to work preparing what is going to be done for her. She reminds him that if he fails, he will pay with his pathetic life. Now, the doctor is not sure if that was the right thing to mention for his greed has put him in a situation. As Sabula's men are carrying Lily out the back door, Sabula looks back and smiles. "Remember, Doctor, no failures," she warns.

Lily was to have surgery but that never happened. Sabula beat her to the punch. Lily was taken to a remote place in the jungle where she was raped and tortured. Sabula remembered the money that Lyle had stashed away and tells Lily it will be a quick death if she gives the account numbers to her.

"Honey, you will not need it where you are going. Let me help you spend it," Sabula suggests.

Lily tells her to fuck off because she is already dead. Sabula's men go to work on Lily to make her talk. If they succeed, they get ten percent of the stash. They start by breaking her arms and then her legs, but she is stubborn. In the end, she welcomes death to join her husband. Lily spits on Sabula wishing she would end it because she cannot understand why she is still alive even after all the beating that she has endured. One thing she won't do is give her the satisfaction of having the money. She already took her husband and now in just a bit Lily will join him.

Sabula says to her, "Look, do you see what he did to me? He took away my beauty." Lily told her that it was an improvement, and some of her men laughed. That is when she brought out the knife and sliced at her face taking away any beauty that was left.

Lily cries out, "You can take my flesh, but you can't take my soul because it belongs to God. Screw you, Sabula!" were her last words.

She was beheaded and left in the jungle as Sabula laughs, "Payback, Bitch. I never did like you." Sabula's men are pissed because Lily didn't break even after all the pain. Lily had the satisfaction and the ten million that Sabula did not get her hands on. In the end, Lily made it to Heaven and met up with Elsa, Nora, and the baby where they served God forevermore in eternal glory. Lily was no dumb woman. She had gone to the bank and made arrangements and told the man in charge that one day a man would show up to claim the money. She was leaving instructions for him, and it was imperative for him to have both the money and the instructions. His name would be Lyle. Two days before she was to have the surgery, she had a dream, if you want to call it that, but to her it was more of a vision. The point is that she was instructed to change everything back to Lyle's name, and she could not fathom why but she had to do it because she had promised. When she woke up, she remembered and didn't question it but went to the bank and did what she had been asked to do.

After breakfast Robert's comrades escorted him to a lab which was very big and modern. They explained some of the biological weapons that they were working on which included anthrax and other germ warfare. They even had a demonstration set up, and the subject is none other than the husband of the red head. Robert turned and looked at him waving goodbye. "Cool. Let's get on with it. The brother is not joining us this morning. I do understand, and I'm not that cold," Robert thinks to himself. They turn the valve on and within minutes it is over, poor bastard. Robert is impressed. They do different applications. It's awesome. Robert tells them that they will be using these methods in the final days. "Because I don't truly want to destroy the whole world, I will need somewhere to unwind. I need to have a little fun so once the air clears, and the buildings are in tact, I will be throwing a big party for the survivors and ruling my subjects by having the time of our lives. I can't wait for the fall of Mankind. All of this gets me horny," he thought.

After their tour, they went to the next level, worldwide telecommunications. I mean they had it laid out. There had to be at least a couple hundred people of all nationalities working side by side. They were in touch with Islam, the extreme fundamentalists. It's awesome. At a moment's notice they can bring up their cells throughout the world. Robert turns and shakes his partner's hand. His henchmen spend the money wisely. They tour the upper floor and watch the people from above. That way they can't see Robert. They spend the rest of the day there for there is much to see and learn. They tell him that as they speak his vehicle is getting retrofitted with the latest technology. They give him a phone that can't be traced. The watch they give him has a panic button, not that he needs it, but he will never tell them that he can't be killed. That's **his** secret. What a wonderful day to be bad. It's a shame that Sabula didn't join them, for this is very fascinating to see. Technology is being used to the fullest, and it's all for his benefit.

After the tour, Robert is ready for food and to play with his woman. Tomorrow or the day after he needs to get back to the states, for he's needed back home. Don't you just love when a plan comes together? Now, it is only a matter of time before he begins, but he needs to check out some things back home before he begins the march to victory? When they arrive at the villa, his honeys are waiting for him like little puppies waiting for their master. He doesn't want to disappoint them so he excuses himself and asks them to call when it's dinner time. The dark haired one's name is Sara. She is the first to drink her milk. She does not spill a drop. When she's done, she licks it clean. Sara is about twenty-one years old, very hyper, about five feet one and weighs about one hundred five pounds. She loves to fuck but still needs to develop the skills that Naomi possesses. In time she will develop into a great fuck. She has short hair, full lips, and a small rack but it complements her body. She has one tight little bubble ass that she's not afraid to use. In addition, she has a gap between her legs that a fist can fit into, and it drives Robert nuts. The red head's name is Naomi, and she enjoys taking her time. She is thirty-five and is five feet eight weighing about one hundred thirty pounds. She's all woman. She has long red hair and full lips with a medium rack and nice upside- down, heart-shaped ass, his favorite. Now red is different. She enjoys cuddling before or after fucking. She enjoys whatever she is doing either by kissing or massaging. She is very passionate, especially when she is sucking you off. She enjoys it, and she lets you know. Robert understands why her husband was pissed. He'd be pissed too but now he has the best of both worlds for these honeys are his, and he's not sharing like in the past.

Robert joins his comrades for dinner. They toast to the new world. Sabula is also there and is pleased to hear that all is going well. All the men stand and toast Sabula, for it is her vision that has inspired the nations that are seated here to come together for this cause. At end of the campaign the world will be divided and each one will be responsible for his own country, but they will all serve Robert. He will be their king. They will be his generals and there will only be one currency. It will have Robert's face on it. On the backside it will have dragons eating flesh. Then, the mark of the beast will be used as a means of tracking individuals. People always assumed that it would be a mark, but in reality it is set forth like animals for each and every one will be required to have a gps-chip installed. If they refuse, they will be sent to camps where in due time they will be turned into slaves or killed in sport. Robert has this dream of bringing back the gladiators; the slaves will build the arena in major cities around the world and then have a process of eliminations. The winner gets his freedom to go where he wants to start a new life.

His comrades agree. They ask Robert if they also are to have chips installed. Robert smiles and says," Do you think that is really needed?" They breathe with a sigh of relief and toast him again. Sabula looks at Robert for she knows that he has his own agendas, and she remembers telling him what they want to hear. She smiles at him, and he winks his eye and smiles back. Robert is good; he can convince anyone that the sky is red when it is blue. He is ready to take over. Many years have passed. He has learned so much. Now, when Sabula sees him she knows he is ready. Just looking at the way he speaks or manipulates these men, she can see that they really believe him. Robert is a greedy man. He is not sharing with anyone, including her. He is only sharing with the dark one because he has to. In the end Sabula feels that they are going to have their problems for neither one likes to share and that could prove fatal. "All my work could be ruined because of these assholes that can't seem to share. Don't get me wrong. I'm just as greedy as the next person, but I do know when to share," she thinks lifting her glass to toast the men. They smile and say that Sabula is the best meanest woman that they have ever met. Then, they all laugh and drink even more. At the end of the meeting they are pretty must toasted. She can't remember when the last time was that she had had such a good time. Even Robert managed to hug her, and he actually kissed her in her mouth and the rest of the men followed. They started playing music, and they were led to the ballroom. She felt alive. They danced and the other women joined them. For the rest of the evening it was wonderful. Robert even asked her to dance with him. He thanked her and said that she had made this all possible. It almost made her cry. A tear did manage to slip by as she hugged him. She didn't care because Robert noticed her. It had been a long time since he had kissed her. She knows that deep down she does love him even after all these years. After all, she had been his first. That night she slept well for the first time in a long time.

The next day they left to return to the states because Robert had to address the nation. He needed to calm the people's fears. They love him. He gives them hope. He has that effect on people. In reality, he could have been the best president since President Obama, but what do you expect? He is the antichrist. Now, he will start making miracles and bringing nations together. He will make crops grow where they normally wouldn't. He will feed the world. They will love him even more. For a couple of years they will live in peace and then when his sheep are asleep, he will strike and men will fall. Robert has it all planned. He will go to every country and demand peace. He will make them destroy their arsenal. That way when it's time, they won't have the means to fight. Robert thinks of every detail. They will look up to him as a savior. They will build statues in his honor. Then, he will make them worship him. The more they worship him, the more traditionally built statues will be taken out until no other statues but his own are left. In the end it will be put into law that anyone caught worshipping another will automatically be put into the prisons awaiting the arenas where they will be used as sport. In addition, people will be paid for snitching on others and with the economy being the way it is, in no time the prisons will be full for the games. It's a win-win situation. The more Robert thinks about it, the more he likes it.

Meanwhile, the people are convinced to have the chips implanted for their own protection. Robert's reason will be to guarantee that there will be no more lost babies, kids, or parents. With a flip of a switch, they will be found. Not all but most of the people will love it. Some will fear it. The strong ones will fear it because of the warning written in the *Book of Revelation* that anyone who has a mark cannot enter Heaven. No matter, they will get their chip, or they will be used to build the arenas and the statues. They will learn to worship Robert. In the end he will be their god.

Then, the dark one joins the party, and he will rule; however, that's when there might be a problem with Robert. There's a possibility that he might have to be taken out. Robert is strong. No one knows his strength. He will join Bruce and Lyle. In the end there can only be one. The dark one will use Robert to fight the Savior. Once he is done with him there will be no need to have Robert around. The dark one will take over. He will finally rule for all the years. Since he has been ousted from Heaven, he will make humanity pay for his wait and his pleasure. Poor Robert, if only he knew all this work is in vain for the dark one will reap his rewards. The dark one at the end will tell him that's how life is. He will let him rule for awhile, but did Robert really think it was just for him? He's a pawn just like the rest. Either he's with him or he joins dear old dad. That's how it is. There is no room for two masters. It all comes down to one.

Steve lays out his clothes and has everything ready. At the end of the day he will come back to shower and shave. Tonight he meets Penny for the first time. Steve has a mild day and at three o'clock he calls in and says that he will catch them Monday and signs off. He calls Dale and says that he has picked up flowers for the women and some candies for the kids. He's on his way home to shower and will be over at five. Dale tells him to call him right before he arrives so he can get the flowers and candies for Lisa. He says he will wait for him by the door and thanks him.

Getting home, he put on the news, and they say another bombing occurred just a little while ago. Again, no one claims responsibility. This time it's in Paris, France, in the middle of rush hour. Many casualties have brought the body count to sixty five, of course, not including the wounded. How can people do such things like killing innocent people for no reason? When will it end? We live in the year 2025 and still we can't seem to live in peace. This world has much to offer, but we refuse to do what is right which is to live in peace like GOD intended us to do? Is Father John right that we need to have the end so the world can start over? That way GOD can guide us and educate us in virtues and morals. Families can be together once more. Most importantly, people will fear GOD to respect him, to honor him, and to give him thanks and praise. If that is what is needed, then let it happen soon. Many feel this way. GOD, we, the people, welcome your return for the glory and peace. We pledge our service to you to the end because without you there is no point in being here.

Penny

Steve finishes dressing and drives to Dale's home. He stops and picks up some wine. Two blocks away he calls Dale. He meets him at the door and tries to seem happy, for the news did indeed bring him down. He puts it behind him because he sees the kids, and they get hugs first. Then, Steve gave them a box of candies as they are being taken to Lisa's mom to spend the night. Their mom is a very charming woman. Of course, she gives Steve a hug and welcomes him to the family. He's caught off guard. She mumbles something, and she smiles as she leaves. Lisa is next to hug him and tells him in his ear that it's good that he irons his clothes. Then, Penny walks out wearing a soft, white dress with red pumps complementing her green eyes and red hair. Wow! She is looking good. Steve shakes her hand like a schoolboy. She pulls him to her and gives him a hug and they all laugh. He gives her the flowers and candies. She tells him that there was no need to bring anything but thanks him. They take their places at the dining room table. Dale gives thanks to GOD. Then, they eat the nice roast with all the trimmings. Lisa asks how they like it.

Steve says, "It's the best so far but what do you expect? You cook with love, Lisa. That sure makes a difference because it makes it all taste good. Don't change the recipe."

She looks over at Penny and says that Penney is the one that prepared the meal. " It's excellent. She can cook but also is organized, responsible, and clean."

"Lisa, in all the years that I have known you, I have never been here where either you or Dale has made excuses about your home or your finances being out of whack. Over the years I've mentioned it to Dale that

I admire you because not only do you deal with the kids but also the home and the finances. Dale prefers you doing the bills and him getting his little cut at the end of the week. He is a happy camper. In the entire years that you have been doing the finances, he's never complained that something was late, or you had to pay late fees or bounce checks. If anything, he said that he'd be lost without you. Not only does he love you, but he relies on you."

Lisa reaches over, gives Dale a kiss, and says she would be lost without him. Steve takes Penny's hand and says if she is anything like her sister, he's sold.

"Not only will I love her, but I will take care of her because it is hard to find a woman with all of the above qualities."

Penny squeezes Steve's hand and says, "Steve, you've grown up. Who would have thought that you could appreciate life the way that you do? People change. Most people welcome it. Some fight it and some never change and those that don't are the ones that always complain. Many times in our young life, we manage to skate on thin ice, but as we get older there is more weight on that thin ice and sooner or later it's not just the cracking of the ice that we hear but our life as it slips into the water, for the weight is so great. Had we figured to stay away from the thin ice and had gone to the safety zone, then we would not worry. We can't expect to be doing things that we did twenty years ago and not feel the repercussions the day after." When they finished dinner, Dale and Steve went outside and had a smoke while they drank a beer.

Steve tells Dale that Penny is a very wonderful woman, but he asked him if he has ever seen her pissed off. "Yes, we went to a lounge where a guy insisted on dancing with her. She tried to be nice dancing with him once, but then he would not stop. I told Lisa that I would tell him something the next time he came around."

Lisa said, "No, watch this, Dale," for she will put him in his place. Penny was sipping on her drink and when the man approached from behind to surprise her, he was the one that got surprised for at the last second she turned around and threw the drink at his face. Then, she stood up fast and kneed him where it hurts. The rest of the evening no one approached her and that guy ran out of there holding on to his balls. "Steve, that's the only time I've seen her get pissed, but what do you expect? She is a red head and takes no crap."

"You know, Steve, that over the years she has brought up your name asking if you were seeing someone. As far has I know, she has not been dating anyone for some time saying she was waiting for mister right."

"Well, Dale, I'm going to ask her out. If she accepts, I will do my best to make her happy. I'm tired of being by myself, and if she will have me, then one day not only will you be my best friend but also my brother-in-law." Dale goes and gets them another beer, and they toast to the future.

The girls call them afterwards to join them. They end up watching a movie and then Penny and Steve excuse themselves and go for a walk. As they are walking, Steve takes her hand and says that he has had a good time and that it would be nice to do this again. They stop at a nearby park and sit talking for awhile. She confesses that she has always liked him. She is also happy that he showed up so where do they go from here?

"Penny, I know that it is our first date but would you consider being my girlfriend?" Penny looks at him and her eyes get watery answering yes. Steve reaches over and gives her a little kiss and they hug. She tells him that she's been waiting for a long time and that she will do her best to make him happy.

"Steve, you know that I've never been married. I don't want you to think that I want to pressure you. If you ever have a problem, tell me. That way we can work it out, I will do the same," Penny told him.

"Okay, Penny, that's a deal. They end up walking some more, but now Steve has his arm around her waist and for the first time in a long time, she feels safe. Steve asks where she works, and she says she has been working at a nearby diner for five years.

"That is odd that I have never stopped to eat there, but if you do not mind, we'll make it a point to stop."

"If you stop by," she tells him," you can meet my boss. He is a very nice man and the staff is pleasant to work with." She gives him directions and tells him that she lives nearby. They exchange information. She tells him that she has been in his apartment with Lisa when Steven was on vacation. She had helped water his plants and was amazed at how clean the apartment was. She had even asked Lisa if Steve had maid service. Lisa told her that this is the way it has always been.

"Steve, we have so much in common. You take pride in your work, home, and finances as I do. What you see is what you get. Would you care to see my place? It's two blocks that way," she informs him.

"Sure, let's go," Steve replies. As they walk, she tells him that her mother made sure that her children knew how to keep house, and the father made sure that they understood finances before they moved out of the house. Steve told her his life was a little different. All that he learned was from the school of hard knocks.

"I did learn, but it took a good while for me to understand reality. I lived in a dream. Once I faced my demons taking control of my life by accepting GOD in my life, it changed me forever. It's odd that it seems so long ago. I welcome change, but then you find out really quickly who your real friends are. Dale is my only true friend. Not only that, but I consider him a little brother that I never had. The rest of my so-called friends fell into the crannies of the floorboards not to be seen again. It's ironic how when you drink or party everyone is around you, but when you stop so does the traffic from the so-called friends. When you find the truth which is GOD, many people don't want to be saved. They feel that what they don't know won't hurt them. Penny, please tell me how you feel about GOD," he concluded.

"Steve, I fear GOD, I love Him, and I accept that He is my Savior. In the morning I wake and pray giving thanks and asking him to watch over my loved ones which from now on will include **you**. I will ask Him to open your eyes, and for you to see me as a woman and as your mate. I've been blessed for here we are." She takes a hold of his hand and says that GOD has made this possible. All day she gives thanks. She's fortunate to be alive. She tells Steve that someday she will be in eternal glory, and that's when she will truly live.

"Penny, I feel the same way because at the end we will have to answer to GOD and explain what we have done to help our fellow man and ourselves. I would love to tell GOD that His blessings are what made me change into a better person by my trusting in his wisdom and keeping the faith. Now, you are here with me, Penny. You know what is important is that we do not forget our past, and we learn from our mistakes. We learn to accept that material goods are needed to an extent, but in the end what really counts is our faith in GOD."

"Penny, I'm glad that you love GOD. Lisa loves Him very much, for I see it in the way the kids are raised. They say their prayers, and they have the kids always give thanks. They respect their elders when adults are speaking. They go to another room without being asked. Lisa has the kids already picking up their toys. When they are done playing with them, they put them away where they belong. Dale Jr. already is taking out the garbage. Lisa is already making them be responsible in life. She told me that she is teaching them the importance of saving money. They get weekly allowances of two bucks for helping around the house. She has them save fifty cents each and every week. Now that the kids are conditioned to that, in the future when they're older and their allowance is more, then the savings will also increase. Dale is a lucky man to have Lisa. That's why he doesn't have gray hair." They laugh.

Penny lives on the second floor. It's a very nice place, clean and orderly. She has only one bedroom, but the kitchen is big, and the living room is also spacious with a nice painting on the wall that complements the furniture. Steve asks her if he can use her bathroom, and she smiles and tells him it's located at the end of the hall on the right. It has a beautiful old porcelain tub and like the rest of the home is clean. Now, Steve is thinking that he is glad that he came for she is the one that he has been asking GOD to put in his path. He will really try to make her happy. He will ask her if she would like to go with him to church on Sunday. That way, Father John can meet her. He stays for awhile, and Penny calls Lisa to tell her not to worry. They watch TV for awhile, and then Steve asks if she would like to go to church.

"Yes, Steve, what time?"

"I will pick you up at seven o'clock. Mass is at eight. Afterwards, we can go and have some breakfast and then to a movie when it opens. It's a date, Steve, but would you mind if I call you tomorrow? I was planning on going to the museum. Would you like to join me?" Penny asks.

"What time?"

"Two o'clock. Afterwards, we can go and get a bite to eat, my treat."

"Okay, Penny, I will call you at noon and will be here at one o'clock." He gives her a kiss as he is leaving. On the way back to Dale's, Steve thanks GOD once more because he is grateful for meeting Penny. With her in his life, it will be complete. It's late when he reaches Dale's house so he just drives on home. Steve reminds himself that tomorrow is another day for which to be thankful because he doesn't have a clue how many more of these they will have.

Address the Nation

Robert is getting ready to address the nation. This morning the camera crews are ready. He is speaking from the oval office.

"Fellow Americans, it is sad to say that the violence continues. Rest assured, it won't continue. After much consideration, I have decided to take matters into my own hands. When a country follows its rules and regulations, then it functions as a unit. If it doesn't, then it's divided. This great country of ours has suffered enough. I speak to Congress, and I can't get them to agree on anything. We are living without laws. There are a number of political figures that think they are above the law. That all changes today. If you get caught, you pay with your life. That's the price. Policemen, you have been warned that you will pay the same price. If you take a bribe or you break the law, you die. I'm taking action. I know that I'm not going to be popular, but if that's the case so be it. We are starting from the top and working our way down. Your lawyers are powerless. There will be no more deals. I will not tolerate this any longer. Anyone caught will be sentenced to death. It's gone on too long. I will put the fear of the justice system back on the right track. Criminals have been walking in and out like it's a revolving door. That all ends today. If you get caught, you will pay with your life. It starts here in the states. I will clean up my back yard first and then move on to the other nations. This country of mine will be the template for the rest of the world to follow. You gang bangers will get caught and anyone involved in such activities will suffer the same fate, which is death. You have been warned. There will be posters erected to disseminate the information so no excuses. Crime will fall in this great nation. The world will see, and other countries will join us in the battle for justice. The program starts immediately. As I speak, the posters are being distributed throughout the country.

"If anyone shoots at a police officer, the officer will shoot back using deadly force. If you rob someone, you will die! If you commit the crime of rape, off with your balls! This country is going to change, and when those pansy-assed politicians don't enforce the law or cry foul, then they we will be given the same opportunity to join the criminals by meeting their same fate. The victims will have justice. Our prisons are overwhelmed with offenders. That will all change. If there is enough evidence, then they will meet their maker. No more prisons are to be built. Like I said, all prisoners will be reviewed. If they are innocent, then out they go. If not, they can count their days, no more years. The violence will end. We will live in peace, for I too have been a victim. My wife was slain." Robert gets chocked up and a tear appears on his cheek. The president continues, "No more, I say. We will take a stand and we will triumph in the end. Hear my words. Work with me to clean up this country of ours. I promise you that all the abandoned homes and other old structures will be torn down so there will be no more hiding places. We will create jobs by hiring clean-up crews to bring down these buildings and that will begin immediately.

"Congress, you're next in line. The fat will be cut out. If you don't work to pass legislation, you're out. There will be no more pay raises until we're in the black. I mean no one. The Senate, that goes double for you. The people elected you so give the people what they want, results. It's a new day in America! You, the people, elected me. Let me do my job. Let me take the necessary steps to insure our safety. One more thing, no more pork spending. That ends right now. If you've received your funding, when it runs out so will you. Anyone caught pushing the pig will be dealt with. You've been warned. We will lead the world once more if you give me this opportunity to reform our system.

"Terrorists, next I'm coming after you, and you will not be able to hide. You don't have to worry any longer. I will bring the fight to you. I will use all means to bring you down, and you will be treated the way you treat the innocent. Regarding their lives, you have shown no mercy. I, President Robert Henry Morgan, promise your death, an eye for an eye. As I speak we are raining down on your country. We are staging our first line of defense using our transformers. They will seek and demolish their prey, and you will not be able to find refuge. Anyone that provides shelter will be considered a threat and will be dealt with accordingly. No more excuses. I will meet with foreign officials to discuss plans to eliminate these individuals, these terrorists. We will move forward! Thank you, my fellow Americans."

Robert walks out of the office and Sabula is there waiting. They go to another part of the wing and toast because it is finally put into motion and there's no turning back. His comrades are there also toasting and Robert drops the bomb.

"We will need to set an example. Tell me who our enemies are, and I will order an air strike," Robert tells them. In the discussion it was established that Syria had been given opportunities to join, but the Syrians had refused because they could not get along with other factions. They agreed that Syria did not try to negotiate with them. They flat out refused to join the cause so Syria is landed the first of many blows. The next is Somali. They disturbed the shipping lanes and have been inflicting heavy loses on corporate offices. Every day they get bolder even sending the president a message that if he were to ever be in the area to stop by, but they never mentioned him leaving. The pirates have been getting really bold, and they needed to be held in check. Finally, Robert's forces will be wiping out the garbage. He will send his transformers and see how they perform in the real world. He will have his drones monitor the progress, and if it turns to their favor, they will send transformers to Syria to do clean up. They will work out a list and then take action for the next two years. They will bring peace. Then when Robert's sheep are asleep, they will strike. Robert tells them all that in the end, they might have to inflict a little pain to other countries in order not to raise any suspicions, but they will be given advance warning. Robert tells them that his forces will try to keep the casualties to a minimum so as not to freak out when it happens.

A secretary knocks on the door and tells Robert to watch the news, for the public and world leaders are responding to his speech. The public blasts the president for his speech, and they are ready to impeach him, for the content of his speech does not reflect the fundamental principles of democracy. The officials blast him asking who he thinks he is. We, the people, will not tolerate what he intends to do. We have laws that govern this country. That is what sets us apart from other countries. World leaders call him a devil. If only they knew how close to the truth they were. For the next couple of days all that is heard is that everyone wants him out of office.

Robert knew this was to be expected, and then he implements his first of many plans. Los Angeles is used as an example. Sleeper cells are planted to charge the State Capital, and in the early hours of the day it's brought down. Many lives are lost. Now, the stage has been set. The people cry out for justice. Of course, they catch a handful of the cells. They will be martyrs. They have been promised that their families will be taken care of. The catch is if they inform anyone, their families will meet the same fate. It's all been staged. Now, Robert has the lawyers defend these criminals involved in the sleeper cell, and they get off on a technicality. The people cry out for justice. How can we let them out, for they have killed Americans? Everywhere on the news people are crying out for justice. Robert stays out of the public's eye and waits.

Two months later in Chicago another blast occurs. This time it's in Daley Plaza on Labor Day in the middle of lunch hour. Many are killed. Once again, the police catch a couple of the extremists. Once again, Robert sends his troops and again they walk scot free.

"How clever!" Sabula tells him for she knows his plan. At first, Robert's name is not so important but once all this started, people wanted justice. Then, Robert planted hecklers to instigate by bringing his name into the game. Now, the momentum is picking up. It's only a matter of time before the people demand action. Then, he will tell them to free his hands and let him do his work.

Robert decides that they need one more example; Atlanta should do the trick. Robert doesn't think it really matters where he does his fighting, for he has many cells at his disposal. This one will get their attention. On Sunday one month to the day in the early morning right after eight o'clock mass, a blast rocks the neighborhood and many are feared dead or trapped under all the rubble. As soon as it happens, Robert is ready to face the camera asking the people if they want to see justice, or if they want what they have been getting. Robert tells them that he has stood back all these months and let the authorities and justice system handle it the old-fashioned way, but it seems that it hasn't been successful. Stressing that if the people let him do it his way, those responsible will pay the price. He tells the people to contact his staff to let them know of their support, and then he will take action; otherwise, he will let the lawyers work out a deal for the terrorists like before. He told the public that he realizes some of them call him the devil, but in the end they want what he wants, justice. Robert tells them that he doesn't care how they look at it, but everybody wants the same result so they should trust him. He tells them that in the end they will thank him.

Meanwhile, the cells that have been captured are detained once more. Now, it's up to the people to decide their fate. Sabula hugs him and calls him the devil, and he finally agrees. He's finally getting what he wants. The people will ask him to do it. News media is out in the streets asking what the people want him to do. His hecklers join the people and begin chanting his name. The other nations are watching to see the outcome. The polls are being set up for the public to decide. There are extra camera crews at the latest bombing showing the massive efforts to save any survivors. It gives Robert a hard on. Sabula, taking a hint, swallows his load. He predicts that his sheep will ask for help, and then it will become easy for him to implement the next phase of his plans.

This time the lawyers are out in force to defend the criminals. As they make their way to the courts, the people object asking when it's enough. These people have killed our mothers, fathers, brothers, and sisters. We want justice. We want what the president wants. If they make bail, they will continue killing our people. It won't ever stop. Let the president do what needs to be done to send a message to these individuals that America doesn't tolerate this behavior. This goes on for the next two weeks. Sabula is keeping the pressure on by sending the news media to the courts and by encouraging them to show survivors in the news. Crumbled ruins are constantly being shown to reinforce Roberts's tactics. It's only a matter of time.

Then, Robert comes up with an idea. Let's take down an airliner. That should do the trick. On Thanksgiving Day one of the worst airline tragedies unfolds. An RPG strikes the fuselage of a jumbo airliner. There are no survivors. Witnesses say that they saw the trail of smoke from the RPG right before impact as the airliner ascended from Kennedy Airport. Debris fell on homes killing families as they were having their Thanksgiving dinner. Two hundred on board and another seventy-five on the ground have lost their lives. Numerous injuries are reported. Also, fires are spreading because the wind has picked up, and it's feeding the fires.

Sabula calls Robert and tells him that all is well. Robert is busy with his two honeys. Now with the good news, the people will ask him to do what is needed to bring order to the country. After hanging up, he opens another bottle of champagne and toasts to the new world, **his** world. Camp David is a wonderful place to party. No one is around on the topside except the staff. It's wonderful. They never ask questions. Robert wants to spend as much time there as he can. One of his aides knocks on the door. Roberts tells him he will be right out. He is naked with his honeys and will need to dress. He tells the women to keep the fire going because this won't take long.

Mr. President, an airliner as been brought down. There are casualties. Our Joint Chiefs of Staff are on their way as we speak. They all make their way to the underground think tank. As they walk in, Robert feels butterflies in his stomach. It is almost too much. He wants to laugh but can't, for it is going better than expected. His people are all wired up. He gets hit from all sides as to whom might have done such a thing. This is just too cool. He should have thought of this sooner.

"Damn, I'm good. The people are going to eat this up. They will tell me to screw Congress and the Senate and all the rest of the judicial system. I can see it now, Robert leading his people likes Moses out of bondage. One day they will call me God, for I intend to rule their world. I also know, however, that one day the dark one will try to reap my rewards. He will find out how strong I am because now he will have to deal with a god. I will kick him back to Hell where he belongs. There can only be one chief and that happens to be me. For now, I will work with him until he is not needed, but after that, 'So long, Sucker!'"

As the rest of Robert's staff arrives, they try to make sense of all these bombings. Are they connected somehow, or are they just random? Again, no one gives a good answer.

"Shit, I'm having trouble sitting for I'm dealing with such incompetence," Robert thinks to himself, "and I can't seem to stop laughing on the inside." These old boys don't have a clue that it's me reading their minds. They are so weak- minded, so easy to read." Then, he raises his voice and demands results, for the country can't continue to function this way. "If this staff can't come up with something, you will be replaced. You'd better start digging under rocks and give me results because this started overseas, but now it's in our own back yard." It's not every day that Robert's staff sees him this angry so they freak out. They are really trying but it seems that every time they try to connect the dots, their minds are manipulated to go to another direction. He puts it in their subconscious to keep looking everywhere else, but in the end it is obvious; therefore, he slams his fist on the table telling them to call him when they have answers.

Going back to his party, he is happy with himself. He knows that he won't be hearing from them until morning. "Poor saps, if only they really knew the truth," he laughs to himself. As he opens his door, his women are waiting for him. Once the people have given him the go-ahead, he will take out his enemies one at a time sending his drones and transformers as planned. After the clean-up, then there will be two years of peace. Meanwhile, he will start to perform miracles having grain and corn growing in countries where it was impossible. His followers will prosper and get fat. Then, when they are full, he will strike. After so many miracles they will call him God. Yes, life is good. Only the strong survive. In the end they will have a champion that will face Robert. Then, he will take any hope that they have left. Once he takes this world, God won't get it back.

The Plan

Steve picks up Penny, and they stay out all day. After going to the museum, they stop to get a bite to eat. They take a long ride not really going anywhere but only for enjoyment. They feel the heat from the summer charging their inner batteries. Talking about their youth, their dreams, and their sorrows, they get to know each other quickly. It's incredible how well they get along. Steve is driving his prized possession, a 1970 Dodge Charger, the last of the v-eight convertibles with a bench seat. Penny sits close to him. As they're taking in the sun, he asks if she is still joining him the next day for church.

"Pick me up. I will be ready. Then, we can spend the rest of the day doing what we are doing now, just cruising around. I have not done this in years."

"Penny, I will be there at seven o'clock, okay? Then, you're right. We can do whatever we want. It's so nice because I don't have to do whatever by myself anymore. By the way, Monday Dale and I go see Father John so I won't see you until Tuesday, but if it is not too late, I will call you when I get home."

"Steve, Lisa mentioned that you and Dale have been spending a lot of time with Father John. Is something going on?"

"Yes, but I do not have all the details, and that is why we are going back. He can fill in the blanks. Maybe later you and Lisa can join us. I will ask Father John what he thinks. Penny, what I can tell you is that something bad is in the works, something that has not been dealt with since the first coming of Jesus Christ. Man will have the chance to redeem himself for the second coming of Our Savior. It's happening as we speak. That's why I asked you if you believed in God. Penny, I do not want to scare you, but if the end comes and we survive, we will see the Savior and all His glory."

"Steve, you are not kidding," she sounded astonished.

"I wish I were because it would be a lot easier. I'll tell you what. After church tomorrow I will ask Father John if you can join us on Monday. Do you want to know more?"

"Steve, didn't they say all this was supposed to happen in 2013? It came and went just like any other year."

"They were wrong, Penny, for no man, woman, or angel knows the time that it will start or end, only God knows. We have clues and some ideas that were found in the *Bible* in *Revelation* about the coming of the antichrist and how he will deceive the people. The manner in which he will perform miracles, how the people will build statues in his honor, and how they will worship him as God are all discussed there. Then, the mark or seal will be placed on the people, and the ones that refuse will not be able to buy food or anything else. All the churches will unite to become only one, and it will worship the antichrist. Penny, we believe that the *Bible* was manipulated over time. We are not sure when it happened, but it did. Someone altered it for his own benefit to throw us off the right track. Father John has been doing research on this theory for some time, as did the priests of the past who formed a secret society in the time of the Crusades. They feel that the higher the hierarchy the more they have to hide, for someone knows the truth and that is who they are after. They are exploring their options. They will seek ways to find the truth to bring it into the light. Over the years, many priests have lost their lives seeking the truth. In the end it will all come out because when Our Savior returns, they will have to face him and explain their reasons for the betrayal. Penny, you may think I'm mad but we have reason to believe that the president is the antichrist, and he is gearing up for the final battle of mankind. The only problem is deciding to know more could put your life in danger. Knowing this, would you still consider learning more?"

"Yes, Steve, if you are by my side we will face this head on. I will do what is required of me. Just tell me that we will win in the end," she seeks reassurance.

"Penny, the only sure thing I know is that God will not let us falter, for he is Our salvation, our light in the dark hours to come. We need to organize in order to fight this evil. Dale and I have been talking about moving out West, getting organized, and then bringing the fight to his forces. Over the years, I've been socking money away and have a nice nest egg. Dale will combine his resources with mine, and we will arm ourselves. We will take a flight to Montana and buy some land near the mountains. Then, we will dig into the mountain and secure it to store supplies and munitions. The more people that joins us, the bigger we will make it. Then, we will branch out and buy land in Wyoming doing the same. Next, we will buy mountainous property in North Dakota. We will continue to purchase near the mountains and have points to hide or to flee. We don't have any idea as to how long this campaign is going to last. We will need to recruit preachers that speak the word of the Father word for word as it is written in the *Bible.* These preachers will give us faith, hope, and courage in the last days as we welcome Our Savior. People of different trades such as doctors, electricians, plumbers, heavy equipment operators, and farmers to teach us how to grow food in the caves and tend our livestock will all be needed. We will also need people that are familiar with geo thermal and solar panels because once we go into the caves for good, that being right at the end, we will be relying on them. The only thing is that we are going to have to be careful and not get anybody's attention. This will be especially tricky when we are blasting or bringing in supplies. Everyone needs to be screened for safety measures. Do you still want to do this, for it's going to be tough. I don't want to lie to you, Penny."

"Steve, I also have a little nest egg so count me in."

"Does Lisa know what you guys are doing?"

"No, but I have a feeling after today she will be informed but don't do it over the phone for big brother has big ears. We never talk over the phone, only in person. Stress that to Lisa," he warns her.

"Steve, I will talk to her tomorrow. You know that she is going to be pissed. Dale should have told her like you're telling me."

"Well, in that department that's where Dale and I differ, but I also understand that he didn't want Lisa to worry until after Monday. He did plan on telling her. When you tell her, don't forget to mention that and tell her not to tell anyone including your mom. We will wait and see what Father John says about how much time we have."

"Steve, not to be forward, but if the end is near will you make an honest woman of me?"

"Well, Penny, I still think we have some time, but if I see it getting ugly, I will do it right then."

She hugs him and he remembers what Dale said, "Watch those red heads, for they are pushy and normally get their way." On the drive home they are both silent, for it's been not only a beautiful day but also productive because things have been brought out in the open, and now there's no turning back.

"God, we ask you to please lead us, guide us, and give us the strength to move forward." Holding Penney makes him feel so comfortable that he doesn't ever want to lose her or the feeling that he feels right at this moment. He turns to look at her, and his heart tells him that she feels the same because she is so close to him that you couldn't get a credit card between them. They get to Penny's home, and he walks her to the door. They kiss goodnight, and he tells her that he will see her in the morning.

On the drive home he thinks it's better that Lisa knows so when they go Monday they will all go together. Dale's is not going to be happy, but sooner or later it has to be done. He parks his car in the garage, puts the cover on it, and then makes his way to his apartment to call it a night. He sleeps peacefully.

In the morning, Steve picks up Penny and drives to church. Afterward, she meets Father John. They hit it off right away. Then, he asks if it's okay to bring Penny and Lisa with them the next day. Father John says it's good, for he has news to tell them that will affect them all. He reminds them not to be late; it will be another long evening. He gives them his blessing and tells them that he is happy that Steve has finally found a good woman. If she is like her sister, Father John thinks Steve will be fine. He has met Lisa before and has always told Dale that he'd better take good care of her because if he doesn't, he will kick his butt. They waved to the father as they drive off. It was a beautiful day so after breakfast they went for a drive, and then she called Lisa and told her that they were headed her way. She asks if they need anything from the market. She hangs up and they drive to Dairy Queen to pick up some ice cream. They are on the porch as Steve and Penny pull up. The kids are waving to them and are happy to see the ice cream that Penny is carrying.

Penny tells Lisa that she'd like to go for a walk so Penny and Lisa leave the kids. As they are walking, Steve takes the opportunity to tell Dale what is happening. He is quiet for a moment.

"Steve, you know Lisa; she is going to get upset. I should be telling her, not Penny."

"Take it easy. Penny's got it covered. I promise you. Have I ever let you down?"

He looks at Steve, but Steve beat him to the punch by saying, "Do not answer that. I spoke to Father John, and he said to bring the women along but not to be late. Tomorrow, I will pick you up at same time, two thirty. Also, Penny will drive Lisa to the church."

"Steve, did you also tell Penny our plans about going out West?"

"Yes, I did and she is all for it."

"Wow, you didn't waste any time telling her so is there anything else I should know about?" Dale wants to know.

"Well, she did mention that if it got bad would I make her an honesty woman."

Dale looks at Steve with a grin. "I told you, but you thought I was lying about those red heads. Once they get their claws into you, that's it, Man. You will never be the same." They both laughed. "They'll be back after awhile so let's play with the kids." Later, when they finally appear, they joined the girls. Lisa looks like a ghost. Dale excuses himself and asks if Penny and Steve can watch the kids while Lisa and he speak. Penny doesn't say too much. Steve asks her how Lisa took the news.

"Not good, but she wants to go tomorrow. She wants to hear it from Father John." Later, Lisa and Dale joined Penny and Steve. Shortly afterwards, Penny and Steve left and stopped to get a bite to eat. Then, Steve dropped off Penny telling her tomorrow they would meet at three o'clock. She gave him a kiss and he left. Driving home, he wonders if he has done the right thing. The rest of the evening is quiet so he retires early.

Rita

Waking up after a couple cups of coffee, Steve picks up his first fare of the day. It's a woman from some network; of course, she is running late and asks him to step on it. Steve drops her off at the United Nations, and she gives him a tip. As he is leaving, he hears someone calling him. It's Dean. Stopping, he gets in and thanks Steve for stopping asking if he bought any stock in Boeing. Steve answers that he did right after Dean gave him the tip.

"Good, for the merger is taking place as we speak, and the stocks are going through the roof," Dean tells him.

"Thank you, Dean, You are a good friend. Where would you like me to take you?"

"To the stock exchange." On their way Dean tells Steve that things are changing so fast. They will start to develop more drones once the merger is complete. Then, he says something that gets Steve's attention.

"Steve, have you heard of transformers like in the movies?"

"Who hasn't? They were in cartoons, and then made into movies, right?"

"Well, they are going into development and will be used to patrol our skies and our streets. They will be equipped with Intel-a-chips. They will be used to track our enemies. They say it will help bring down the casualties. I worry because we rely too much on technology. Have you noticed that people are being replaced with machines? Can you remember when the last time was that you saw an aircraft pilot because it's been years since the Iran war. Shortly afterwards is when they started to replace them with drones. What would happen if they were programmed by someone that hacks into the Defense Department? Steve, computers have come a long way, but they are still accessible to hackers. There are no real safeguards. It worries me because I'm participating in all this and so are you but no one questions it. In the old days they will have public input, but now that's a thing of the past. This country has changed so much and not for the better." Stopping at the Stock Exchange, Dean reaches over to pay his fare, and Steve tell him that it's on him.

"Steve, I owe you."

"No you don't. One thing, Dean, if you were to ever know that this world was on its last days, what would you do?"

"Well, I would try to find a way to save it," Dean replied.

"Do you trust in God?"

"Where are you going with this?"

"You did not answer my question," Steve points out. "Do you trust in God?

"Of course I do; he is my salvation," Dean affirms.

Steve writes down his number and tells Dean that he will be hearing from him in the next few days but keep this conversation between them. As Dean leaves, Steve doesn't know if he has done the right thing, but it seems to be okay. He will let his heart decide in future days if the end is near. They will need troops to take a stand. Steve decides that he will call Dean later in the week and see where he stands on this issue. The rest of the day is normal and at two-thirty, Steve picks up Dale.

He is quiet on the drive to the church, but Steve understands with Lisa knowing and all that Father John has told them. Steve is surprised that they are not all crazy.

"Dale, you okay," he asks.

"Yes, Steve, but last night I didn't get much sleep. Lisa wouldn't shut up. She kept asking me if there was any hope for Mankind and what would happen to the kids. Then, she dropped the bomb on me that she is pregnant."

"What? Did you just say that she is pregnant?"

"Yes, any other time I would be happy, but with this going on it messed me up."

"What do plan on doing"? Steven asks.

"Well, to start with I'm taking her to the doctor and then buying diapers. After that, I'll take it from there."

"Congratulations, Dale! Maybe you'll name this one after me. How about it?"

"Shut up, Steve. I'm not in the mood. Don't push it and don't mention it to Lisa, for she will let you know in due time," Dale responds emphatically. As they pull up to the church, the girls are waiting for them, and Father John is with them. They go into his study and take a seat. Father John wastes no time telling them about Rita.

As the story goes, when Rita met Robert she fell head over heels for the man. He was all that she wanted in a man. For many years she was by his side. She worshipped him, and they would often go out for weekends, but Robert didn't seem in any rush to get married. Robert had met her parents, and they liked him, for he was well-mannered and had a bright future. Frank often commented to Rita that he was a good catch. The mother, Carla, thought he was cute, and that they would have some good-looking kids. After many years passed, they were happy to hear that the couple was getting married. They planned a big wedding and all the big wigs were invited. They had about four hundred people attending. Rita was so happy that Robert had asked Frank for Rita's hand in marriage. She would make him happy because they got along just fine. After the honeymoon, they went everywhere and Rita felt she was walking on clouds. This lasted for about two years, and then when she pushed him to run for public office, it all started to change.

Robert didn't have the time that he had before. He was busy learning the ropes. Frank at one time had been the governor of Rhode Island. He still had connections. They met with Robert, and they liked the way he carried himself. With Frank's help, Robert's career was launched. Then came the fundraisers and all the different functions involved with running a campaign. Because of this, he had less time to spend with Rita. She understood because it was not new to her. She had grown up in a house where her father was almost non existent. It did not mean that her father did not love her. On the contrary, she was his joy. Frank knew that when he returned home, Rita and Carla would be there waiting for him with open arms. He was a good father and a caring governor. His public loved him because he cared. Getting results and having the satisfaction of making a difference is the bottom line.

When he decided to back Robert, he advised him, "Do not let the people down because they are the ones that put you here, and they have the power to take you out. As long as you remember that, you will serve for as long as you desire."

Robert asked him if that was the case with him. "I served as long as I felt fit for the public because they expect a lot out of you, and they should.

I retired because it was my time. I felt that for the last thirty years I gave the public what I promised, results. Now, Robert, I spend all my time with my loved ones and would not have it any other way. In the end, it will be up to you what you do with all the power. I suggest that you use it wisely because with power comes more responsibilities, and did I mention back stabbers that will lie to your face? Over time, you will be able to read people because if you don't, you will fail. Are you still interested? It's not too late to find some other way to help the public."

"Frank, I will do my best to make you proud. I thank you for all the advice and for all that you have done for me, but let me reassure you that I will not fail. If that were to happen, how could I be president one day?" Frank was not expecting his answer because Frank had never thought of running for president.

"Are you serious?" Frank asked surprised.

"Yes, Frank. Today, it's the governor's office, tomorrow the White House. Mark my words, and I won't take no for an answer because you will help me to attain it."

As Election Day draws near, anticipation as to the outcome of electing a new governor is all the people are talking about. Who is this Robert Morgan? Can he make a difference? Can he take us out of the red and put us in the black? Will he be a caring governor and bring justice back to give people hope? Frank is pushing to influence the people to vote for Robert promising reform and more programs for the unemployed. Some of the programs include opening more day care centers to provide for single parents. Another offers tax incentives for employers who hire single parents. Robert makes his rounds at the schools, homeless shelters, and at community centers promising change if elected. Are you tired of the way things are? Then vote for me, and you will see the difference in the way things are being handled. Look at my record; it speaks for itself. Do you really want another eight years of no results? Look around. What has he accomplished? How has the public benefited? I promise results if you vote for me. Rita and Carla campaign for Robert. They hit the streets and don't let up. They are seen everywhere promising change. The public loves that she is caring, warm, and understanding. As the days fly by, the day for voting draws near.

They are ready for Election Day. So many hours have been invested. Now, they will see if it pays off. It's odd but Robert is poised waiting because he already knows the outcome even before the polls close. Rita is by his side along with Frank and Carla.

Frank is nervous and asks Robert, "How can you be so calm?"

"Well, I believe we have done all we can. Now, I wait for them to announce me as the winner," he replied in a matter-of-fact tone.

"Robert, you are so sure. How can that be?"

"I'm a positive thinker, and this is just a stepping stone. You know what comes after this Frank? The announcement is made a short time later that by a small margin the state has elected a new governor, Governor Robert Henry Morgan. The precinct goes crazy. Robert makes a speech thanking his father-in- law, wife, and public for their support. Robert kisses Rita and hugs Frank and Carla. They open the champagne and toast the new governor. Robert calls the governor that lost and tells him not to feel so bad. He has been in office for eight years. The people wanted new blood in the office, but he wishes the lame-duck governor well.

His career begins. Robert, after serving two terms, takes his leap into the books as governor. He mandates reform and brings the state out of the red in just two terms. The public loves his tactics because Robert will not back down. He makes things happen. He has a gift for speaking in front of people. He has the ability to calm them despite the problems. Rita is always close. She is in the public eye working the food banks and distributing literature to help the unemployed find work. She also works with kids and once is even asked by one of the kids if she plans on having kids. She answers, "If God wants us to, I would welcome the addition."

That day on the way back to her home, she thought about her answer wondering why they never have had kids. It is weird that in all this time she never thought about it until now. When she got home, she called the doctor and made an appointment for the following day. She would get checked out before she brings this subject up to Robert. Rita and Robert were always in the sack, and she did not take any pills and Robert did not wear any protection, but she had not become pregnant even after ten years of marriage. Why hadn't she ever thought about this before? It really bothers her. She calls her mom and asks if her mom thinks something could be wrong. She decides she will go to the doctor tomorrow and take her mom with her. She tells her mom that she will be picking her up on the way to the doctor's. The appointment is at ten in the morning.

When Robert got home that evening, Rita was quiet, and he asked if she was feeling okay. She tried to downplay the situation by saying that she was just a little tired and was going to bed. She told him that she doesn't feel so well, and that her mom is going with her tomorrow to get a check up. She assures him that she will let him know what the doctor says. Robert gives her a pat on the butt. She leaves him in the study where he goes over papers concerning the upcoming election.

Meanwhile, Frank is preparing for his next campaign because it will be his biggest challenge to date. He is focusing on getting Robert elected, and Frank is tying up loose ends for there is much to do. They have their office set up, and the volunteers are waiting for their orders and scheduled fundraisers to attend. Yes, there is much to do, for this is for the big one. Robert is getting closer to implementing his plans for world destruction. Once he is in office, then his generals will join his ranks, but for now they lie in wait in the shadows. All this careful planning and time involved will finally pay off. Sabula was right. Now, he is glad that he listened. In a few more years everything would be his. At that time Sabula will get hers. The dark one can be a problem, but Robert feels he will be stronger by then so he is ready for the challenge. Robert goes back to working on his speech, but it's also important to keep events that will come to pass in the back of his mind because he doesn't plan on sharing his power.

Rita picks up her mom, and they talk abut her dilemma telling her not to worry. They will leave it in God's hand, for He knows what's best and they trust in his decision. As they enter the doctor's office, he is happy to see them, for he has been her doctor since she was a child It's rare for Rita to get sick. The doctor says they will run some tests and check to make sure that everything is working as it should be. Then, he will call her with the results. Rita feels better. After leaving, they stop for some lunch. She drops off her mom and tells her that she will call her when she gets the results.

Three days later the doctor calls her to come back and is happy to tell her that she is fine and not to worry. He will need Robert to make an appointment so he can run tests on him to determine if anything is wrong. Robert has not been sick in all the time that Rita has known him. Just to be on the safe side, though, the doctor tells her to have him come in. They will take a sperm sample, and then he will let him know the results in a matter of days. Rita calls her mom on the way home telling her the good news including that Robert will need to be tested next. That evening Rita tells Robert about the results and that he needs to go and have the tests because she would love to have his child to make her life complete. In all the time they have been married, they never really spoke about children. It's time to address that subject. At first, Robert says that he has never been sick, not even a cold, but if that will make her happy he will go.

"Robert, I figured that so you have an appointment for tomorrow at ten in the morning. Would you like me to go with you?" she offers.

"No, that's fine. On my way to the campaign office, I will stop and do the deed. I'll call you later in the day so don't worry." That night Rita makes it extra special for Robert. She does not refuse anything because she just wants to please him.

The next morning Robert stops and sees the doctor. After taking samples, he reminds the doctor to vote for him in the next election. "Robert, I will call you with the results in the next few days, but so far is all looks good." On the way to the office he calls Rita telling her that he will get the results in a couple of days and not to worry. That evening they go to a political function, and they have a real nice time. On the way home they see the first of many billboards. Vote for change. Vote for Robert Morgan. Rita gives his hand a squeeze. You will be our next president. Robert, you are the best candidate. I'm proud of you." When they get home, Rita goes to work on Robert. He is delighted to have such a wonderful wife, and what makes this even better, is that Rita lets him do what he desires. Robert is not timid about trying new things with her.

Two days later Robert gets the call from the doctor. The doctor says Robert needs to stop by the office because he needs to ask him something.

"Okay, I am on my way."

After signing in at the front desk, the doctor is waiting for Robert. "Please close the door and have a seat. "Robert, I'm happy to tell you that you are in excellent health. We ran your blood, and it seems that none of my colleagues had ever seen your type of blood. We don't have any records of anyone with your blood type. We will need to run more tests. Being that you have never been sick, we will need to study you more closely. The only thing that we did find is that you are sterile. Sorry about that, but when can you return because it's fascinating how your blood works. Tell me you will come back. While you are here, let me take another sample. We need to examine why your blood is different from everyone else's."

Now, Robert freaks out because this is the first time in his life that he has ever heard that his blood is different. He looks at the doctor, goes to work on his mind, and asks where they keep the samples and the rest of his information. The doctor tells him that it's all in the computers, and the samples are in his lab. Go and bring me the samples and all the hard data that you have on me. The doctor is in a trance and obeys. Shortly afterwards, he returns giving him all that he has. Then, he asks the doctor to delete his files. When it is done, he tells the doctor to remember only that Robert is sterile and that's it. Robert also requests that the doctor write down the names of anyone else who knows this information. Robert realizes he will have to deal with them too. Two doctors all in the vicinity are the ones that have called this to his doctor's attention.

"Do they know who I am?" Robert asks.

"Yes, they know your name."

"You will not remember any of this, understand?" Robert admonishes him. Then, Robert puts the items away in his jacket and brings the doctor out of the state of hypnosis. The doctor tells Robert that he is so sorry about Robert's not being able to have children. He tells Robert to call if he can be of any assistance.

Shaking his hand, Robert leaves the office and calls Sabula to tell her they have a problem. He tells her to meet him at the park because they have to talk. On the way down there he starts planning how to deal with this problem. It needs to be addressed today, right now. Sabula is waiting at the park. She gets into his car, and they drive off. Robert is thinking that the best way to handle it is to burn down their facilities and make sure these doctors are included in the inferno.

"What is wrong, Robert? My blood is unique. That's what's wrong. These assholes want to study me like some guinea pig. By the way, I can't reproduce. When the fuck were you going to mention this to me?" he demands of Sabula.

"Well, Robert, you never asked. Tell me that you never noticed the women in your life, not one, coming back telling you that you're going to be a daddy. Nothing happens except the screwing? Blanks are what you have. How many years have you been married and no kids? Come on. You can't be that naïve about the blood. Well, you can thank your daddy for that. He made it all possible. Remember, you are not all human but half evil. How easily we forget. You blend in real well, but you will never be one of them because you are like me. I took all the necessary ingredients and molded you taking pride when you were made that you turn out okay," she said proudly.

"What do you mean 'When I was made'?"

"Robert, you were not born like normal children. You were hatched like an egg. Then, we slipped you into your momma and here you are. Go figure."

"Sabula, I can kill you. You know that one day you kept pushing me and I ……Well, get your men and do this. No screw-ups and report to me when it's done. You know election is in three months. We need no skeletons in the closet appearing at the last minute. If the public knew, it would ruin our plans. We are getting close. We need to be extra careful," Robert warned.

Dropping Sabula back at the park, Robert made his way to the office all the while thinking, "Fuckin' shit! I'll never go back to any doctor. How was I to know that I was hatched like an egg? You'd better not be lying, Sabula. If that's the case, and if I'm so unique, that will really come in handy at the end of my plan, but right now I need to make certain that it ends here. No proof can be left anywhere. One thing for sure, Sabula has not let me down in all these years and the good doctor did delete the files, but I still can't take a chance. I must call Sabula back to tell her to include the last one that I mentioned into her agenda for peace of mind."

After he hangs up from talking to Sabula, he calls home and breaks the bad news to Rita. She feels so bad about the news. He tells her that he would understand if she decided to leave him because her clock is ticking, and she's not going to be able to have children with him. He tells her that they will talk more when he gets home, but he was keeping his promise to call her as soon as he found out.

"Rita, maybe we can get away for a few days. It's still warm, only the second week of August. Let's go somewhere and get far from all this. Your dad is more than happy to take charge while we're gone. Check into it and let me know. We can adopt later on if you like."

When he is off the phone, he thinks about adopting. "Yea, like that's really going to happen," he is more honest with himself. "Me raising some asshole's kid?" He needed to tell Rita but that will change when he gets home. He will do his magic on her like he did on the doctor. She won't ever bring that up again and neither will Robert.

Rita, on the other hand, is devastated feeling so empty. She loves Robert but thinks staying with this man means no kids. He did say that they could adopt. Maybe that is their solution. Even if the baby didn't come from her but they raised the child, over time it would grow to love her. She knew she would love it as if it indeed had come from her. That gave Rita some comfort. She decided that she would call her mom and ask for her opinion.

Right before she picked up the phone, it rang and it was one of the doctors from the lab. "I'd like to speak to Robert. This is Doctor Carter," states the voice on the other end.

"Robert is not here, but I'm his wife. Can I be of some help?"

"Well, I'd like to speak to him concerning the tests that we did on him. The results are incredible. We would like him to come and talk to us.

We would also like it if you joined him, for we also need more blood from you. Mrs. Morgan, can you come down right now, and then we can speak more freely? Here is our address. We will be waiting, okay?"

"Fine, I'll be there in twenty minutes. She hangs up and leaves forgetting to call her mom.

On her way, she wonders why they need more blood. Is there something that Robert fails to mention? She parks and makes her way to the lab. She checks in with the receptionist and asks for the doctor. After a few minutes he asks her to join him in his office. Then, he tells her about the blood samples. He has two vials of blood and tells her that he has checked both; the results are the same. Robert's blood is unique. She is confused and does not understand what he means about it being unique. They go to the lab, and he tells her to look and see for herself. It's nothing like she as ever seen in her life. The cells are all wrong. They are arranged differently. Then, he takes a sample of her blood and puts it in the slide. He looks first and then compares them. He tells her that her blood is normal. Next, he puts them side by side up on a monitor. He asks her to compare them. He then asks her to watch the screen. He slices one of Robert's cells. It slices fine, but right afterwards it bonds right back and then multiplies. Then he takes some of Robert's cells and puts them into Rita's sample. What they see floors her. They start killing her cells and growing at a fast pace. Within minutes her cells are no more. Only Robert's cells can be seen on the monitor.

"Mrs. Morgan, we need to notify the Disease Control Center. Something is very wrong. He gives her the results telling her that Robert is not human. We don't know what to make of all this," the doctor concludes.

"Doctor, can your machine be wrong? Robert is my husband, and I love him very much. He is very human to me. He was the governor, and now he is running for president. I can't accept this. Your machine is wrong. We need to see him to get to the bottom of all this. If I made a mistake regarding his blood sample, then I owe you both an apology. If not, then we need to notify the disease center. It's my obligation to national security. I have guidelines that need to be followed," he explains.

"Please, Doctor Carter, wait until he comes, and you get another sample. If the news media were to get wind of this, they would have a field day. I will return tomorrow about this time, and you will see that it was just a mistake. Do I have your word that you will wait?"

"Fine. Tomorrow make sure he comes in because if he does not, then my hands are tied," he says adamantly. Rita thanks him. As she walks back to her car, she barely opens the door and loses it. She cries and can't believe what has just taken place. She looks at the documents and vial of blood. She can't believe her eyes.

The doctor was concerned about having both vials, and instead thought it best to give her one and the documents for safe keeping. He didn't tell her, but he is scared and doesn't know why. He does know that something is very wrong. Now, he is second-guessing if he has done the right thing. Deciding to take back the documents and the vile, he makes his way outside. By the time he reaches the door, she is already driving off.

Rita wonders what she should do. Finding out that the person she has been living with is perhaps not who he says he is has been devastating and perplexing. Who is he? It's not a matter of false identity in the usual sense. If he is not even human, **what** is he? What are his intentions? Rita decides to play along. She will get her answers but what about the papers? She needs to put these in her safe deposit box and tell no one. She takes the vial home, and hides it in the refrigerator. It's seldom that Robert looks in the back close on the bottom shelf. She wraps it in paper towels with the cilantro. After she goes to the bank, she stops by her mom's house staying for awhile and drinking some coffee. She leaves but never mentions anything that just happened. She fears for her parents, but first she wants to ask Robert some questions before she jumps the gun so she drives to Robert's office.

She asks Robert to take a break, and they go for a walk. She tells Robert not to worry, for they don't need kids to be happy. She loves him either way and that won't change. They talk about different things. She realizes this is not the right time to bring up such a delicate subject so she decides that she has kept him long enough because he has a very busy political schedule. Robert does say to her that he feels so bad about his condition, but that it is nothing more. They stop walking and she gives him a kiss and says that she has kept him long enough. They walk back to the office. She stays with him for awhile helping answering phones, and then she runs into her father. They speak for awhile, and he asks her what she thinks about the campaign. He is certain that Robert will be the country's next president. In only a few months they will be celebrating his victory. Rita kisses her dad goodbye and tells Robert she will see him at home. She will tell him later that evening about the next day.

Robert thinks how well she took the news. He wouldn't have to do the magic on her. This weekend he plans to do something special for her. She is a good woman and her dad is a hard worker. Robert is glad her dad is on his side. Robert is still waiting to hear from Sabula. It's close to four o'clock. They need to get rid of the doctors and the paper trail today before they leave. About a half hour later Robert's TV comes alive with breaking news. There's been a massive explosion at a nearby lab, and there are no survivors. The explosion was so massive that it leveled the building. The authorities are blaming it on a gas leak from the building where flammables were stored. They suspect a leak occurred causing the explosion. No one can be sure until the investigation is completed Twenty people lost their lives as they were getting ready to go home for the day. Frank tells everyone to bow his or her head and to pray for the lives taken.

Robert is happy. Sabula came through once again, two down and one to go. That is all he could think of. Life is good. Life is wonderful. "Ask me for more blood," Robert thinks chuckling inside. Forty-five minutes later another life is lost, for Doctor Carter is run down walking to his car. There were no witnesses. Police are investigating. Doctor Carter died from massive head wounds on the way to the hospital, but no further details are available at this time. Sabula called a short time later, asked him if he is pleased, and then hung up. Robert once more got his way. He is thinking that he really needs to celebrate because too much excitement is giving him a hard on, but that will have to wait until he gets home. He will pick up flowers and candies to make it special.

Rita is finishing her workout and running her bath water when the news comes on. They have news crews at the location standing by for live coverage. In the background she sees the remains of the building. Her heart sinks. She holds on to the bedpost because her legs are weak from the news. Listening, she hears that there are no survivors.

"Dear, God, please do not let Robert be involved in this." They say it will take months to determine the exact cause of the explosion. As she is about to turn off the TV, she hears Doctor Carter is dead on arrival from head injuries caused from a hit and run. Anyone with information is asked to call the authorities. His wife and son survive him. Arrangements are being made for the funeral.

Rita does not know what to think. All this in one day! Is it a coincidence or was it intended to hide the truth? Robert has a lot to explain when he gets home.

"I will get the truth so help me. People are dead for no reason. Why did I ever have to push him to go and get checked? We were happy but now I'm scared. I'm not even sure who is sleeping in my bed. God, help me find the truth. I must be sure that I'm not going nuts. My blood is fine, but Robert's is way different so what do I do about it? The results are safe at the bank for the time being, but if he is lying, then I will need to protect myself and my parents. We will need to leave," she decides.

Then, Rita remembers the priest who has helped her all her life. He has been an inspiration to her, and he will know what to do. She will show him the results, ask him what he thinks, and ask him not to let Robert know that she has his test results. Rita decides to call the priest and ask if she can stop in the morning to speak to him about a sensitive subject. Father Mike tells her nine would be a good time and that he would see her then. Father Mike baptized her when she was one year old, and she did her communion at the age of eight. She has been active in the church for many years helping with the less fortunate kids by providing them with extracurricular programs which will help them become better individuals. Now she feels better because she has the beginning of a plan. Tomorrow, she will stop at the bank and then go and meet him at nine.

Robert gets home a little early and surprises Rita more than he knows. He gives her the flowers and candies. They kiss and he tells her he'd like to go upstairs and get a little crazy. He leads her to the bedroom even though she is not in the mood. She needs to play along for now. Tomorrow Father Mike will calm her down. Hopefully, he will explain that it's all a mistake and their lives will go back to normal and that's it. In the bedroom Robert is an animal that just cannot seem to get enough. By the time they were done, Rita could not walk. Her legs were all screwed up. "He had me like a pretzel," she thinks. Not that she was complaining because many women wish they had this problem. She wonders what got into him. Reflecting, she hopes she's wrong because as they lie in bed and she looks at him, she realizes how much she loves this man. There is nothing that she wouldn't do for him. After dinner, she tells him that she's turning in early because Father Mike wants her to be at church early in the morning to plan some activities for the kids. She kisses Robert and goes upstairs to sleep.

Robert has a couple of drinks. He is satisfied with how his day has gone. A lot has been accomplished. The news is wonderful. Rita is back to her old self now. He can concentrate on matters that are more important. He has three months left. Then, he takes office. He will be addressed as Mister President. That has a nice ring to it. He has been waiting for a long time, and now it is all coming together like a puzzle. He will need to see Sabula, thank her in person, and give her a good fuck. It's been way too long since they were last intimate. Tomorrow while Rita goes to church, he will spend some time with Sabula. She knows how to push his buttons but in the end, she is loyal. He gives her a quick call.

"Sabula, I call to thank you. I will see you tomorrow at ten in the morning. Wear something sexy. I hope you are horny because I am. Also, give me all the details on our successful plan as crafted and let me know if we've missed anything. Chow!"

Rita leaves early while Robert is still asleep. She stops at the bank and drives to the church. Father Mike is happy to see her. He gives her a hug, and they go to his study.

"Now, my child, what seems to be brothering you," he asks concerned.

"Well, Father Mike, I don't know where to start. Okay, let me start from the beginning. I had to have some blood work done at the doctor's office and here are my results," she says handing him the paper. He looks it over.

"Rita, I'm not a doctor but the results seem normal." "Yes," Rita responds, "but Robert had to have the same test done and here are **his** results.

With a stunned look on his face, he asks, "Are you sure these are correct because they are not normal or even close to anything that I have ever seen? Rita, I have a brother that works with blood. He would be better at answering you. If you do not mind, let me call him. He does not live far from here," he suggests.

"Father Mike, please don't tell anyone else, but if your brother can join us right now, I will wait." she agrees. After the quick call, he tells her that his brother will be there in about twenty minutes.

"Rita, have you heard of the antichrist? It's written that he will deceive the world. Some say that he lives among us. I don't want to scare you, but we have proof that he does exist. I'm not quite sure who he is, but in due time we'll find out."

"Father Mike, why does this have to happen?"

"Rita, in order for us to live in God's grace, we will have to endure the antichrist for as long as it takes until the arrival of our Salvation. Then and only then will we live in peace. This all has to happen, but it's not going to be decided in the Middle East. It will be here in our own back yard."

"You're wrong, Father. The *Bible* states that Armageddon will be fought close to Israel. The nations will gather for the final battle. Then, Our Savior will return and crush the enemies. Then, we will all live in peace for a thousand years," she states confidently.

"What if the *Bible* was changed, manipulated? How would you know, Rita? Everything else is true except where the final battle will be fought. It's so critical because then we could prepare for what is to come. Mankind has been fooled, blinded. We need to expose this threat. Rita, we've been studying this dilemma for many years and have concluded that it will be fought in New York City. All the nations will gather against us. We will take a stance and fight for our lives. The antichrist will be here promising us hope by doing miracles and once again deceiving us. It will be all lies, and then the mark of the beast will be placed on us. We will be required to worship him. Listen to what I say. We still have a choice. It's not too late. Take the blinds off. We need to wake before it's too late. Only God can save us. Rita, it's going to take all of us to sacrifice whatever means we have in order for us to have a chance. Our numbers are growing. Although we are expanding, there is still a lot work and effort that needs to be completed. We are investing in technology, munitions, and supplies. I trust that you won't divulge this information to anyone. We need your help," he pleaded.

"Yes, if that's what it takes to secure our future, count me in," she agreed pledging her support.

Tim knocks on the door and comes in. "This is my brother Tim. This is Rita," he shakes her hand. "What can I do for you?" Rita hands him the results. He studies them for awhile and then shakes his head. "Rita, are you sure that these are correct?"

"Yes, Tim, we had them done by the same doctor who is now dead. The people from the lab are also dead because the building exploded. My results were normal so Robert went to have his blood and semen tested to see if anything was wrong. We were thinking about starting a family. That's what started this nightmare," she explains.

"Rita, his blood is off the charts. Never in all my career have I encountered anything close to this. We need to run tests. Father Mike shows him pictures of the slide that Rita brought with her. Again they look as Robert's cells attacking Rita's. Tim is dumbfounded. "He's not human. Rita, do you know if he has ever had any x-rays or Cat scans? It's important."

"No, not that I remember, but in all the time that I've know him, he has never been sick. I asked him about it before, and all he said was that he has good genes. Tim, Robert is not aware that I have this, not any of this." She takes out the vial of blood and asks him if this will do.

"Mike, I need to use your lab," he says hastily.

"By all means." Rita looks puzzled by his reply.

"You have a lab?" she asks surprised.

"I did say that we invested in technology. It's in the basement," Father Mike explains. As they walk in, Rita is amazed at all the stations and equipment. Tim takes charge by putting the samples on a slide. Then, he asks them to look at the monitor. They see how Robert's blood cells multiple when Tim slices them. Then, he magnifies them, and they are all amazed. Robert's cells are not only red and white but also purple. How can this be possible? Tim takes a purple cell and puts it in another slide. Then they watch as it grows on its own. He then puts a sample of Rita's blood in the slide. It eats her cells. Then as it reproduces, it starts to make its own red and white cells, which is impossible!

Father Mike seats them, wipes his forehead, and says they have found him. Tim asks whom they have found. Father Mike says it is the antichrist for whom they've been searching since the nineteen seventies. That was when he was to be born.

"Are you crazy?" Tim asks.

"I wish, but how much more proof do you need?" Father Mike replies.

Rita freaks out, "You've got to be kidding me. Maybe I should leave and forget this ever happened," she says in denial.

"Hold on. Relax. Breathe. Tell me when he was born."

"It was October 13, 1973, in Chicago, Illinois. Then, he was taken back to live in England. They moved to the states when Robert was one year old," Rita told them.

"Rita, your life could be in danger. You must leave him," Tim warns.

"Easier said than done, Tim. He's running for president. Don't you watch the news?" she chides him.

"No, not really, but that will change. We need to plan an escape for you," Tim says. Father Mike agrees that if Robert gets into office that will start a chain of events. Their days as they know them are numbered.

"Rita, do you feel safe to return home and pretend that all is fine," Father Mike asks.

"Yes, what choice do I have? I know that you want me to do something for you. What is it?" Rita asks.

"Keep an eye on him but don't make it obvious. Then return and report back to me or Tim. We will notify our network that he has been found, and we will take measures to prepare for the final battle. If it ever gets to the point that you want out, come here and bring any members of your family who believe in God. They will be safe here until they are relocated. Rita, you are not alone. Remember that we love you, and God wants us to be here when he returns," Father Michael concludes. Tim writes his number on a card that says "flowers for peace."

"What is with the flowers?" she enquires.

"Rita, it is for your protection. That way if he were to ever see it, he will not get suspicious," Tim explains to her.

"That makes sense. You guys think of everything."

"We try but we're not perfect. Keep it close by.

"I need to go. Robert will be waiting for me. Please let me know when you are sure who he is," Father Mike gives her a hug and tells Rita that he will be in touch. Tim hugs her too and she leaves.

On the drive home Rita's body shakes. "I will need a good drink to calm me down. I'm glad that I went to see Father Mike and Tim. Also, it's better that they have the paperwork and the blood sample. If it is true what they say, they will need it to combat Robert. Now, I need to pretend and there is no need to alarm my parents until I'm sure. In all my years, I have never gotten into Roberts's things until now, but I will be careful to put it all back in order," she thinks to herself. Looking over his things, Rita finds nothing out of the ordinary. She was thinking that it was just as well because Robert would be home in awhile, and she needed to get ready because they had an evening function to attend. All the big wigs would be there.

Robert calls her at two and says he's been detained but will be home at four. Rita reminds him not to be late because they have an engagement. Robert had forgotten. He was planning to wine and dine Rita, but that would have to wait until tomorrow. "See you at four o'clock." He tells Rita to call her dad and tell him to bring anything that they might need for the function.

Robert turns over and Sabula asks him if all is well as she goes down on him. It has been quite some time since he has spent quality time with Sabula, but she is up to the challenge. As always, she is eager to please him. Deep down she loves this man. After they shower Robert asks if there were any problems yesterday. Are they sure that it can't be traced back to Robert?

"Robert, we brought the building down just to be sure, and we deleted all files before that and destroyed the blood sample," she stated confidently.

"Did you say blood sample?" he asked.

"Yes, Robert, there was only one. I made sure to destroy it myself."

"Sabula, they took two vials of blood from me," he stated.

"Robert, all I found was the one. Besides, if we miss it then it's under the rubble. Don't worry. It's all good. Doctor Carter will not be a problem either. He met his maker, and we made sure later that evening to return and destroy all the data on his computers. Then, we set fire to the office and made sure it looked as if one of the computers shorted out. I've got you covered. Please relax. No need to be paranoid. There is no proof, and I suggest no more doctors or blood work," Sabula reaffirmed.

Robert and Rita go to the function and it's a success. The people chant Mr. President and cheer for him. He holds Rita's hand and thanks his followers. Then he gives thanks to Frank. " He has made this all possible. He believed in me. People of this wonderful country I promise to be the best that I can be, but I will always need your help to implement policies. Help me turn this country around and move it forward. We can do it if we work hand-in-hand, but we will need to sacrifice and tighten our belts to control our spending." They clap and whistle. Afterwards, they mingle with the people. They enjoyed his speech telling him that they need change and no more empty promises because that's what they have in office right now. Senator Carl Hines will support him. He is a good friend of Frank, but he tells Robert to look him in the eye and promise not to bend like the one in office because he is weak. Spending is out of control.

"We need someone that's not afraid to stand up to these individuals and take charge. When I voted for this current president, he said it all just like you. Then, as soon as he took office, the economy took a nose dive. He is incapable of tying his shoes, let alone running the country. Robert, we need results. Please, can you do it?" the senator asks him.

"Yes, Senator Hines, in just my first term you will see how this great country will be turned around. I have the capacity and audacity to make a difference. I do not negotiate," Robert stated determinedly. Again, the people clapped because they were listening as Robert answered the senator's question. Music started playing. Robert took Rita's hand and led her to the dance floor. The rest joined in. For the latter part of the evening they enjoyed the music. Rita is very happy, even forgetting for awhile about her dilemma. On the drive home, Robert laughs telling Rita that her dad made this all possible. "You are looking at the next president, and I'm looking at the next first lady," he said and they both laughed.

The next few months raced by. Then, on election night they all gathered at the campaign office waiting for the results. It's been so far a close presidential race. At the end Robert wins by a small margin. Robert calls President George H. Collins and tells him it was a good race. Then, the nationwide parties start. The party supporters open the champagne and begin to celebrate. Rita and Frank are pushed a little from the limelight. In all the time Robert has run for office, he's mentioned Frank's name giving him thanks, but this time it's not been the case. Frank mentions it to Rita, and she defends her husband saying to give him a break.

"It's Robert's moment so just let him shine. Father, tomorrow I will mention it, and I'm sure he will apologize to you," Rita reassures him. At the very end of the night Robert does thank Frank and Rita for making this possible. Frank acknowledged him, but he is not as happy as he once was because he feels he has been used.

The secret service was dispatched as soon as the results were known. Now, Robert and Rita are protected for the rest of their lives. They are driven home after the celebrations, and Robert finally has gotten his dream. Now, it only a matter of time before his plan is implemented. Rita is on a good buzz drinking too much champagne. She will pay tomorrow. The headache that will follow will keep her in bed for most of the morning, but that's okay because if it had not been for her father, this would not be possible. Robert won. That is what this is about, his moment. Now, we will see what he does next. They arrive home and are both exhausted, but Robert will not let Rita sleep until he as his way with her. Robert turns into an animal and screws Rita in the mouth, the pussy, and then comes in her ass. Then he sleeps.

The next morning Robert tells her that they well need to start packing. They have three months but with all the ceremonies time flies by. She has been busy getting things ready because she had the feeling that he was going to win the election.

"Robert, if you don't need me for the day, then I can use the time to pack the rest of the little stuff to get things ready for the movers," she tells him.

"Rita, I've decided to sell this home. Don't plan on coming back any more. Talk to a realtor and have them put it on the market. Do not forget to mention that your husband grew up here and now is the president," he advises her.

"Yes, Mr. President. Is there anything else?" she teases and then salutes him.

"Today, I will need you by my side but tomorrow you can start talking to the staff to let them know that in three months we're moving, and they are no longer needed. Tell them that we will pay them for three months' work and give them my thanks. Let's go have breakfast and get ready to leave. It's going to be a long day."

The news crews are gathering outside the perimeter, and their cameras create a multitude of flashes capturing the first photos of the newly-elected president and first lady. They, along with their caravan of secret service agents, drive all over town giving speeches, thanking the public, promising to reform the government, and pledging to bring stability and growth. The people cheered him on chanting his name. The next couple of months were extraordinary. They toured the White House, and Robert told Rita that this is the moment they have been waiting for. Next week they will move into this his castle, and he will rule with an iron fist. It's Robert's turn at the helm. He will take this country where it's never been before.

Robert prepares to make his speech because in a matter of minutes he will be sworn in. Rita is by his side. Frank, at the last minute, has decided not to attend saying he was under the weather, and Carla was to care for him. Robert was not surprised on election night. He notices the change in Frank but blows it off. Now, Frank is faking it. Robert doesn't know why but thinks, "Screw him because it's not important. Old Man, I used you. I screwed your daughter, and she swallows my load so fuck you. I bet Carla does not do that for you or take it up the ass. By the way, Frank, I have your boys working for me, and they'll jump hurdles if I ask them, weak-minded fucks," Robert laughs inside. After being sworn in, they go party and party all night.

Robert manages to sneak away from Rita and gets a blowjob from Sabula. You know she would not miss it for the world. All the years of planning and now it's finally here. As she swallows his load, she looks up at him saying, "Was that good for you, Mr. President?"

Robert's body shakes with excitement. " You're good, Sabula."

Then, he returns the favor lifting up her dress and is not surprised that she is not wearing panties. He's goes to work on her until she lets loose, and she grabs him from the back of the head and tells him not to move. Robert doesn't listen. His tongue is still doing its magic, and she comes again, this time with convulsions following close behind. "Now, you can brag that you have been eaten out by the president and he licked you clean," Robert jokes.

Father Mike and Tim watch with amazement as Robert is sworn in. They can't believe their eyes. The antichrist is now in office, and it's only a matter of time before he shows his true colors. The last three months have been rough from trying to determine if they can introduce a virus to fight Roberts's blood to making it break down. Roberts's blood fights everything they throw at it, and it grows even more harmful cells such as numerous varieties of cancer, including leukemia. It also carries a strain of the Ebola virus. They have continually bombarded it but with no results. Father Mike tells Tim that they will find something at the right time to fight this evil. Tim wishes he could believe that but with all the science that is available and nothing working so far, it makes him wonder. Rita has only called once since the incident to report that she found nothing. She also told them that she will stay by his side for as long as it takes. She asks them not to forget her parents in case something were to happen to her. Rita is a strong woman. They do want to keep an eye on her but know with the secret service it will be even harder although not impossible.

Father Mike for the last couple of months has been notifying the priests from the secret society that Robert is the antichrist. They are trying to find a way to prepare to combat it immediately. They need to purchase land in the West and prepare for the final days. They need more manpower. Doctors are also in great demand. Father Mike is to meet Father John and some of his followers to discuss their options in the next couple of days. They need to be extra careful because they have been betrayed within the church, and to this day they wait for the traitor to surface. It's a sad day when one of God's servants betrays Him not only as he has been betrayed in the past but now also in the future. Its sucks to think someone can promise vanity and "bling" and that's supposed to do it. Why pretend to follow? One day they will have to answer to God and explain what was so important for them to betray His church. Then, they will burn in fire for eternity. Just ask anybody that was promised from below how long they had their dream. God offers us eternal life with no catches and no small print. All he wants is what we all want, to be loved and not to be used. Is that too much to ask?

Father Mike asks Tim to contact Rita when he returns from New York City. They will be able to tell her where her parents can find refuge. Also, they must tell her about the blood tests. "Tim, I need you to send a little blood sample to Berkley, California. Here is the address. Send it FedEx to Charles McLain. He is a renowned scientist of hematology and pathology. Send him our tests and all the data. Ask him to notify us if he gets any different results from introducing different parasites. Let him know whom we are dealing with and to get his people ready because time is at hand. Our Savior returns. We know not the hour but we wait for His arrival.

Tim, I'm leaving in the morning and will be back in a week. Here are the sites that fit our needs. Check them out. Fly down and survey the area. Check for minerals, water, and anything else that can be useful. Take Barb with you. She is the geologist who can prove to be very useful. I spoke to her yesterday and said you would be calling her. There's one more thing. She is a very attractive woman. Don't let that fool you. She is smarter than both of us. If the land meets our criteria, buy it and go to the next one. Notify the construction crews as soon as you find out, for they can begin working on fortifying the structure. You need to tell them also that we are not only going to have people but also livestock and greenhouses. Send them a list of our needs, okay? Do not forget to tell them that we will need an escape route coming in and going out. It's imperative that they know that. It needs to be built first and camouflaged. Only certain people will know of it, for it can save our lives one day. Tell Barb not to overlook anything. Our lives are in her hands. Tim, I need to finish packing. Will you join me for dinner?" Father Mike concludes.

"Mike, I need to run an errand but will be right back. What time is dinner? In about one hour Julie is making a roast with all the trimmings. Don't be late."

Frank is happy for Robert, but lately he is not happy with how Robert acts. He has changed. Carla tells him he will be alright and just to let it slide. It's not every day that one of the family is chosen to be the president of the United States. She reminds him that Robert has been under a lot of pressure, and he did thank Frank at the end.

"Carla, Robert used to thank me in the beginning and all that changed. It hurt my feelings. He was a nobody when we met him. Now, he's too good for us. Even my friends in politics have taken his side telling me that Robert knows best," Frank complained.

"What did you think that he was supposed to do, ask you for your opinion for the rest of the time he is in office? It seems Robert has learned to make his own decisions. By doing so, I feel that he will do this country well by bringing reform. Frank, let's give him a chance and see for ourselves. Look at Rita; she seems happy. Let's be happy for her. It's her time to shine," she advises him.

Rita dances with politicians, speaks to the wives, and wonders where Robert is. He's been gone for about one hour. He said he'd be right back. He is supposed to be here entertaining the people. Rita decided to go and look for him. She excuses herself and goes from room to room. At one of the last doors she hears moans and peaks in but it's not Robert. It's the manager and one of the staff. Rita feels foolish and decides to go back and join the party. By the time she returns, Robert is talking to the news media. He motions her to join him. Robert gives her a kiss, and she smells the scent of sex as he gives her a hug and tells her that he loves her in front of the cameras. How could Robert do such a thing? After all these years, he waits until tonight to do something like this. Rita feels like she could kill this man; however, Rita is a true professional. She stays close to him for the rest of the night, but she is hurting because she has been betrayed. All the years they have been married she has had plenty of opportunities with men but never accepted. Some of the men were not just cute but looked like models. She thanked them and would say that if she were not married it be different. When she took the vows for good or bad till death do you part, she was serious and figured that Robert felt the same. Therefore, for the rest of the evening she would do her best not to ruin his party. Rita gets drunk and puts it out of her mind. After awhile they dance and mingle, and she forgets for now.

Robert does not leave her side anymore. He tells her that when they get home, he will have his way with her. When they leave for home, Rita is in good spirits. Not only did she drink booze but also did shots. She is incredible. It amazes Robert that she can handle her liquor because she did not slur or embarrass him in any way. She deserves to be first lady because she is a first class woman. He considers himself lucky to have her. He wonders if she smelled Sabula. He had not had time to wash up, but she never let on so he just reminds himself to be more careful.

They move into the White House. Rita picks out new colors for the paint and curtains. She wants different styles that brighten the rooms because they are so dark. Robert is busy picking his new staff, and when Rita is not attending some function, she gets her new home in order. She flies back to their home and supervises the packing telling the movers what goes to storage and what is going back with her. They have been living in the White House going on two weeks. She wants to complete the packing and storing today. That way, on the way home she can call the realtor and have her staffs do the final cleanup. Then, they will drop the keys off with the realtor. Rita tells the movers when they are done to leave, and she stays behind walking throughout the house one last time to make sure that nothing is left behind. As she walks through the house which is now empty, Rita remembers the good times they had here. Her staff is almost done with the cleaning so she might as well just stop in the realtor's office and drop the keys off herself. Rita walks to her bedroom for the last time.

She opens the closet door, and then she notices a small door. She does not ever remember that door. It's odd all these years, and now here it is. She opens the door and it's a small room with some boxes. She wonders if Robert forgot about these? "Let me take a look," she says to herself. One box is full of trophies and another box is full of plaques from the schools that he attended. Then, she notices a small box. She opens it and there is a book. As she takes it out of the box, she realizes that it's old. Opening the book she sees writing that she has never seen before and remembers Father Mike. He will need this. "I'll stop at the church before I go to the realtor," she says. She flips over a couple of pages and is dumbfounded. This book is about rituals and spells. The pictures are amazing. They show people flying and some look as if they are teleporting. Another picture shows how to hypnotize a person. Then, she sees the signature at the end of the book. Her heart sinks. It has the same marking that Robert has on his hand. Then at the bottom, it has "Lucifer" written on it. She calls Father Mike from her cell phone to tell him about this finding, but he is out of town. She remembers that Tim gave her his card so she calls him. He answers on the second ring. "Tim, it's imperative that I see you right now. Where can we meet?"

"Rita, you have the secret service with you. Tell them to take you to the church. Do not let on that we are meeting. Once inside, go to the confession booth, the first one. I will be waiting for you inside, and then we can talk in private. Tell them that you need a little privacy, for it is the last time in awhile that you get to confess in this church. They will understand." After hanging up, Rita puts everything back minus the book. As she is walking back with the book, she can't hide it so she tucks it under her arm and tells them that she is ready to leave. It's a good thing that she told the staff goodbye earlier before she made her last round because she gave them hugs and kisses. It would have made it awkward with the book. She locks the door as they leave.

Then, she tells her security staff that she needs to stop at the church because she wants to say her goodbyes and to confess for the last time at the church. Then, they will go to the realtor to drop off the keys. She complains that she is tired, but after this then there is no need for her to return for awhile. They seem to understand. They go with her to the church, and she asks if they can wait outside. One of the secret services agents agrees, but first he needs to check it out. He cannot be too careful. On his return, they escort her to the door. Then, one goes to each entrance, and they give her the okay to go in. She walks to the first confession booth, goes in, and sits down. Tim is on the other side waiting for her, and he asks what the problem is. "Tim, I found this old book and it has important information inside. You will need it take it. Tim opens the divider and takes the book. I need to leave in a few minutes, but they know that I walked in with a book. I need to replace it with another one. Please give me one that resembles it," she explains.

"I'll be right back," Tim says and returns in a few minutes to give her a book. Then, he tells her that the blood was sent to Berkley to be examined by Charles McLain. She writes down her mother's number and her new number.

"Call me when you know more about the blood and the book. I must leave. Promise me that you won't forget my parents. They are all I have."

"Rita, I promise to take good care of them, but you need to be very careful. Better that you start thinking about the near future. Your life will be in danger. You well need to run. You can call here, or you can reach me by calling the card number that I gave you. We will come and take you to safety. Go with God," Tim tells her.

Rita leaves and is truly scared but can't show it. They drop off the keys with the realtor, and then they fly back home. Robert is waiting for her. They have dinner, and he asks about the house. She tells him that it is all done. The realtor will call when it sells. "I also did mention to her what you said about the president living there," she says. Robert is pleased, and they have a quiet evening. Rita is exhausted and turns in early.

Robert talks to the secret service and asks how Rita's day was. They explain it was quiet, and that once they locked up the house, they stopped at the church because Rita wanted to confess before they dropped off the keys. Joe tells him that the only thing Rita brought back was a book. It was odd because she could have packed it with the rest. Robert asks him what the book was about. " It looked like an old book," Joe said.

"Do you remember anything else?" Robert asks.

"No, that's it, but she did bring it back. It's in the parlor. Do you want me to get it for you?"

"Please," Robert responds. When he returns, he gives it to Robert. It's *Tom Sawyer.*

"Joe, I thought you said it was old. Well, it looked old when I first saw it, but I could be wrong."

"Okay, next time pay more attention, or it's your ass, understand?" Robert has a couple more drinks. Then, he remembers the book. "**My** book? Where is it? Where did I leave it? It's been many years since I've needed it," thinks Robert. "Could it be the same book?" He picks up *Tom Sawyer* and reads a couple of pages. Then it comes back to him. "Shit, I left it in the room in the closet. I need to fly back tomorrow." He calls one of his assistants to schedule a flight for tomorrow. Then, he goes upstairs taking the book and lays it next to Rita's night stand.

Rita wakes up. The first thing she sees is the book and it frightens her. Robert is already up and brings her some coffee. He asks her about the book. She tells him that she never read it but was interested in reading it. He then tells her that he will be flying back to the house, and if she wants to join him for old times' sake, she's welcome to go with him. She tells him that the movers are scheduled to come today. She tells him that she is sorry, but she cannot go and asks Robert to take some pictures for the album. "Okay. I'll see you in the evening. I'll call you on the way home," and he gives her a kiss and leaves.

Rita is freaking out. "Why is he going back? Did he remember the book?" she wonders. "Well, I'll stay busy and see what he says when he returns. If he does not mention it, good; if he does, I will deny it. Then, the first opportunity that I have, I will run out of here just as fast as I can. I need to call Tim and make arrangements but that will have to wait until tomorrow. Then, I will take it from there." The movers arrive at ten in the morning, but by the time they leave it's five o'clock. Rita also has been busy while the movers are distracting the security. She manages to pack a suitcase with her passport and some cash and put it in the trunk of her car. Then at the right moment, she gets hold of one of the movers and asks if he could do her a favor and park her car in a nearby parking lot. She gives him one hundred dollars and the address. "Please leave the keys under the seat and lock the doors. Tell no one, for I'm playing a joke on my husband." Just in case, better to be ready. She as no clue how much longer she can stay here.

Robert calls at five-thirty and sounds upset. He asks if she was in the closet of their room. "Of course I was. Don't be silly. How do you think they pack our stuff? I told the movers that the boxes were going to storage. The clothes were coming here. They arrived today, and the clothes are already hanging in the closet. You need to check in storage if something was misplaced," she explains.

"Rita, I'm missing something, and the only thing that bothers me is that in the closet there is a small storage inside. Opening the door there was a set of footprints, but they weren't from a man. Rita, you did go in the little room so where is it," he demands.

"Where is what? I do not have a clue as to what you are talking about. What are you missing? Tell me. Then, maybe I can help you find it, or maybe one of the movers took it," she states calmly.

"Bitch, are you trying to pull my chain? Give me my fucking book before you regret you were born. I'm coming home, and I don't want *Tom Sawyer.* You understand me? You will pay for lying to me. Just wait for me to get home because the honeymoon is over, and your ass is mine," he yells angrily.

After Rita hangs up she calls her parents and explains what is happening, not all of it, but a quick summary. She tells them to find shelter with Father Mike or Tim. She gives them the numbers. "I will call you in a few days. I fear for my life and need to get away!" Rita does not have much time left. She needs to leave but they won't let her, or they will follow her. She needs a distraction. She puts on some jeans, sneakers, and a jacket with a cap. With her keys in her hand, she starts a fire in her bedroom and waits for the fire alarm to go off. Then at the right moment, she runs out with the staff because they are yelling as they are running outside. She does not stop but continues until she clears the gates. Then she walks fast, never looking back. Once she gets to the parking lot, she looks for her car. After about twenty minutes she spots it. She opens the car but right before she leaves she remember her license plates. It will be easy for them to spot her. She remembers her dad always kept some tools in the trunk. Once she finds the screw driver, she takes off her plate and starts looking for another plate. She found plates from a car that is similar to hers and did the switch. Now, she feels more secure with them on the car.

She then drives to her parents' home and talks to her dad. He gives her the keys to his second car. He tells her that her car will be easy to trace with the tracking device but tells her that she did well by changing the plate. He will ditch the car and tells her not worry for when they do find it, she will be long gone. She leaves the state of Washington and remembers that Father Mike told her that they have safe houses in the western part of the country so she heads west towards the Dakotas. After driving for eight hours straight, she needs a break. She stops in Toledo, Ohio. She finds a Wal-Mart and buys a cell phone. One of them is pay-as- you-go. Then, she stocks up on some supplies: TV dinners, juices, and bread. She buys hair color and anything that might help hide her identity. Then, she gets a room with a kitchen, pays up front, and asks if she can leave the key in the room because she is leaving early. That way they do not see her new disguise. She is not taking any chances. While the TV dinner is cooking, she cuts her hair short and what used to be black is now auburn. She looks in the mirror and is amazed at the difference. Wow, she still looks hot. After a quick shower, she switches on the TV while eating dinner. Sure enough, there is a massive manhunt for her.

Robert is pleading to the public for her return or any information as to her whereabouts. "Rita, if you see this please call home. I worry about you. Your parents are being flown to the White House as we speak. Rita, if for whatever reason you are not able to call, please have someone call for you. We need to hear from you. Rita, whatever is wrong can be fixed. Remember that your parents are not in the best of health. Your mother is taking this very hard. You do care about your mother and her well-being, don't you? Just call and tell her you're safe. I ask you as a husband, not as your president. We all have our differences. That's what makes us human," he pleads as he wipes a tear from his face. Then, he signs off.

"You are not human, Robert. How can you justify that, you monster, especially after you said you are going to hurt me? No way I'm going back. Why would Robert say such things, he knows that I found out about his book," she concludes.

Rita calls Tim. He is happy when he answers. " I feared for you. Please tell me that you are not using your cell phone," he says.

"No, Tim, I left it at home. I've watched enough TV to know better. What happened, Rita?"

"Well, for starters he knows that I have his book. He wants it back. He told me that he is going to hurt me for lying to him; therefore, I decided not to take any chances after taking the book. I packed a suitcase earlier in the day. Then, I had a mover park my car in a garage, and I even changed plates," she informs him.

"Tim, did my parents call you?"

"Yes. They called. We were making arrangements, but we got cut off. Then, the news came on that they were being flown to the White House for their safety."

"Tim, you mentioned you had a safe house in North Dakota. Let them know where. I'm on my way."

"Rita, you need to keep a low profile. Please be careful because Mike said it's only a matter of time before it begins, the downfall of Mankind. Call me tomorrow. I will have an address for you. Rita, you did see the news. They have your parents. It's only a matter a time before they use them to bargain with you. What do you plan on doing?"

"If I give him the book, we do not have a chance to defeat him. Tim,

I love my parents but what about humanity? What should I do?" she asks, her voice revealing the stress.

"Let me talk to my brother. We will figure something out. Get some rest and promise to keep a low profile," he advises her.

After Rita hangs up, she cries herself to sleep. In the early morning it's all over the news that she has disappeared. She drives to Wisconsin after getting a room in Portage In. She waits for the evening to call Tim, but before that, she tries calling her mom, but she didn't answer. Then while waiting, she watches the news, and her parents are both pleading for her to return. Looking closely at their eyes, however, she realizes that something isn't right. They appear not to be crying, but they have fear in their eyes. "God, give me the strength to do the right thing. Please let them be safe and allow no harm to come to them," she prays.

Robert, meanwhile, is talking to the parents. "Come now. You know where she is. She would not leave without first telling you. We had a little spat just like normal people. It's not making me look good in the public eye. This has never happened to any president. The citizens will lose faith in me, and this country cannot afford a fiasco. "Frank, tell her to come home. You know how women get. I love Rita. You both know that I'm lost without her. I admit it was my fault. Carla, please tell her it's all right and I'm sorry. I've been under so much pressure, but it won't happen again," Robert pleads.

Carla starts crying. Frank sits next to her and puts his arm around her and looks at Robert and tells him they are leaving. "Frank, that's not a good idea because what would happen if she has been taken by force? I mean I could be wrong and then what? You stay here until she returns just to be on the safe side. Then, you can both leave." An aide comes and whispers something to Robert, and he tells them he will return shortly.

Sabula is in another room and tells him that they have her number. Carla's phone was the answer. They have it on memory. When Rita called earlier, it came up anonymous and that was determined to be her. Next time she makes a call, they will trace it back to her. She also tells him about the call that was made afterwards from Carla's phone. The redial was from Tim Summers. They have surveillance on him. As soon as he leaves home, they will search it. Robert tells her to find everything they can on him, family members, and friends. He says he wanted it yesterday, okay? "Sabula, you know that we are going to eliminate Rita after all this? After we get my book back, start planning something that will get me sympathy from the public. Make it bloody and do not leave anything to chance including this Tim Summers and anyone that might have any ties to him, understand?"

"When do you want to kill Tim, before or after?" Sabula enquires.

"Wait and see. If she contacts him again, then take him to the safe house and do your magic. See what else he knows. Sabula, you do understand this bitch is trying to ruin my career. I need to stop her."

"How about her parents? What are you going to do to them?"

"Nothing for now but that could change in the future, especially for Frank. I don't like him and would like to see him have an accident," Robert responds matter-of-factly.

Tim worries after hanging up with Rita. She is a sweet person, and he fears for her life. When he goes outside to throw the garbage, he notices a van parked by the curb. It's odd that he never has noticed it before. Then, he decides to take a walk. As he is passing by it, he looks over, but it's hard to see inside. The windows have a heavy tint so no one can see inside. On his return, he memorizes the plate number. Then, he approaches the van and knocks on the door, but it drives off. Once inside his house, he writes the number down leaving it by the phone. If it returns, he will call the cops. He then calls Mike and tells him about Rita and the van. Mike tells him to wait for Rita's call and leave for a safe house because it has begun. There is no turning back. Mike tells Tim that they will be coming for him. It's only a matter of time.

Tim looks outside and tells Mike that the van has not returned. "Tim, leave and meet me at the park. Bring only what you can carry and all your immediate information. Do not forget the plate number. I'll meet you in forty-five minutes." Tim gathers his personal belongings and loads up his car in the garage. Then a look outside reveals the van is back. He calls the cops telling them that it looks suspicious, and in no time, they are there. As the police arrive, the van hurries to leave but is stopped. That's Tim's chance to leave. Opening the garage door, he leaves trying not to draw their attention, but one of the Robert's spies spots him as the garage door is closing. Tim wants to burn out but can't. As soon as he gets a chance, he will take off. As the police ask the spy for some ID, that's his chance. He drives off. Knowing he cannot return, he fears for his life and for Mike's. All they have is each other.

Mike is waiting for him at the park. They load Tim's stuff in the trunk and leave the car. As they drive around, the phone rings. It's Rita telling Tim that she is worried that they will harm her parents. Tim tells her what just happened, and that he will dispose of the phone right after the call because he knows that they are tracing it, and it's better for her to do the same. "Buy another phone. Then, call this other number. We'll be waiting for your call," he assures her.

Then, Mike tells Tim that Rita could be in jeopardy. If the van was parked outside, then what's to tell them that Robert's "perps" don't have her number or have an idea of her whereabouts? "Tim, we also need to wait for her to call back and discard this other phone after she calls us back. Meanwhile, remove your battery and toss it out the window with your phone. Tim, while we wait let's take a ride to the church. We'll drop you off and you get the book and my Rolodex. We'll send it to Father John. The FedEx is still open, and if we hurry, we can still send it tonight," Mike suggests. Mike drops Tim off, circles around, and waits for him to return. A few minutes later he returns. Then, straight to the FedEx they go. Once it's in the mail, they breathe a little easier, but now they worry because Rita has not called back. They drive for the rest of the night waiting for a call that they never get. In the early hours, they ditch the phone and disappear into a safe house, one after the other, until they arrive in North Dakota.

Rita's plan was to go to a Wal-Mart, buy another phone, and call back. It was simple but on the way over there, they caught up to her. They ran her off the road. Her car got stuck, and they took her in the van. The pain began. Sabula was there to supervise. Rita recognized her. "You can't touch me," Rita told her. When I tell Robert what you are doing to me, he will have your ass!"

Sabula laughs out loud. "Bitch, your husband is the reason that I'm here. I never liked you Rita, you snotty bitch. You act like your shit don't stink. Oh, by the way, Robert prefers to screw me. The only reason he fucks you is because he feels sorry for you." Then, Sabula punches her in the mouth and blood trickles from the right side of her mouth. Rita covers her mouth and then tells her that if it was just one-on-one it would be a different fight, but she is a coward just like Robert.

"I know what has been going on for a while. You think I'm that stupid? On election night I knew what you were doing. I can't prove it, but my heart doesn't lie." Rita has one clean shot at Sabula and takes it. She strikes her in the face with all her might catching Sabula off guard. Sabula's men look in disbelief. They grab her arms and hold her. Sabula doesn't waste a minute. The pain starts. She hits Rita so hard on the left side of her face that it rattles her eardrum. Blood starts seeping out of her ear, but Rita doesn't have the time to worry about that now. One of the men punches her in the stomach and another in the legs and arms. In a matter of minutes

Rita's features have changed and as the beating continues, she prays. What is sad is that it's only the beginning. Sabula asks again where the book is. "I don't know what you're talking about. You've got to believe me," Rita tries to convince her.

"Believe you? Why do you think I'm here? Robert said that if you give it back, you would get an easy death, but if you refuse, it will be awhile before you meet your maker so what's it going be? Rita, you know I have the power to let you live. I could easily tell Robert that you gave in, and then you escaped as long as he has the book. Maybe it would buy you some time. Then, you can recover from your little incident and disappear." Then, Sabula rubs her legs and asks her, What do you think, Honey? We can maybe stay in touch, and I can show you the time of your life. Think about it. You and I, I bet you've never been with another woman. After me you won't want a man . Sabula licks her lips and tells her not to worry. Leave it up to me. I can convince Robert into believing anything I want. Ain't that right, Boys?" and they all agree. Rita looks up and spits in Sabula's face. "Oh, you want to have more fun? Okay, so you like to spit. Sabula cleans her face with her fingers, and she licks them afterward. Boys, how do we teach a woman not to spit? She instructs one of the men to put his cock in her mouth and not to take it out until she swallows. They force her mouth open by punching her in the stomach, and they start taking turns. They grab her by the hair and don't let up. Poor Rita, she wishes it would just be a bad dream and that she could wake up. Then she feels the first one coming in her mouth, and there is nothing that she can do to stop it. The second is the same. They force her and Sabula laughs and tells her to get used to it. As they get ready to leave for the airport, two of Sabula's men get Rita's car out from where it was stuck and leave. They go back to the hotel and clean it up leaving no trace. They drive the car back to Washington. Sabula has a plan and it includes the car. Robert would be proud of her. Sabula tells Rita that she like the new look. Had it not been for the phone call to Tim, they would not have triangulated her position. It's amazing how technology evolves and with a touch of a finger, here you are.

"Now, Rita, let's get down to business. The book is where and please don't pretend?" Sabula warns her.

"I don't have it. I threw it out. I figured it was an old book of no importance, so there. Sabula gets close to her, strikes her in the face again, and asks Rita the question again.

"I told you. I threw it out," Rita repeats. Sabula tells one of her men to hold Rita's right hand to the door panel. The other man pulls out a hammer and strikes her pinky finger, and it explodes blood gushing everywhere. Her petite hands will never be the same. She asks again and gets the same results. Rita loses another finger. In less then twenty minutes she lost her right fingers, and then they start with the left hand. Rita's prays to God for a fast death but death does not come easily. After she passes out the first time, they let her be. They bandage her hands and load her on the plane. Once more they wake her and begin asking about Tim. She tells Sabula that he has been a friend for a long time. Sabula tells her that Robert has never met him, and he knows all her friends. "Not this one, but what is the big deal? He is no one but a friend," Rita tries to assure her.

"Then why did you call him?" Sabula demands to know.

"I called to tell him that I was going to fix him up with a friend of mine for a date," Rita tries to convince her.

Sabula tells her, "You have sweet mouth. You have an answer for everything." One of the men tells Sabula that they will be landing in a few minutes. "Rita, take a break for you will need all your strength once we land. Then, you're all mine, and my men will do as they please because the next time Robert sees you, you will be in the morgue."

After landing, they put her in a van and drive to a warehouse. This time the men take turns raping her while Sabula watches. Even Sabula gets into the action. After seeing her men, she gets horny and joins in. She forces Rita to go down on her while her men watch. After she has her way with her, she invites her men to join in, and they screw her in the ass while Rita has her face between Sabula's legs. Sabula asks her men how it feels to screw the first lady. They laugh, but they also want her to swallow so they take turns forcing her mouth open but the last one is not lucky for Rita knows that she's already dead so she does what is not expected and bites off his cock. The poor bastard bleeds to death, and they laugh as Rita spits it out, and then the pain begins once more. They take turns punching her face breaking her jaw and nose. Next, it's her right arm. The brother of the unfortunate mishap wants some payback. He takes out a drill, puts on the biggest bit, and goes to work on her pussy. Meanwhile, Sabula is asking about the book. There is blood everywhere. Sabula gets her tools and cuts off one of Rita's breasts, but Rita doesn't die. She spits at Sabula and tells her that she is on her way to Heaven to meet her Savior. Then, Sabula removes one of her eyes, and Rita finally dies. She never revealed anything about the book or about Tim. Robert is not going to be happy, but wait. She still has her plan. They will plant the body in the car, riddle it with bullets, set it on fire, and then blame it on some scapegoat. That's it.

The next morning the news headline is that the first lady has been killed in a drive by as she was returning home. A massive manhunt is underway. There are few details at this time, according to the press, but they will keep the public informed. The flags are all to be flown at half mast. A statement is issued by the authorities in charge of the investigation, "We regret the passing of a good woman, and our hearts go out to the president and the rest of the family. If anyone has any information, there is a big reward. We need to have justice. Never in the history of the presidency have we buried a wife that's been murdered. We demand to bring these criminals and all parties involved to justice. Then and only then can our president morn his loss of ten years."

Robert is pleased about the news but is pissed off because Rita didn't reveal the whereabouts of his book. Tim disappears along with his brother leaving no trace. Tim worked for a blood bank. His boss said he never showed up for work and never called back. He still has his last check. His brother is a priest at Our Savior Church. They have no information as to where he went. They said that he became displeased with the church and left. They are watching the church in case he returns. Regarding Sabula, the secret service said that on the last day Rita stopped at the church and was carrying a book.

"Sabula, what if Rita managed to get a sample of my blood to Father Mike along with the book?" Robert asks. "It could be devastating because in the book there are not only many ways to manipulate my blood to enhance it but also there is a way to make it normal. I did not read the whole book, but what I read scared me. It makes me vulnerable," he lamented.

Sabula looks at him and for once in his life, he is truly scared. What if she got hold of the book? She could use it to her advantage, and at the right time, Bam! She could take over after all the work is done. "Robert, you're being paranoid. They know nothing, but we will continue to look for the book. I promise you if they have the book, we'll get it back, and I will make them pay just like Rita, okay?"

Robert wonders if it was a good idea for Sabula to know his weakness, but it's too late. "How I ever forgot the book is beyond me. For many years it was close to me. Now, it's lost or it's in the wrong hands and could be used to fight me," he thinks to himself. "Sabula, use all means to find the book. Go back to the church and tear it apart. Do what you do best. I want results. Get me names, addresses, and anything that can be helpful. Send your best men. Leave no trace. Burn it down when you're done. Someone knows something so find out who and make him talk. Now back to Rita. Tell me you have a good plan and how it will get me sympathy," Robert demands.

"Well, for starters we are planning to use bikers as scapegoats; these bikers should do the trick because they have a long record. They will not be missed. At the right time we will plant DNA on them, and we have bullet casings and her ID. That should be the icing on the cake. There will be no prisoners. It's an empty warehouse. My men have them under surveillance as we speak."

"How many bikers are there?" Robert asks.

"They counted twenty men and women. They've been living there for the last week. Send a squad of men. Plant the evidence and call when it's over. Do not fail me again, Sabula, for I'm keeping track. You already have two strikes against you," he reminds her adamantly. "How about Rita's body? How was it found?"

"I think a closed casket should do the trick. I had the parents identify the body. They were devastated. I had some camera men close by to capture the moment. They had to use dental records to identify the body," she reports.

"Splendid, you did well," Robert finally compliments her.

"Her parents are staying here only for the funeral, and then they want to leave. I don't think we'll have any problems with them."

"Sabula, once in awhile I still want you to check on them just in case."

"Robert, pictures of Rita are being posted on the Internet. You will get even more sympathy then. We will cry out that someone leaked them."

"Sabula, I'm glad you're on my side," and they laugh. "By the way, I send a group of my men to the church where Father Mike and his brother Tim disappeared. They left no trace. We did find computers, but they've been wiped clean. All the memory was deleted and a virus was left so when we plug it in, there is nothing but contaminated files. We are still having problems. They are using nano technology. Robert, they are organizing. We need to strike at the heart because if we don't, it could have consequences. We don't need them having hope. The clergy that were at the church were tortured but did not revel anything we do not know already. As of right now, the brothers have not used any credit cards; also, they are not driving any vehicles that are registered in their names."

Hearing the news, Tim and Mike pray for her soul. They see the pictures on the Internet and can't believe it's Rita. She was very pretty.

They now know that they can't ever show their faces. They will be in hiding for the rest of their lives. Father John has the book and is working on deciphering it. They scan the book and send it to their safe houses. Maybe someone can find a use for it to combat the antichrist. They will have someone watching the parents; thereby, keeping their promise to Rita. Father John told them when the time is right they will be relocated out West. Meanwhile, Charles McLain is still working on the blood but said that it will be awhile before they can crack the code. Robert's blood is so powerful it could take years to crack, but he promises not to give up. He said maybe once they crack it, then they can be manipulated and bond it with ordinarily blood and use it on a volunteer to enhance his abilities. That is all speculation for now, but there is hope and with the book, it raises their chances for survival.

Frank and Carla are devastated when they see their daughter. They will put her to rest and leave this place. Frank is sure that Robert is behind all this but can't prove it. He remembers that Rita told him Robert was the antichrist. How does he fight a demon? Frank is sure that their phone is being tapped, and they are being followed. How can they escape and who will believe them? Father Mike said that he would contact them or have another acquaintance get in touch, but they have to wait awhile for everyone to calm down. Carla wanted to have Rita buried at home, but Robert refused saying his wife was to be buried in Washington and that was final. They both feared Robert, and all they wanted at this point was to leave to go home, pack, and disappear. Robert had never even told them how sorry he was to lose his wife. When they heard the news that she had been killed, they both cried but Robert did not even flinch until he was on the podium giving the news that his wife had been killed. That was the only time that he had shed a tear. "This man does not have a heart. Had I known back then what I know now, I would have killed him myself. He took my Rita, my life. This man is not just a demon but a coward. " Please, God, I pray to you that my Rita did not suffer much and that she is in your eternal glory. Give us the strength not to give into this demon. God, I ask you for forgiveness for helping this man get into power. Now, I understand that it's only a matter of time before the world sees his true colors. The *Bible* stated that the end of times would be fought in the Middle East, but I'm not sure now because no one ever said that the antichrist would be president of the United States. We welcome your return to save us from destruction. Please give us faith, courage, and hope.

The bikers are getting ready to eat the woman, and some men have been busy cooking. They've been staying here for the last week. With the economy being so bad even the ones that want to work are not able. Mind you, some have records but some just lost everything and had been forced into this type of living. They banded together. Some did odd jobs, and they put all the money in a kitty to buy food and things that they needed. It's been a hard life but when you run out of resources, you do just about anything to survive. The state refuses to help them. Their unemployment ran out and many lost their homes. With many companies closed down, it was difficult to find employment, but they were thankful because they still ate and no one bothered them here at the empty warehouse. People thought because they were bikers they were all bad, but that's not true. Even the bad ones always gave thanks to God. They were trying to change. Among them were some that did practice what they preached, and they encouraged the rest to follow suit so for the most part they were all changing for the better. They are just sitting down to give thanks when all hell breaks loose. Gunfire rains on them from all sides. Some manage to get to their guns, but they are no match. Sabula's men completely surround them, and no mercy is shown in their death. Sabula is watching from a distance and marvels at her men, and the way they take action. It makes her horny just watching the blood and the bodies. After her men take the bikers down, they go back and shoot them again just to make sure they're dead. Women are treated like men, no mercy. Even the one with child met the same fate. Then, when the dust settles, they plant the evidence, clean the area, and make it look like animals were living here. Afterwards, the media is called as a witness to the massacre. They cheer for they have justice. Now, the country can mourn the death of the first lady and move forward. Robert got what he wanted. Now, Sabula and he can concentrate on finding the book.

After the funeral, Frank and Carla leave back to Hartford and wait for the call because they now have closure and can disappear. In their hearts, they know that the bikers were not the real killers, just scapegoats. Robert never even thanked them for identifying the body. He did not even shed a tear for their daughter at the funeral. Frank again regrets ever getting involved with Robert, but one day Robert will get his, and Frank hopes to be alive to witness the downfall. Robert took Frank's little girl, and it does not end here. Frank treated him like a son, and now he watches his wife in pain. It eats him from the inside. He blames himself for her death, but Rita never expressed any trouble or fear until the end. What could he have done differently?

Father John tells his followers that Rita is the one that is giving them hope. He shows them the old book. "We've been working on this book for awhile, and we have clues so that's a start. Steve, I fear that the worst is yet to come because the president announces that they will start using robots to fight conflicts overseas, and they will also be used here in the states for civil unrest. They are being supplied to every major city. They are equipped with the Intel-a-chip and smart batteries which give them the capability to run for years before they need maintenance. We are looking for ways to fight these machines. It's not going to be easy because they are using titanium armor now, but who knows what they will be using next. We have resources on the inside, and they speculate that there are at least one hundred thousand already built. That's on the ground, not counting air. Everything coming out of production is unmanned. We are in the works of finding the main hub. That way we can introduce a virus and use nano technology to take them off line disrupting communications. Even though they are using the Intel-a-chip, they still need to be given orders. Once we infiltrate, then we mobilize our units and start waging the war for humanity. Believe me, it's not going to be easy, but with God's help, we will win especially with the arrival of Our Savior. We need to be strong putting our faith in the Lord. He will be our armor. We need to resist temptation in order for us to triumph.

"We still have a bit of time but you need to consider your families, your friends, and the helpless. We cannot leave anyone behind that believes. Out West, we have started building shelters, but we are going to need resources to accommodate the people. We need doctors and medical supplies, smart batteries to run generators for lighting and livestock, fresh water holding tanks, dry goods, munitions, and steel to fortify the caves. We need heavy equipment to dig the caves, fluids for the equipment, and plenty of petrol to run our machines. Do not get me wrong. Over the years we have managed to stockpile drones, for they will be our eyes in the night. They will help target their bases. We are equipping them with smart bombs and nano technology to disrupt their communications. We do have a fighting chance, but we will need more because we don't know how long this conflict will last. Once it starts, no one will be able to buy if they do not have the mark. It's for our benefit to stockpile now. We need snipers and more ground troops, people with a military background to train our men and woman.

"Steve and the rest of you, I'm sorry for the bad news, but it's the truth. What do you want to do wait for it to happen and be caught sitting down or prepare for the worst and have a chance to live and fight until the return of Our Savior? When you leave tonight, sleep on it. Once you make up your mind, there is no turning back."

"Father John, before we leave would you marry us because we don't want to live in sin, and if this is the end, well, I think Penny feels the same," Steve requested. When Steve takes her hand, she looks at him, and they bow their heads. Penny has been caught off guard but in her heart, she feels the same. Father John immediately honors their request and they are married. Steve says, "We love God and welcome him into our lives." After the ceremony, they all left and celebrated, but it is different now because their future is unknown. They do not have a clue when it ends because it's already begun.

www.ingramcontent.com/pod-product-compliance
Ingram Content Group UK Ltd.
Pitfield, Milton Keynes, MK11 3LW, UK
UKHW041946190726
13854UKWH00004B/1819

9 781452 098142